Veronica Stallwood was born in London, educated abroad and now lives near Oxford. In the past she has worked in the Bodleian Library and more recently in Lincoln College library. Her first crime novel, DEATHSPELL, was published to great critical acclaim and became a local bestseller, as did both her next novels, DEATH AND THE OXFORD BOX, and OXFORD EXIT. OXFORD MOURNING is the third novel to feature Kate Ivory, and she has recently completed a fourth.

When she is not writing, Veronica Stallwood enjoys going for long walks, talking and eating with friends, and gazing out at the peaceful Oxfordshire countryside from the windows of her cottage.

Oxford Mourning

Veronica Stallwood

HEADLINE

First published in 1995
by Macmillan London Limited

First published in paperback in 1996
by HEADLINE BOOK PUBLISHING

10 9 8 7 6 5 4 3 2 1

ISBN 0 7472 5343 9

Printed and bound in Great Britain by
Cox & Wyman Ltd, Reading, Berks

HEADLINE BOOK PUBLISHING
A division of Hodder Headline PLC
338 Euston Road
London NW1 3BH

For Robert McNeil

ACKNOWLEDGEMENTS

With heartfelt thanks to:

Colin Harris of the Department of Western Manuscripts, Bodleian Library, for finding the illegible manuscripts.

Robert McNeil, Head of the Hispanic Section, Bodleian Library, for taking me on the roof of the Radcliffe Camera and scaring me witless.

Ruth Gosling, formerly of the Department of Western Manuscripts, Bodleian Library, for explaining how to read illegible handwriting.

Ann Bowes, formerly College Secretary, Lincoln College, Oxford, for information both on college administration and on Indie chart rock groups. *Jesus ama Los Swervies*, as they say.

Barbara Peters, of the Poisoned Pen Bookstore, Scottsdale, Az., for cutting up the lamb chops and reminding me what a wonderful place Oxford is.

Hugh Griffith, for sorting out the T-shirts and identifying the loose ends, but most of all for teaching me the Alexander Technique.

Annabel Stogdon for everything else.

The book that is nearly referred to a number of times in the text is *The Invisible Woman* by Claire Tomalin, published in London by Viking, 1990. It is a lot more informative, and accurate, about the lives of Maria and Ellen Ternan than either *Oxford Mourning* or the lurid piece of historical fiction that Kate Ivory is currently writing.

Chapter 1

Oxford awake! The land hath borne too long
The senseless jingling of thy drowsy song...
G. V. Cox, *Black Gowns and Red Coats*, 1834

Two small knights in blue tunics and gilded helmets advanced with a whirring and clacking of machinery. There was a moment of silence and then they struck their golden bells to inform the citizens of Oxford that it was six o'clock.

On the street below Carfax Tower, the home-going crowds wearily pushed their way through the damp October air towards their bus queues, and ignored them. Everyone, that is, except for a woman of about thirty, with short bright hair and round grey eyes: this was a novelist, Kate Ivory.

As the first bell chimed, she paused at the crossroads to look upwards, causing a minor traffic jam on the pavement. 'Sorry!' she cried to the people who crashed into her. But Look! she wanted to say. Don't you see what's here? This city is full of ancient delights, which we no longer notice. All we see is the new autumn display in the window of Marks & Spencer, and the headline on the newsstand.

1

She mentally removed the buses and the commuters and sent herself back in time to 1865. This is what you should be concentrating on, she told herself. Keep you mind on your work and then come up with a bright idea, the one that will make all the difference to your new book.

Nothing. Just the sound of the bells high above the noise of the traffic.

She shrugged, pushed her hands through her short blonde hair in the gesture that her hairdresser hated, and walked on through the anonymous crowd. Along Queen Street she strode. She passed the prison and the Castle mound. Then she turned towards the railway station. The newspaper headline screamed, *Oxford Woman's Shock Find!*

But Kate Ivory walked on, oblivious to its message. And thus she failed to buy a newspaper, since she didn't imagine that its front-page story had anything to do with her.

Liam Ross, in his rooms in college, raised his head as the Mourning Bell, rung by the head porter, chimed eleven times. The flag above the lodge was flying at half mast, and he remembered that some long-retired, and mostly forgotten, elderly Fellow of the college had recently died. He knew him only as a stooped, rather deaf old man, who had spent most of the previous Gaudy complaining about the food. Liam pushed the memory to the back of his mind, with the ease of someone who has another fifty years to go before worrying about senility. He checked his watch. Just past six fifteen. He could work for another hour and still have time for a shower and a change of clothes before his lover had dinner ready for him.

Life was good. He had managed to have some very satisfying relationships without taking on any boring commitments. And for the next few years he was quite content to let his life continue in the same way. He closed the book he had been reading and added it to the tottering pile already standing on his desk. One of these days he must tidy the place up, he thought, looking around hopelessly at the folders that spilled out their contents, the heaps of music, the computer disks that punctuated the whole clutter. Another time, perhaps. His scout grumbled about the mess, but he rather liked it, himself. This, he considered, was how a real academic should live.

The sound of the bells carried through the noise of the traffic. It floated past Magdalen College, drifted over Magdalen Bridge and up a small green hill. There, it reached a group of people sitting on the grass. They stared down into the blue haze, at the view of domes and towers, trees and spires, and listened to the sound of the bells.

Slightly apart from the others, the young woman they called Angel turned her back on the charming view. She sat with rigid shoulders and gazed instead at a terrace of Edwardian houses which marched down the hill, veiling their windows with net curtains.

'Oxford!' said Ant, in her ear, lifting up the flap of pale hair that hid her face from the others. 'Aren't you excited, Angel? City of dreaming spires and golden opportunities. Think of the romance, the legend!'

Angel closed her eyes. 'Piss off, Ant,' she said.

'No swearing,' said Dime, overhearing. 'Ant's rule.'

'Dime's right,' said Ant. 'What do you say, Angel?'

'Sorry, Ant,' she said, dutifully, but still kept her face

turned away from him. 'I meant to say, it's lovely. Really, Ant, I do think it's lovely. It's just that it's not the place I want to be at the moment.' Ant let the strands of her hair fall and moved away from her.

It wasn't that she wanted to snub them, not after the way they had befriended her without expecting anything in return. But what they were saying meant nothing to her. She had to hold on to her own vision, and that took all her energy and all her concentration. She felt so tired from the effort that she could fall asleep there on the hillside, among the discarded Pepsi cans and the old hamburger boxes. And their constant sympathy got on her nerves. For the moment she needed their support, so she agreed to follow their rules. But she was sick of being forever grateful to Ant and the family. And something more than weariness was making her feel low. She had somewhere else that she needed to get to, and they – Ant, Gren, Dime and Coffin – were supposed to be taking her there. The trouble was, they were doing it at their own pace, and to her it was agonizingly slow. Hold on, get your strength back, she told herself. Get strong for what you have to do.

Coffin took a whistle from the velvet-lined black box where he kept his collection, and started to play some haunting Celtic tune. Dime came to sit very close to Angel and pushed his round face near hers, so that she could smell the last pizza he had eaten.

'Are you cold?' he asked. 'You can borrow my sweater if you like.' Dime's sweater, like Dime himself, smelled of old food, and Angel shook her head.

'Leave me be,' she said.

'Don't you worry, Angel,' he said. 'We'll get you there.'

He frowned his puzzled frown. 'What was the place you wanted to get to?'

Angel sighed. 'Leicester,' she said. 'I have to get to Leicester.' It seemed as if she had repeated this sentence a hundred times in the past few weeks. If Dime asked her once more, she might hit him. She imagined the look of surprise on his round red face, and smiled. Dime, happy to see her pleasure, smiled back at her.

In fact they were all glad to sit or sprawl on the grass at the top of the hill, enjoying the view, allowing themselves to be taken in by its charm. They formed a rough triangle, with Ant at its apex. He was dressed, as usual, in black: jeans, boots, T-shirt with the sleeves ripped out. His hair had grown quite long during the summer, and he had pulled it back off his face into a pony tail.

'Here though, Ant,' said Gren, his voice taking on the whine of a tired child. 'Where are we going to kip tonight? You got a place for us to crash out?' He took out the piece of cardboard which he always had hidden inside his clothing and read the words written on it. *Hungry and homeless*. He held it up for Ant to see, then put it back. Angel could never understand how he could hide it away like that. Gren was so thin, his clothes so meagre, yet always, hidden about his person, he carried an assortment of things that might come in useful.

'Give me twenty minutes,' said Ant. 'I'll find us somewhere. No problem.'

Coffin played a more cheerful tune on his whistle. They could all rely on Ant, thought Angel. They had been relying on him for ages, maybe more than a year. Coffin had told her about it, but he had lost count of the months. Ant was their leader, said Coffin, the one they believed in. They followed his rules and he looked after them. Life was simple if you belonged to Ant's family. She looked over at him.

'Stay here,' said Ant, standing up. 'I'll be back within the hour.' He checked that everything he needed was in his small blue backpack, then hefted it over his shoulder.

'It'll be dark soon,' said Dime, lifting a worried face. 'You sure you'll find us a place?'

'When did I ever let you down? I'll be back before dark,' said Ant. 'Trust me.'

Kate Ivory reached her small house in the suburb of Fridesley. Before making herself a cup of tea and cutting a slice of cheese to eat with it, she went down to her workroom and looked through the notes she had made that morning for her new book. Something's missing, she thought. It's not so much that the material is thin, but it's over-familiar. There's nothing new, nothing to surprise the reader. I need something meatier, something that isn't in the books I've been reading and that my readers won't have seen, either. I need an angle.

But where to find it? She had tried the Bodleian's catalogues and had read up everything about Maria Susanna Taylor and her sister, Ellen Ternan. There hadn't been a lot. She had then read a couple of biographies of Ellen's lover, Charles Dickens. They had been discreet on the subject of his amours, giving as excuse the fact that he had destroyed nearly all his diaries, and torched his correspondence in one great bonfire in 1860. After that, he destroyed all personal correspondence as he received it. But recently there had been murmurings in the Sunday supplements, bringing the subject up again, hinting at spicy revelations. What she needed was a meeting with someone in the know. Unfortunately, she did not live in that world. She needed a contact.

At that moment the phone rang.

'Kate? Andrew here.'

Andrew Grove, her friend at the Bodleian. He owed her a favour or ten. She had done a small job for him five months ago which had involved a lot of boring cataloguing work, and had nearly resulted in her death at the hands of a psychopath.

'I wondered whether you'd like to come to a concert with me next week. Very pretty music. In Bartlemas chapel.'

'Doesn't Isabel want to go with you?' Andrew knew Kate's opinion of his girlfriend, Isabel Ryan: an airhead, and twenty years too young for him.

'I admit that I bought the tickets with the idea of introducing Isabel to some simple classical music.'

'How simple?'

'Oh, you know. Pachelbel's *Canon*. Vivaldi's *Gloria*. Something by Handel with lots of jolly trumpets.'

'And she didn't buy it?'

'She said she'd come with me if in return I accompanied her to a concert given by some people she admired called Swervedriver. She said they were big in something called the Indie charts, whatever that might mean.'

Kate laughed. 'You should have accepted. You might have enjoyed it.'

Kate could feel Andrew's shudder all the way down the phone line, and she relented. Andrew was too easy to tease to make it worthwhile.

'I'd love to come with you to the concert. Just tell me the time and the place.'

When he had told her, and as he was about to wind up

the conversation, she said, 'Andrew, do you know anything about Charles Dickens and Ellen Ternan?'

'His little actress friend? You need to read that book by—'

'Yes, I know. I have read it. I was hoping for something that wasn't published yet.'

'Ah! You've seen the newspaper headlines.'

'Sorry?'

' "Oxford Woman's Shock Find".'

'Now that sounds more my intellectual level.'

'The paper's got hold of the fact that the English Tutor at one of the colleges is transcribing a collection of notebooks and letters that were found recently in the Bartlemas library. They had been in the possession of Nelly Ternan's sister, Maria. I'm sure you know that she married an Oxford brewer and lived here in the Banbury Road.' Once off the subject of heavy rock music, Andrew could be relied on to return to his customary self-confidence.

'Yes, I'm very interested in Maria,' said Kate. 'A woman after my own heart.'

'Artistic, independent. A writer. Yes, I suppose you would be. It all sounds so restless to me.' Andrew liked his life to be calm and predictable, and not punctuated by the demands of a New Woman. Or even by a fan of the Swervies. Kate didn't give much for Isabel's chances of remaining in his life after this latest incident.

'Well, how do I go about getting my hands on this material?' she asked.

'I doubt whether you do. Why don't you try writing to the academic in question? It's possible that she'd give you something, but I shouldn't bank on it.'

'Good idea. Have you got her name and college?'

'Unfortunately, I've already thrown my newspaper out. But I can check on it for you. I'll get back to you.'

That was a start, anyway.

The woman picked up the sheet of paper and read it.

What did you do with the child? You know that I would have taken it from you and brought it up as my own. No one would have known that it wasn't mine. Couldn't you trust me? Tell me, what did you do with the child?

She read it again, slowly, making a small adjustment to the punctuation. Yes, she was sure she had it right now. She turned it face down on a pile of similar leaves, and picked up the next. She started to write on the pad in front of her, then shook her pen in irritation and tried again.

She worked on for another twenty minutes, then put her work to one side and went to put on a jacket and pick up her handbag and keys.

Ant walked off down the hill, thin legs in black jeans swinging fast towards the city. He took the first turning to the left so that he was soon out of sight of the family, and only then did he allow himself to slow down. He hunched his shoulders and muttered under his breath. 'Fuck the van. Fuck this town. Fuck the lot of them.' He grinned. ' "No swearing. Ant's rule." ' What do you say, Ant? ' "Sorry, Ant." ' Just the one small blip of rebellion. Even he was allowed that. Then he had to follow the rules again. If he expected the rest of them to obey, he had to give the lead.

It was good, though, to be free of them for a while. Good

to rid himself of the responsibility for their survival. Everyone knew that you had to have laws and had to obey them, if you wanted to form a proper community. This discipline was what set them apart from other travellers. No dreadlocks, he had told them. No dogs. No getting drunk and fighting. No women, at least not yet. And we don't do drugs. Coffin had looked a bit sour at that one, and Ant had caught him a couple of times smoking a joint. But mostly they obeyed because they wanted to belong to Ant's family. No fear of ending up sleeping in a cardboard box if you belonged with Ant. He had tried to introduce them to the idea of a group language: something that would set them apart, give them a special identity. But Dime, though willing, could never remember it, Gren couldn't be bothered, and Coffin just shrugged and picked up one of his whistles and started to play.

And sometimes, like now, Ant felt a temptation to cut free and make off on his own. He didn't do it, though. He knew himself well enough to recognize that he enjoyed the power he had over the others.

Ant turned right into a side street that branched off at an angle and climbed higher up the hill. After a short distance, he turned right again, following his instincts, crossed another road and plunged left into a side street. Here the houses grew tall and clustered together, filled with the transient population of a two-university town. Somewhere here he would find the house he wanted, and neighbours who took no notice if strangers moved in. He started looking out for For Sale signs, uncurtained windows and uncut grass. Thirty yards down, he thought he had found what he was looking for: an unkempt front garden, with a vine climbing up to obscure the front porch and shade the cloudy ground-floor windows. A couple of large envelopes stuck out of the letter-box. A notice under a grubby milk bottle read: *No more milk until further notice.* No For Sale board, but it looked as though the owner had been away for a few days. Promising. Ant looked up and down the road. Nothing. No one interested in him. He carried on with his survey.

Two good locks on the front door, one of them a deadlock. All the windows closed, and locked too, by the look of them. Not as simple as he had thought at first sight. He would have to investigate round the back. Still no one was taking any notice of him and he tried the latch on the gate that led to the back door. Locked, too. This householder was more careful than he had expected. Another quick look round. An overhanging tree sheltered him from the next-door garden. Sweat started to trickle down Ant's back, and he felt his neck begin to itch. This was hardly a Neighbourhood Watch area, nor the sort of place where old women spent their days twitching at net curtains. He was probably safe enough from discovery, but still he felt edgy and nervous until he could get inside the house and out of sight of possible objectors. He would have to take his chance.

The gate was high, but Ant had his hands on the top and had climbed it in seconds. He landed on two dustbins and swore, rubbing at his shins. They made a horrible noise and he held his breath for a moment. Still no one came to look at what he was doing.

Sitting apart from the others, Angel leafed through the note-book. She stopped at a page and re-read what was written there. The handwriting was difficult, and the individual words

11

hard to make out, but she understood the sense of the passage, and her imagination filled in what her eyes could not see.

The room is filled with the scent of lilies. A sweet, heavy smell, pervading every space, creeping down into hollows and crevices like a sickly miasma: like some treacherous, poisonous, insidious vapour. They are huge hungry things with gaping mouths. The mouth of the infant, screaming and purple. Toothless and roaring like a primitive instrument.

If some stranger reads this, he will believe that I am insane. It will confirm his opinion that a woman without a child will turn mad. And perhaps he is right. Perhaps my mind has curdled in here in my calm, silent room with its grey walls and its view out to the green hill.

The lilies are white, like the little bonnet she wore, with its frill of white lace and the long ribbons. She shouldn't have worn it in January. Now she will wear it for ever.

The lilies are alive, in their dark blue vase, there on the table by the window. Swollen white animals, breathing out their scented vapours, filling my room with memories.

Of course, they put lilies on her coffin, didn't they? Large white madonna lilies, sprays of lily-of-the-valley. They kept me alive, left me in ignorance, to sleep.

Bury them. Bury them deep. Lose them for ever.

'What're you doing?' asked Coffin.

'Nothing. Just reading,' answered Angel.

'Looks like writing,' said Coffin. 'Did you write it?'

'I don't know,' said Angel. 'Perhaps. I was trying to make sense of it. But I can't.'

'Give it up,' said Coffin. 'It's only making you unhappy. It's best to live in the present with us, and maybe look to the future sometimes. You should get rid of anything that holds you back.'

'I don't think I can get rid of it until I understand what it is. You can't go forwards if you don't know what's gone before. You're stuck in a continual present.'

Coffin shook his head and picked out a whistle and played her a tripping tune that made her close the notebook and put it back in her pocket.

Ant investigated methodically, as always. Solid back door, solid lock. Next, french windows: thick glass, more locks. But the kitchen was more vulnerable: a rectangular thumb sticking out into the back garden, a late addition to the house, and it had a flat roof. Above this roof was a frosted-glass window – belonging to a bathroom, probably – and someone had left the top of it ajar. Not much room to get in, but Ant was thin, and if his shoulders would fit through, the rest of him could follow.

'Come on, Ant, get yourself inside. It's safer in there than out here.' You could convince yourself of almost anything if you told yourself it, out loud, Ant had found.

It wasn't difficult to get on the roof, then force the top half of the window open and wriggle himself in, 'like an eel out of water', he thought, and laughed uneasily. He was really sweating with nerves by now: the whole operation had taken longer than he liked. He landed upside-down between the lavatory and the bath, but with nothing worse than a bruised shoulder for his trouble. He was in. He felt the adrenalin start to subside. He got to his feet, sniffed at the faint smell of mould, scowled at the ring of grime

around the bath, and tipped a toothmug of water into the
sad brown spider plant.

'Be of good cheer,' he told it. 'Thrive and grow: you're
about to become part of a whole new family.'

Ant used the lavatory and flushed it. Now to work, he told
himself, and set about the next most important thing after
getting himself in: securing his exit. Assuming that the householder had taken his own keys away with him, there should
still be a set of spares. Where had he hidden them?

The answer to that question didn't take long to find. They
were on a board by the back door, looped over hooks and
labelled neatly – Front door, Windows, French windows,
Back door. Couldn't have been better, really. He unbolted
the back door and tested the key labelled 'Back door'. It
worked. He put it in his pocket in case he needed to get out
of the place in a hurry, and set about exploring the rest of
the house. He needed to know that it would be empty for the
next couple of days, while Gren found them a secondhand
drive shaft and fitted it. Only then could they consider the
next part of their journey.

The woman came out of the house and got into her car. She
had a set, purposeful expression on her face as though she
was about to leave on a long and arduous journey, or commit
a crime.

She drove into the centre of Oxford, then took the road
west towards Botley. She followed the wide, anonymous
road until a row of shops that looked like warehouses loomed
their grey concrete shapes on her left. She pulled into the
huge expanse of a car park. She set her steering lock and
got out of the car.

Ahead of her a harassed woman with a toddler in a push-chair and an older child with a hot pink face and a petulant mouth pushed through the door and into the shop. There must be shop assistants, other customers, even. But all she could see were the tall, wide aisles filled with toys of all descriptions, shouting at her from their bright plastic packages. She started searching for what she wanted, saw a sign hanging from the ceiling twenty yards away and walked towards the back of the hangar-like expanse.

Dolls. Cute dolls, ethnic dolls, politically correct dolls with discreet genitals: she walked past them all and stopped by the old-fashioned dolls with realistic faces and soft, cuddly bodies. Toddler dolls. Baby dolls. One baby doll lying on its side in a blue silken box, its eyes closed, its limbs limp. Asleep or dead? She walked on.

White broderie anglaise bonnet, inflated pink cheeks, eyes of the unfocused blue that she knew from staring into other women's prams. Her doll. She recognized it. Biscuit-coloured face, wispy blonde hair, short chubby limbs, soft leather boots. She picked it up gently, as though it were a real baby, and cradled it in her hands: even the weight seemed familiar. She could tuck it under her jacket and walk out past the cash desks to her car. She could cradle its soft body and sing to it so that it closed its blue eyes and slept against her shoulder. She would claim it as her own. She didn't need to pay anyone for what had always belonged to her. Above her the signs told her that she was being tracked by closed-circuit television, that all the stock was electronically tagged. All for your protection, she murmured to the baby. She put it inside its box. Then she took it over to the cash desk.

'How do you want to pay?' asked the assistant, whose eyes

followed the badly behaved toddler as it tore the wrappings from another toy on the shelf.

A pause before answering. 'Cash. Thank you.' And she tendered ten-pound notes in payment. She stood and stared out into the grey anonymity of the road until the package was wrapped and handed to her.

She carried the white box carefully, so as not to turn the doll on its face or upside-down. She set it on the back seat and pulled the seat belt around the box so that it could not fall on to the floor if she took a corner too quickly. Then she drove as cautiously as if she had a real live baby on the seat, back to her own house.

As she drove through Oxford, she heard the first of the bells start to ring. The sound followed her through the town, increasing all the way, as porters tugged on ropes, or mechanical hammers struck on bronze. She wished they would stop.

'It sounds like a funeral,' she said to the baby in the box. 'That's wrong, isn't it? They should be welcoming the new life, not saying goodbye to the dead.'

Once inside her house, the woman lifted the baby from its wrappings, ran her finger down its cool cheek, held its soft body to her shoulder, cooed to it. Then she took it upstairs to her bedroom and opened a cupboard door. Inside, in the dim light, on the shelves, ten more babies sat and looked at her, holding up their stiff hands in supplication. Each wore a white cotton bonnet, each had its fixed blue eyes turned upon her.

'Here you are,' she said to the latest arrival. 'You'll be safe now.' And she placed it among the others. She drew her hand along the row of dolls, stopping at each waxen face to speak a few words.

'I didn't want to lose you. It wasn't my fault. But now I'll care for you. I promise I'll look after you.' Down the row she passed, until she reached her newest baby. 'Sleep well, now,' she said to it, and touched its cheek in farewell.

'Good night,' she said to them all. 'Look after your new sister.' And she closed the door.

Chapter 2

The Scholars who are appointed to the duty of study-
ing in the College are to have a common table, and
to dress as nearly alike as possible, and are to take
a care each for all.

Leicester College Statutes

Ant had found what he needed. A downstairs room fitted
out with a computer, printer, a wall full of books and a huge
square desk piled high with papers was obviously the owner's
study. A yearly planner was pinned to the wall above the
computer, and according to this, the owner was at the
moment attending a conference in Atlanta, Georgia. When
that ended, he was moving on to New Mexico for a further
week, flying to Colorado for three days, then back to Oxford.
They had twelve days, minimum. Ant could relax: he certainly had time to take a good look round the house.

To the right of the computer stood an upright piano,
covered with dust. On top of that stood three old valve
radios, their insides spilling over the surface of the piano
top. Ant whistled softly through his teeth as he went through

the rest of the house. There were things here that could come in handy. A long cabinet in the dining room was loaded with oil lamps in various states of disrepair, and the components of a dozen old coffee-makers. Wonder if you even know what you've got here, mate? said Ant to himself. Taken an inventory lately, have you? If Gren spent several days mending the van and if they could convince Angel to put her hysteria on hold, then there might be a penny or two to make here in Oxford. Ant turned over ideas in his mind as he went through the house.

The air had the dead feel of a place that had been empty for a while. The only danger was that a neighbour or someone might have a key and come in to dust, to turn on the central heating, to feed the fish and water the plants. But he didn't think so. It didn't feel like that sort of place. The fish tank was packed with something that looked like thick green fur. What was it? Weed? Algae? Ant peered in through the glass, but could make out nothing. What did he keep in there anyway? Piranha?

The two or three houseplants were already dry and dead, and the place didn't seem to have a resident woman. Ant pulled the two tell-tale envelopes through the mail box, but left the message for the milkman. In the rooms at the front of the house he drew the curtains part of the way across the windows. Now it would not be obvious that people were inside and moving around.

A couple of brass taps, some items that looked like part of a car engine, three volumes of a nineteenth-century encyclopedia. Opportunities for an entrepreneur, that's what it offered, this house.

Kate's phone rang. It was Andrew.

'I've rooted through the rubbish bin in the Common Room, Kate dear, and found the newspaper article you wanted. I did think, as I picked my way through used teabags and old sweet wrappers, that it might have been easier if you had popped down to Mrs Clack's and bought your own copy.'

'Mrs Clack closed her doors an hour ago, Andrew. And you've paid off one of the little favours you owe me.'

'Now, have you got your pencil and paper to hand?'

'Yes.'

'Well, the woman you want is called Dr Olivia Blacket, and she teaches English at Leicester College.'

'Isn't that your college? Do you know her?'

'I'm afraid not. I don't often go in these days. I do find the conversation at High Table a little tedious.'

'You're being suspiciously reticent, Andrew. What's the dirt on her?'

'None,' he said, too quickly. 'But she does have the reputation for being a tiny bit difficult.'

'Does that mean she has a filthy temper, or is permanently legless? Drugs, maybe?'

'Your imagination is overdoing it as usual, Kate. She is an exceptionally good-looking woman. Tall, slim, blonde. Beautifully dressed. Elegant, I think you would call her. But apart from that, I'm afraid that you'll have to find out for yourself what Dr Blacket is like.'

'So, I turn up at Leicester College and ask to see this Doctor woman, and wait for her to bite me on the ankle with her exquisitely pearl-like teeth?'

Andrew ignored her exaggeration. 'It would be better if you had an introduction. Perhaps that friend of yours' – Andrew would never bring himself to say the name of her lover – 'might be able to help.'

'Yes. I'll try asking Liam. How's Isabel, by the way?'

'As lovely as ever.'

'I'll see you at the concert. Goodbye, Andrew. And thanks.'

Liam Ross. His subject was music, but he spent so much of his time at his college that he must know someone there who specialized in the literature of the nineteenth century. Surely this was just the sort of thing academics chatted about at High Table. Liam said that they talked about their defective central-heating systems and the latest football results just like anybody else, but she didn't want to believe him.

She checked her watch. Liam should be free and in his room at college. She rang his number. He answered on the second ring.

'Ross.'

He was busy. He was working. He did not want to be interrupted. It was all there in the monosyllable. Kate turned on her warmest, most ingratiating voice.

'Hallo, Liam, it's me. Kate.'

'Mmm?'

She could see him at his desk, long limbs sprawled over the red and brown kilim rug. The fingers of his right hand would be keeping his place on the page of the work he had been reading when she interrupted.

'I need your help with my book.'

She heard him sigh. 'I'm a musician, if you remember. I deal in notes, not words.'

'I know that,' she snapped back. 'But you can still help.' When she asked him to help her with her book, she was offering him an important piece of her secret life, something for him to share. He shouldn't turn it away like that. Really, Andrew had been much easier to deal with.

She continued, 'To be specific, I need some background information on a nineteenth-century literary figure.'

'Try the Bodleian,' he said, dismissively. She thought she heard a page turn at his end of the phone.

'I already have. I was hoping to get to something more recent. Something unpublished.' Take some notice of me, she wanted to cry down the phone. Don't just fob me off like this with answers I could provide myself. Put your book down, give me all your attention, just for a couple of minutes.

'Not my field.'

'Did I tell you I was busy when you rang to complain about the lousy management at the theatre where you were trying to put on your opera? Did I tell you it didn't matter, since you were all amateurs anyway? So listen to me. Help me.'

'Go on.'

'I've heard that there's an English tutor at your college who has got her hands on some letters and notebooks that belonged to Maria Susanna Taylor.'

'Who?'

She sighed. 'Charles Dickens had a long-standing friendship, or whatever, with an actress called Ellen Ternan. Known as Nelly. And Nelly had a sister, Maria, who married an Oxford brewer, Rowland Taylor.' She was getting good at giving the background in thirty words. She hoped she'd be able to expand it to over a hundred thousand for her book. She knew she had told Liam about Maria and Nelly before. She hoped he would manage to remember who they were for another day or two, until the next time.

Another pause from Liam. 'Oh yes, I think I did hear

23

about it. We might have someone who's involved.'

'So, please can I have an introduction to her.'

'I'll see what I can do.'

'Soon?'

'As soon as I can.'

'Fine. Thanks. See you at the weekend?'

'Yes. I expect so.' And he put the phone down.

It was ridiculous to take his lack of interest personally. She reminded herself that they were getting on so well at the moment. She was even considering asking him to move in with her – well, for part of the week, anyway. This was just a small hesitation in the smooth flow of their relationship. He was probably in the middle of an important piece of work. She was short-tempered herself if someone interrupted her work, and there was no reason to treat Liam's as less important than her own. But however hard she tried to convince herself that all was well, she still felt dissatisfied with their conversation. Couldn't he have committed himself to their weekend with a little more enthusiasm?

Liam Ross logged off his computer and picked up a couple of student essays, humming a tuneful snatch of a Vivaldi concerto under his breath as he did so. Time to depart for a pleasant relaxing evening in North Oxford. He was about to lock his door and leave, when the telephone rang and he had his unsatisfactory conversation with Kate Ivory.

Four minutes later, Liam walked through the creeper-clad front quadrangle to where he had left his bicycle. As he unlocked the bike and rode off slowly northwards, he was no longer singing.

There were three bedrooms on the first floor, and the top

floor had been converted into one big room, now used as a workshop. As well as the cloakroom on the ground floor, there was the bathroom on the first floor where Ant had climbed in. In the basement he found a utility room with a washing machine and dryer. Good, it was about time they laundered their stuff: the smell of Dime's clothes was starting to get on his nerves.

When Dime had asked to join the family, Ant had taken him to one side and impressed the idea of personal hygiene on him. Dime was willing to comply, but had little experience of what 'clean' smelled like. He had sniffed appreciatively at Coffin one day when he had bathed using expensive rose-scented soap in their current home. 'Nice,' he had said, nuzzling up against Coffin's pale ears, 'Really nice.' Coffin had said 'Geroff!' and pushed him away, and even after his own bath, Dime had continued to smell of week-old sweat and last night's chips. Ant had yet to convince him that a bath should be followed by a change of clothes.

The owner of this house wasn't as particular about his housekeeping as Ant would have liked: apart from the film of dust over everything, no one had vacuumed the stairs for a long time by the look of it. There were balls of fluff, old scrumpled Kleenex, and a few odd socks under the beds. The kitchen wasn't too bad though: the washing-up had been done, even if no one had cleaned the stove for a year or two. Angel would scrub down the bathroom for them. Ant was particular about hairs in the bath, and wouldn't get into a bath with a grimy ring round it like the one upstairs.

The man should be grateful to us, he thought. We'll leave the place better than we found it. Not too clean, though, he reminded himself. We don't want him to suspect that someone's been in here. In his experience people did not remember too clearly the state in which they left their house when they went away. They were usually disagreeably surprised by the level of grime when they returned after even a short break, forgetting that that was how they usually lived. The family could clean the place up a bit without the houseowner being any the wiser.

On the other hand, Ant mused, there was little doubt that he would notice the other changes that Ant planned for the place. He stood for a moment in the hall, dreaming of the future. It was getting dark, though, and he could hardly see anything without putting lights on. Time to get back to the others.

Usually, after he moved the family into a new place, he changed the locks. But they would only be here for a few days and the owner was unlikely to return before they left. If they kept the front door bolted all the time they were here, no one could walk in unexpectedly, even if they had a key.

Before leaving to fetch the rest of the family, Ant went down into the basement again. Might as well have a bit of heating on, he thought. It could get chilly this evening, and it does Angel good to keep warm. He finished locking up (remembering to close the bathroom window) and let himself quietly out of the front door. He would have liked to clean the grubby fingerprints off the paintwork and polish the brass letterbox, but knew that it would be a bad idea.

He slipped the keys into his pocket and set off up the road like a grey shadow in the grey dusk. His mind was still on Angel. First they would go to Leicester and do whatever it was that she had to do there, but then she could commit herself to them and to their joint future. He hadn't told

Angel about his plans for her, yet. He was waiting till she grew stronger and understood better what they were about.

He would be back with the others within an hour of leaving them, in the short blue twilight. As he had promised.

It was important for Ant to keep his promises.

In her workroom, sitting at her computer, Kate Ivory was composing a letter to someone she had never met. She had found the name, O. R. Blacket, and the list of her degrees, in the Leicester College Memorandum, the booklet which listed all the senior college members, with their degrees, areas of responsibilities, and the year they were appointed, together with the College Calendar for the year, and its rules and regulations. She addressed it to Dr Blacket at Leicester College and she chose her words carefully, indicating that they had a common acquaintance, Liam, and interests that they both shared. She asked whether they could meet and talk.

When she was satisfied with the letter, she printed it out, addressed it, stamped it and posted it in the box on the corner of the Fridesley Road.

October was Liam's favourite time of year in Oxford. The crowds of tourists and language-school students had left, the undergraduates had just arrived and were still full of enthusiasm and good intentions. His workload, at the beginning of the new academic year, was bearable.

The sky had been a clear, uncluttered blue all day, deepening now in the evening to cobalt and pewter grey. Broken chestnut hulls lay on the pavements where the children had been thwacking the trees with sticks. It had been a mild, sunny autumn so far, and the bright leaves still adorned the trees. The lavatera and Michaelmas daisies sprayed their flowers over walls and fences as though they could go on blooming for ever, but cotoneaster and rose bushes were bright with scarlet berries to warn that summer was over.

Cycling up St Giles and on through the back streets of North Oxford, he sniffed appreciatively at the autumn air, with its hint of woodsmoke behind the car fumes. His earlier sense of unease as he had left his college had departed. He was free and unmarried and could do what he liked. And if he had two women in his life, rather than one, what did that matter? Just as long as they didn't find out about one another. He answered to no one. He pushed to the back of his mind the thought that these decisions of his were one-sided and arrived at without the agreement of either of the other people involved. Discussion would only cause argument and ill-feeling, he told himself. People were happier when they lived in ignorance. It was much better to keep his life in separate compartments. And on this note, he secured his bicycle to the iron railings outside a small house in a prosperous-looking road.

It stood in the middle of a row of similar houses, where all the paintwork gleamed, the gardens were well-kept, and the cars shone. Beside the front door, a clematis climbed up a wooden trellis, and terracotta pots spilled out their scarlet geraniums and trails of blue and white lobelia. After admiring the pleasing neatness of the street, Liam could not quite stop himself from checking quickly to left and right before letting himself in through the front door with his own key.

As soon as he opened the door, he was greeted – if that

is the right word – by a snarling, muscular mass of beige fur.

'Down, Ludo!' he said, and waited for the fangs and claws to retire a couple of feet before calling out, 'Olivia! Are you in?'

'Do you need rescuing?' She stood behind the dog, a tall, slim woman with fair hair drawn back from her face and fixed in some sort of knot on the back of her head. 'Basket, Ludo!' she said to the dog. 'Liam, you're early for once.' She sounded pleased. 'Sorry about Ludo,' she said. 'Brendan is in London for a couple of days and asked me to look after him while he's away.'

'Just because Brendan's the head of your department, doesn't mean you should allow him to dump his bloody dog on you every time he has to leave town,' grumbled Liam. He sneezed.

'I'll shut him in the kitchen while you're here,' she said. 'And a woman has to do what she must to further her career in our business.' She removed his jacket and led him into her comfortable, cluttered, sitting room. Already, a coal fire glowed in the grate. Welcoming, he thought. He felt at home in the muddle of books and papers that littered the surfaces. There was something clinical and unfriendly about a tidy house, he had always thought.

She removed his tie. 'How long can you stay?' she asked.

'I have a tutorial to give at ten tomorrow morning,' he answered, and sneezed again. 'Bloody dog!' he said, and moved nearer the fire, where he helped her to remove several more articles of clothing.

'There you are, Angel,' said Dime again. 'Don't you want to look at it?'

He spoke as though the city belonged to him, and he offered it to her as he might have offered a bag of sweets: spires, towers, domes and trees, gift-wrapped in pale blue mist, highlighted with pink evening sunlight and spread out below them for her approval.

'My feet hurt,' said Angel.

'That's because you're tired,' said Dime, sinking down beside her, his face concerned as he pulled aside the veil of her pale hair and tried to peer into her eyes. 'That was a long walk for a skinny little thing like you. I offered to get us some new wheels,' he said, wistfully.

'We've all had to give something up,' said Gren. 'You know you're not allowed to nick cars any more.'

'Could have come in useful today,' said Coffin. 'With the van packing up, and all.'

'Don't worry,' said Gren. 'I'll have it back on the road, no problem.'

'And what did you give up?' Dime asked Coffin.

'Boozing and fighting,' said Coffin. 'But what are we going to do about Angel?'

'She'll be all right after a cup of tea and a cheese roll,' said Gren. 'Soon as Ant gets back we'll take her to our new house and get a meal. Give her a few minutes' rest and she'll be fine. Won't you, Angel?'

Angel turned her head briefly to acknowledge his concern before retiring behind the blank wall of her face. One day she would escape from this cloying consideration of theirs. But for the present she needed them and she had to go along with it. When she was stronger, she would be able to leave them behind. For now, just like the others, she would depend on Ant. All they had to do was to wait for Ant to return.

Ant would solve all their problems for them.

The light was fading from the sky, and still Ant hadn't returned. Coffin, as Coffin always did, had taken out his whistle and was playing softly: something plaintive and probably Irish. He wore a green knitted hat with a rolled brim that he pulled down over his forehead so that it rested on his protuberant brow ridges. His curling hair bristled out over his ears. When he saw that Angel was looking at him, he grinned at her.

'Where did you get the box?' she asked him, idly.

'Used to have a flute,' he said.

'What happened to it?'

'I was hungry, so I sold it,' he answered.

Angel looked away again.

'Here he comes,' said Gren.

Coffin moved into a few bars of 'Conquering Hero' before returning to his former mournful tune. Even Angel looked up through her fall of hair to watch Ant coming up the hill towards them. There was something in the way he walked that let them all know that he had succeeded in finding a place for them to stay.

'Well?' asked Gren, when Ant reached them.

Ant pulled the door key out of his pocket and held it up. 'Your rooms are waiting for you,' he said.

'Now?' asked Dime. 'Can we go now?'

'I'm hungry,' said Gren.

'Wait just a short while,' said Ant. 'Sun's down. It'll soon be dark.'

'Dark's best,' said Gren, agreeing in spite of his hunger. 'We could get our things together, though.'

Somehow in the time they had been there, their belongings

31

had scattered over the grass, making them look more like a gypsy encampment than ever. The five of them bent down and gathered up their gear, stuffing things back into their bags, pulling on sweaters and scarves.

'Reckon it's a good place for busking,' said Coffin, looking down towards the town. 'Tourists. Students. They can be very generous, can students. They're not cynical about buskers the way older people are.'

'They can be competition, though,' said Gren. 'Playing classical rubbish on fiddles and that.'

'Worth a try,' said Ant. 'If we have to stay for a day or two, we might as well earn our keep.'

'But I still think,' said Coffin to Ant, continuing a conversation they had had many times, 'that I'd do better if I had a dog.'

'No,' said Ant.

'The punters love a dog,' said Gren. 'They stop and pat its head, and give you another fifty pence for dog food.'

'No,' said Ant.

Their belongings were now all stuffed into plastic supermarket bags, and they were still in possession of a large corner of the park. They watched as, in the twilight, a woman took her toddler by the hand and pushed her baby in a buggy in a wide circle round them. While she gave them a wide berth, her liver-and-white spaniel came across and sniffed at the bags.

'Here, fella,' said Coffin, and whistled through his teeth. The dog stuck its nose in Coffin's ear and licked his chin.

'Why do you have to do that?' asked Angel, irritably, as the dog investigated the rest of the group. 'You know Ant won't allow dogs.' She leant her body away from the spaniel as it came up to her. 'Piss off!' she said.

'That's not very nice,' said Coffin, reaching out a hand in apology to the dog, and stroking its ears.

'Sorry, Ant,' said Angel, before Dime could remind her about her swearing.

'Tanner! Come back *here*, Tanner!' the dog's owner called in a high, nervous voice.

The dog gave one last yearning look at the rest of their possessions, lifted a parting leg against a nearby bush and then trotted off after its owner.

Angel said, 'What are we going to do without the van? How are we going to get to Leicester?'

'Don't you worry,' said Dime. 'We'll get you there somehow. We promised, didn't we?'

Angel nodded and retired back into her own pale, angry world.

The van had broken down on the bypass. Gren had opened the bonnet and looked inside at the engine and closed it again, then had slid his long thin body underneath to look.

'Drive shaft's knackered,' he said, when he re-emerged. 'Going to need to find a secondhand one somewhere.'

'Will it get us as far as Leicester?' Angel had asked.

'It will when I've replaced the drive shaft,' said Gren. So they had had to leave it in a layby, stuff their most important possessions into every available bag, shoulder them and walk down into the city.

Ant turned back from the view and watched Angel. Once, she had had a different identity and a different life. He didn't know what they were, and Angel herself couldn't remember, not yet. But, gradually, with time and patience, he was helping her to find them. Ant wouldn't forget the day they had found her, and how he had felt when he first saw her.

There had often been suggestions that they should find themselves a woman. Dime in particular had felt the need for one. They hadn't wanted some scrubber, though. More a communal wife that they would look after and protect and who would care for them in return. Someone who would take their washing down to the launderette and heat up their food when they came back in the evening. Someone who would create a real home for them.

'What you're wanting is a mother,' Coffin had said, last time they had talked about it. And he was right, in a way. They wanted a mother and a wife. Angel had seemed an unlikely candidate for either job, but they had all agreed that she must be the one. At the moment, though, she was neither, just their child, their mascot.

The only coherent thing she had said, the thing that she had always insisted upon, was that she wanted to get to Leicester. She didn't seem clear as to the why, but she certainly knew about the where. But here they were, stuck in Oxford until they could get the van going again.

'How you doing then, Angel?' he said, by way of encouragement to her.

She gave him her wan little smile. 'I'm fine,' she said. 'Really, I'm fine.'

They both knew that she wasn't, but he and the rest of the family were working on bringing her back into the real world. And meanwhile that white face of hers, that underfed, submissive expression, would earn her share of the family's pizzas of an evening.

'Right,' said Ant, standing up. 'Let's move into our new home, shall we?'

Chapter 3

The Porters and other Servants of the College are
hereby instructed to prevent the entrance to the
College and its grounds and quadrangles of all beggars, all persons in ragged or very dirty clothes, all
players of portable musical instruments, persons of
improper character or who are not decent in appear-
ance and behaviour; and to prevent indecent, rude,
or disorderly conduct of every description.

Leicester College Statutes

It was Coffin's turn to make breakfast. His hair was still
damp and curled lower on his forehead than ever, but his
thick fingers were as deft with cups and plates as they were
with his musical instruments. The family were sitting round
the table in the dining room, with mugs in front of them,
and bowls for their cereal. Coffin had done his best to find
a matching set, because he knew that was what Ant liked,
but the mugs were all different, the bowls came in two
different patterns, and one of them was chipped.

'Put a mat on the table for that teapot,' said Ant.

35

Angel buried her face in her mug of tea. Ant looked around the table. They were all clean after their baths, and the third load of washing was on the go in the basement. He had found a powerful tumble dryer down there too, so the completed loads were already dry and folded in the bedrooms upstairs. It might show up on the electricity bill, but what the hell? No one would be able to prove anything against them by then.

Ant and Gren had done their best with the dining room, removing the assortment of junk that cluttered the table, and stacking the sideboard neatly with it. Angel had found a ragged duster under the sink and cleaned the top layer of grime from the furniture. What could the owner complain to the police about when he returned? 'Please, sir, these yobs broke into my house and tidied it, cleaned it up for me, then watered my plants. I want to lodge a complaint against them.' They'd just laugh at him.

Tired and nervous as they were when they arrived yesterday evening, they had all helped to get the place a bit more civilized. Angel had scrubbed out the bath when he had asked her, while Gren had dusted and hoovered their bedrooms. They would all make their own beds when they had finished their breakfast, after they had cleaned their teeth. The man ought to be paying them to housesit for him. Even Dime was getting the hang of the routine. The smell from his side of the table was a lot nearer to neutral than usual.

'What we doing today, Ant?' asked Dime.

'We're doing the tour,' said Ant.

'I'm off,' said Gren. 'Be back later.'

'Done your chores yet?' asked Ant.

'Yeah,' said Gren.

'Where are you going?' asked Dime.

'Out,' said Gren. 'Got work to do.' And he left.

Ant sent Dime upstairs to wash his face and hands again, while Coffin and Angel shared the washing-up.

'Were you really a musician, Coffin?' asked Angel.

There was a silence while they both remembered that it wasn't right to talk about life before the family. But Ant was still out of the kitchen.

'I played the flute,' said Coffin. 'Studied it, like. When I was good enough, I wanted to be a professional in an orchestra, or standing up on a concert platform, doing gigs on my own like James Galway.'

'You need money behind you for that,' said Angel, and she handed him back a spoon that wasn't clean enough.

'I was all right till I got the money,' said Coffin. 'There was this old bloke, fancied me, I suppose. And he gave me a room at his place to live in, which was good. But then, when he died, he left me the money so everything should have been great. But it fell apart, somehow. I used to get up at midday, go down the pub with me mates. Never got round to practising any more. I got through the money in six months. Sold all me belongings. Had to give up the bedsit. Even sold the flute.'

'Then he joined the family,' said Ant, who had come in while Coffin was speaking. He sent Dime back upstairs to comb his hair while the other two waited patiently in the hall.

Ant led them down the Cowley Road and over Magdalen Bridge.

'Right,' said Ant. 'This is where it starts. This is your main route into Oxford. This bridge—'

'What's it called?' interrupted Angel.

'What's it matter?' said Dime. 'It's just some old bridge.'

'Pay attention,' said Ant. 'Now, like I was saying, you might think this was a good place to start. Put Coffin, say, here with his tin whistle to catch the early morning commuters and the shoppers.'

'Nice view,' said Coffin, ignoring the river and the lush green spread of meadow. 'You could see the police coming in either direction and be off over the bridge before they could ask you to move on.'

'Nice view all right,' said Ant. 'But this site's not for us. I took a look here yesterday evening, and this place is full of tramps arguing over cans of beer and bottles of sherry. I saw four mangy dogs and a woman who was so paralytic she was shouting abuse at the punters. Now, that's no good for business. So we give this place a miss. The first lesson in trade is to find the right location. And this isn't it.'

'I dunno how he knows it all,' said Dime to Angel. 'He's a marvel, inne?'

They walked over the bridge and towards the centre of Oxford. As they got further into town, they had to keep pulling Dime away from shop windows, especially the expensive delicatessen in the High Street.

'You're worse than a five-year-old,' said Ant, as he retrieved Dime from a display of sticky cakes.

'I wouldn't know anything about five-year-olds,' said Angel, and kicked Dime sharply on the ankle while Ant wasn't looking.

'Come on,' said Ant. 'This way.'

'Just a minute,' said Coffin, stopping on the corner and listening critically for a moment to a fiddle player. 'Not bad,' he said. 'But the weather's getting a bit cold for fiddles. They go out of tune too quick.'

'How much had he made?' asked Ant.

'Not a lot,' said Coffin. 'Couple of quid, maybe.'

'He's not properly organized,' said Ant. 'Not like us.'

'Not got the right location,' said Dime, knowingly.

They followed Ant down a side street and stepped suddenly into medieval Oxford. Grey stone walls towered over them and black iron lamps drooped from their brackets.

'I'm bored,' said Angel. 'And I want to go to Leicester.'

'We're going to look at the colleges,' said Ant. 'And the theatre thing, and the round thing with the dome that you see on all the postcards.'

'I thought you were just looking for good busking sites,' said Angel.

'I told you, this is a day out for the family.'

Ant led them through tiny lanes that traversed a pub garden, where Dime sniffed appreciatively at the smell of beer and cooking. Ant and Coffin had to take his arms and march him past the open bar door, and back along a narrow, winding lane under the old city walls. They emerged at last into an open cobbled square with a circular domed building in the middle of it, like an oversized pepperpot. On their left, a college built in golden stone, decorated like a wedding cake with twin tiers, stood behind an ornamental metal gate. Coffin put his nose up to the ironwork and stared inside.

'What's this place?' he asked.

'It's old, isn't it?' said Ant. 'It must be one of the colleges, then.'

'And the round thing in the middle of the square?' asked Coffin.

'That's another college,' said Ant, with authority. The pepperpot building had a look of St Paul's Cathedral about it, though it was a lot smaller. 'Or maybe a church,' he conceded.

Behind them a tower and spire surmounted another old building.

'And that?' asked Angel, pointing. She had never seen so much architecture crammed into one small space.

'They're all colleges, aren't they?' said Ant. 'Or else, they're churches. Now pay attention, this is important.'

'Hey,' said Angel, who had wandered away from the others. 'There's a real tour going on here.'

'Take no notice of them. This tour's the real one,' said Ant. But Angel and Coffin had joined the group around the official tour guide, and Dime and Ant had to attach themselves to it as well if they didn't want to be left on their own.

The tour party was led by a young man dressed in a striped blazer and a straw boater, who was aiming for the *Brideshead Revisited* look. He waved a furled golfing umbrella above his head to secure the attention of his charges and launched into his account of their surroundings.

'In front of us is the Radcliffe Camera,' he began, giving the latest additions to his group a startled look. He was about to ask whether they had purchased tickets for the tour, then caught the snarl on Ant's face and changed his mind. 'This is the earliest circular library in the country, and was designed by James Gibbs.'

'The place is full of people reading books,' said Coffin, in disbelief, peering in at one of the windows.

'The thing about this square,' said Ant, 'is that it is unofficially controlled by the heavies employed by the big old library over there. Door security services. Bouncers. But what you have to remember is that they have no real power over you, not unless you belong to the university. So look around you, weigh up the potential.'

'And here on the other side is the Bodleian Library,' said the tour guide, raising his voice to drown out Ant, 'founded by Sir Thomas Bodley during the reign of Queen Elizabeth the First.'

'Now,' said Ant, ignoring the interruption, 'anyone who's come to look round Oxford, they're going to arrive in this square, aren't they? Stands to reason. Best-looking square in the country, this is. So we put Coffin over there, under that wall, with his penny whistle and his box for contributions from the public. And Gren can sit on the pavement over there, with his *Hungry and homeless* notice. It'll make a nice contrast to the size and wealth of the college behind him.'

Looking pale and thin was Gren's speciality when he wasn't looking after their transport. His long, bony toes poked through the holes in his trainers, his ears jutted out from his skull-like face, his ragged sleeves drooped on his thin arms. On a cold wet morning, Gren could bring in nearly as much in an hour as Coffin on his whistle. And the *Hungry and homeless* sign wasn't a complete lie: Gren was always hungry, however much he ate. His body seemed to burn up all the food he fed into it. And as for a home, well, it was with his family, and not defined by any particular roof over his head.

'We may have trouble with the competition,' said Ant. 'Since this is one of the prime sites in the city for our business, you can be sure that other traders and buskers will have their eyes on it. Leave it to me and Dime to watch your backs for you. And of course we'll use the normal routine for regular banking of the takings.'

'The Bodleian Library,' the guide was announcing grandly, 'has a copy of every single book ever published in the English language.'

A young woman who was passing at that moment, and who overheard the remark, laughed out loud. 'Where did he get that from?' she asked Angel. 'I've just been trying to get hold of a book by Maria Taylor, and they say they'll have to get it from Rome!'

Angel looked at her blankly. What was this woman on about, and why was she talking to *her*? She had never even heard of Maria Taylor.

Kate Ivory (for it was she, indulging her habit of addressing strangers in the street) was unnerved for a moment at the expression on Angel's face. It wasn't just incomprehension, it was as if the tenant of the mind was absent. 'Sorry,' she said. 'Enjoy the rest of the tour, and don't mind me.'

'Here, Angel!' Ant was irritated. 'I've told you we don't mix with outsiders. Get back here with Coffin.'

'Don't let yourself be bullied like that!' hissed Kate in her other ear. 'You make your own decisions. Believe me, it's easier in the long run.'

Angel shook her head, but she gave Kate her shadowy smile before turning back to see what the others were doing. Ant, who was still talking to Coffin, watched Kate leave the square and disappear up Brasenose Lane.

'What's that place over there?' Dime had stopped listening to Ant, who was always on about something, and to Ant's disgust was talking to the tour guide. They were losing all their discipline this morning.

'All Souls,' said the guide, speaking to Dime, glad that at least one of his flock was interested in what he was saying.

'And yes, the one with the dome is the Radcliffe Camera.'

'I wish I had a camera,' said Dime. 'I could take a picture of Angel if I had a camera.'

'And now for the Bodleian Library,' called the tour guide, who was finding Dime's line of thought difficult to follow. He led with his umbrella into a golden quadrangle, whose walls were furnished with huge windows, and in which stood a bronze statue that looked like Charles the First, but wasn't. His charges, including Ant and the family, all said 'Shh!' very loudly to each other, and then giggled, gathering some disapproving frowns from a passing porter.

'Nothing here for us,' said Ant, as their guide answered questions from the rest of the party in a hoarse whisper. 'We'd only get moved on if we tried to work here.'

'What about me?' asked Angel. 'What job am I going to do?'

'I'll show you when we get out on the other side,' said Ant, who had been up at dawn and out doing his homework before the others were awake.

They all crunched across the gravel on the far side of the Bodleian Library, in the wake of their guide.

The theatre thing was apparently called the Sheldonian, and used by university people for fancy-dress parties. 'Built by Sir Christopher Wren,' the guide confided to Dime, whom he had put down as his most appreciative follower. 'And those are the heads of Roman emperors,' he told him. Dime goggled at them as they emerged into Broad Street, but didn't like to ask whether they were real or not.

'Over there, that's your pitch,' said Ant to Angel. 'Outside Blackwell's.'

'The world-famous book shop,' as their guide put it.

'Just to the left of centre,' said Ant. 'In front of that black door. It'll set you off nicely, if you wear a clean white dress. We'll have you sitting there, reminding the punters of the fragility and mortality of all human life. Gren's got a nice line in make-up for you.'

'What do I have to do?' asked Angel, doubtfully.

'You don't have to do anything,' said Ant. 'You just sit on the pavement, and they give you money because you make them feel guilty.'

'Follow me!' cried their guide at this moment, and led them across the Broad and on to the pavement in front of Blackwell's, and just beside Angel's black door.

'Where does it lead to?' asked Angel.

The guide heard her. 'Now that's quite an interesting point,' he said. 'I'm glad you brought that up. The main part of the college is round the corner, in Parks Road. But this is, if you like, their back door. I'm afraid they wouldn't let us go through it: only their Fellows have keys to this entrance. We'll have to enter through the lodge, opposite Wadham. But the college is an interesting mixture of the original medieval foundation, with its Clifford Quad, and the eighteenth-century buildings, the New Quad. There is a rather dull Victorian addition, the Arnold Building, it's called, that is now used as student accommodation. An elegant Warden's lodging, built in the eighteenth century. A rather pretty Fellows' garden, I believe. And then, of course, there is the distinguished modern library, for those who have a good head for heights.'

He turned away from them to answer another question from one of the paying customers, so that Angel nearly missed his next remarks.

'Yes, that's right,' he was saying to some know-it-all who had stumped up a fiver to hear these facts. 'The college was founded in the fourteen-twenties by the Bishop of London, Richard Clifford, and later fell into obscurity. It was re-founded in the fifteen-seventies by the then Chancellor of the University, the Earl of Leicester, Queen Elizabeth's favourite. That is why the college is named after him. He gave the place financial stability, so that now it is one of the wealthiest in the university.'

'What did you say it was called?' Angel's voice sounded quite strange.

'Didn't I say?' And with an air of a magician producing a particularly plump rabbit from his hat, he said, 'This is Leicester.' Then he stopped suddenly. 'Oh, I say, is your little friend feeling all right?' he said to Ant.

'She's all right. She's just practising for her new job,' said Ant.

For Angel was sitting on the pavement in front of the black door, and it was clear that she needed none of Gren's expertise with make-up to render her face a startling shade of white.

Maria picked up her pen and continued writing to her sister.

I read today in the newspaper of an incident that would have interested our dear friend Mr Tringham, though perhaps these unfortunate occurrences are common in London. Here in Oxford, our criminal classes are less imaginative in their illegal acts, or perhaps less hardened in their wickedness. The incident of which I read this morning had to do with an unfortunate child who was

*robbed of its clothing. They call it, I believe, 'skinning'.
A young child, separated for a few minutes from its
nursemaid, who was momentarily distracted by conversation with a friend, was seized by two evil women,
divested of all its clothing, and sent naked back to its
distracted family.*

In France, Nelly would enjoy reading the latest news from
Oxford. It must be a lonely life for her, in a foreign land,
cut off from society.

All the way back to their house, Dime was trying to work
out what was happening. In the months since they had found
Angel and brought her into the family, he had stopped trying
to understand her, and had taken it for granted, like the rest
of the family, that she was a bit strange in the head. She'd
improve, they thought, and get used to the family and her
part in it. Dime knew what he thought that part should be.
He had known it since the first day, when they'd found their
Angel. Back in London, that had been. They'd had a nice
place at Notting Hill to live in, and were working the West
End. It was a mild but damp day in March, and the three of
them were going to meet Coffin at the tube station. Ant
would bank the takings, and Gren would take over his pitch.
Dime was going along with Ant to try to learn something
about the business.

Ant was talking. More like making a speech, thought
Dime. Ant's head swayed from side to side as he walked.
Gren, who was walking close beside him, their shoulders
touching, could hear all he was saying. Dime, who trailed a
pace or so behind, heard only the few words that blew over

Ant's shoulder as his head turned in his direction.

Ant's voice floated back to Dime through the thin drizzle that coated their skin and hair with an oily film. This drizzle seemed to absorb Ant's words like blotting paper.

Ant and Gren were so immersed in what Ant was saying that they didn't notice the girl, and it was Dime who saw her first. That's what he always said afterwards, anyway. 'It was me what found her,' he told Coffin. 'I saw her first, so I found her. And finders keepers. Isn't that right?'

'If you say so,' said Coffin. 'Finders keepers. And then again, losers weepers.'

Coffin often came up with rhymes like that, and Dime never knew what he was on about. He was a funny bloke. Maybe it was because he was Irish, or so he said, though he sounded normal London to Dime.

'I've got to get to Leicester,' said the girl, sitting down abruptly on dirty concrete. She had reached the third step from the bottom of the first flight leading down into the underground station, but it didn't look as if she could get any further that day.

'Here, Ant. Look at this,' called Dime, pulling at Ant's sleeve, wishing he would stop making a speech and start noticing what was happening in the real world. Ant turned reluctantly and looked down at the girl.

'You all right, darling?' he asked.

'I said I've got to get to Leicester.' It sounded as though she had said it a thousand times before, and no one had listened.

'Leicester? Don't be daft. You must mean Leicester Square,' said Ant. He looked down at the heap of rags at his feet. 'You're there already, dear. Pick yourself up, won't you? It's disgusting down there on the concrete.' He prodded at her with a toe. She kicked out at him and caught him on the ankle.

'She's barmy,' said Gren. 'Leave her alone.'

The girl's eyes shot open. They were a bright blue, though the whites were bloodshot, and brilliant against her grey face.

Further down the steps, round the corner, they could hear Coffin's tin whistle. They knew it must be Coffin because he was playing 'Whiskey in the Jar'.

But Dime seemed reluctant to leave the girl. He was standing close to her, and still talking, as Ant and Gren moved off.

'Where you from, love?' he asked.

The girl took no notice.

But Dime wouldn't move. He just stood by her side, and stared down at her, till at last Ant said, 'Oh, all right. We'll take her. Help me to get her to her feet.'

'She's a ruffian,' he said, as she kicked out again with her filthy feet at his legs in their clean jeans. 'We'll have to get her up the stairs between us, if we're going to get her back to our place.'

'She hasn't even got a name,' said Gren.

'She's my ruffian on the stair,' said Ant. 'And I shall call her Angel.' He grasped the girl by the upper arm. 'Grab her other arm, Gren. We're taking her home.'

'Her breath smells,' said Gren, 'she's worse than Dime.' But he did as he was told.

'You take her a minute, Dime,' said Ant. 'I'd better tell Coffin what's happening. Explain why Gren's not taking over from him.'

He was back a couple of minutes later and took Angel's arm. The four figures moved slowly back down St Martin's Lane. Behind them, Coffin lifted his whistle to his lips again and started to play 'She Moved through the Fair'.

Chapter 4

Neither rope-dancers nor players (who go on the stage for gain's sake), nor sword-matches, or sword players are to be permitted within the University of Oxford. All stage-players, rope-dancers and fencers trangressing are to be incarcerated.

Laud's Code, 1636

This should be one of the most beautiful times of the year in Oxford, thought Kate. Last week, the leaves turned to gold and red and brown. And then, two days ago, the clouds came rolling in, the rain lashed down, the wind rose and there were the leaves, dead, sodden and pulpy on the pavement. The tourists have departed and the students have returned. It should be a time of hope and renewal. But the faces are the same every year; only the names change.

She stared morosely around at her sitting room. Yesterday it was tidy, bright with sunlight, warm, welcoming. Today, what? Ruined. She liked to live with everything under control. She liked to sit on her sofa and admire a vase filled with a simple arrangement of flowers. She even liked to drink a cup of China tea and notice how there was no dust on the ornaments on her mantelpiece. She had to admit that this sort of thing didn't often happen to her, since she spent most of her time in her workroom, typing away at her latest book. Her neat, orderly workroom, she reminded herself.

Only a man could reduce a room to chaos in so short a time. Didn't he notice? Didn't he *care*? Were all men like it, or was it just this particular man?

Kate was entertaining her friend, and sometimes lover, Liam Ross. It was Sunday, and Liam was sitting on Kate's pink velvet sofa, reading the Sunday papers. He had bought two, which added up to an awful lot of newspaper. He had divided them into their separate sections, and these were littering the floor and the table, and were spread over the sofa itself, so that Kate feared that its pink surface would soon be marred by black smears of ink. She longed to gather up the scattered sheets and fold them and put them in a single heap on the table, but she knew that this would irritate Liam, so she stopped herself. They had just finished drinking Earl Grey tea and eating home-baked scones dripping with butter and piled high with strawberry jam. Liam's cup and saucer, and his plate and knife, had disappeared somewhere into the layers of newspaper.

What was particularly irritating to Kate was the fact that Liam hadn't bothered to speak to her for the past half-hour, apart from asking her to pass him the last scone. She had made a couple of half-hearted attempts to start a conversation, but had been rebuffed each time. There were two subjects that she wanted to talk to him about, but Liam had ignored her overtures, as if he knew what they were and wished to avoid talking about them. She picked up a handful of newspaper, folded it and put it on the table and decided to try again. It was time to prod him out of silence.

'You won't mind if I go to your college and talk to this woman myself?'

At last she had his attention. He looked up from the Arts pages of the Sunday paper with an expression of amazement. Kate never intruded in his place of work. 'What was that?'

'I rang you about it last week, but you took no notice. And I've been trying to talk to you for the past half-hour. I could introduce myself to her by saying that I'm a friend of yours.' She didn't tell him that in her letter to Olivia Blacket she had already done just that.

'I'm not sure that's a good idea. You know what academics are like. They live in their own world, and feel threatened when approached by outsiders. What is this all about, anyway?'

'My new book, if you remember, is about Maria Susanna Taylor—'

'Who?'

'Married Rowland Taylor, an Oxford brewer. Her sister was Nelly Ternan, close friend and constant companion of Charles Dickens.' There, she'd got it down to twenty words this time.

'Why bother with the nineteenth century? There's all that sleaze and more in today's papers.' Liam turned back to his paper.

'Libel laws. And anyway, I'm a historical novelist.' She wished that Liam could at least pretend to take some interest in her work. The proceeds from it had bought the food for their lunch, after all, and paid for the comfortable room they were sitting in. 'Perhaps we could meet for lunch after I've seen her.'

'So why do you need to go to my college?' This was the

one thing that would keep Liam's attention on her.

'I'm sure I told you all about it on the telephone.' Didn't he listen to *anything* she said?

'Tell me again.'

'Dr Olivia Blacket, of Leicester College, has been given the newly discovered notebooks and correspondence of Maria Taylor to edit. I'd like to know if there is just one whiff of scandal that I could use in my new book.'

'Ah,' said Liam. 'I'm starting to understand. There was talk at High Table, in between the criticism of the food and discussion of the wine, and interest in the latest football scores. I believe someone did mention the work that Dr Blacket was doing. And I remember now that you said something about it last week.' She had the impression that he remembered very well, but did not want to acknowledge the fact. 'Don't nag me about it. Give me time, I'll get on to Dr Blacket next week. These things shouldn't be hurried. They have to be led up to, gently. She—'

'Next week will be too late. I've already written to introduce myself, actually, and asked for a meeting with her. And I was hoping that you would have a word with her before then. Tell her that you had this friend – this *close* friend – who would be absolutely fascinated to hear all that she had managed to find out about Maria Taylor and her sister Nelly. Or if not all, perhaps just one fascinating snippet. Explain how we are sisters united against the male-dominated institutions, trying to earn an honest living.'

'And you think she's likely to share her findings with you?' He pretended a deep interest in a review of an exhibition of paintings in Glasgow. 'If you think that, you don't understand the academic world at all.' His tone indicated that the conversation was at an end. Maybe this treatment worked with undergraduates, but she was not going to be put off so easily.

'The trouble with you, Liam – *one* of the troubles with you – is that you like to keep your life divided up and filed in separate boxes.'

'What on earth are you on about? I do wish you'd get rid of the chip on your shoulder about your education, or lack of it.'

'You don't want to introduce me to your Dr Blacket because we belong to different compartments of your life,' said Kate, ignoring this. 'You think of her as work. College. Whatever. And me as . . .'

'Yes?'

'Oh, I don't know. Rest and relaxation. Carnal recreation. And you don't count what I do as real work, do you?'

'I think you've moved off the main point of your argument now. Are you complaining because I don't like to mix my professional life with my personal relationships? Or are you back on the grievance that I don't take those ridiculous books of yours seriously enough?'

'There is nothing ridiculous about a book that pays the mortgage.' Kate held on to her temper with difficulty. What was more ridiculous than spending your life immersed in the music of the dullest composers of the eighteenth century? She spoke as calmly as she could, but she could hear her voice start to rise in an unattractively vehement manner.

'I think the two are related. I think you're embarrassed to admit to a colleague that your partner writes popular romantic fiction,' she said.

'That's untrue, and quite unfair.' There was something shifty about the way he wouldn't meet her eyes. Was he ashamed of the popular fiction, or was it perhaps the term 'partner' that he objected to?

'Well, how about inviting me to dinner at Leicester and introducing me to your colleague in the English department, over sherry?'

'It wouldn't work. She hardly ever dines in Hall.'

'Unconvincing, Liam. So take me to tea, then. You did once take me to tea in the Senior Common Room, I remember. And I didn't entirely disgrace myself. Couldn't we do it again?'

'I'm sure I can arrange something, if you'll just stop going on about it.'

'So you'll speak to her for me?'

'Hmm.'

It didn't sound promising. 'Tomorrow?'

'Hmm. Yes. Perhaps. Next week.'

She wasn't reassured. She didn't trust Liam when he was being this slippery.

'Actually, the word from you needs to be right now, Liam. In my letter I've asked whether I can see her this Tuesday. If you could put in a word for me tomorrow, it would be really useful. But if you leave it longer than that, you can just forget it.'

Now she had his full attention. There had been a hint of an ultimatum in that last phrase. A small gamble, but probably worth it. She could tell by the set of his lips that he was furious. She could really go off him when he looked like that. Sometimes she wondered how well she knew this man, after all. Had she just been too busy writing a book over the past few months to find out what he was really like? Had she invented him, like one of her characters, and then expected him to live up to the script she had written for him? She said:

'Don't you think that she'd find it odd that I should go to see her, and that you hadn't mentioned my existence to her? I know I am ignorant of the workings of the academic mind, but in the normal world outside, that's how it would appear.'

'How would she know that we were friends?'

'I would tell her.'

He straightened the newspaper with an irritable crack. 'All right. That's enough. I'll speak to Olivia tomorrow, and inform her of what you want. But in future I would prefer it if you didn't approach members of my college with any more of your crackpot requests.'

No, she didn't know this man. He wasn't working to his given script one little bit. She would like to have a row with him over this Dr Blacket business, get some straight answers. But she knew that he would refuse to join in, and she would end up angry and frustrated, and he would just get on his bike and cycle back to his college, avoiding any unpleasantness. He would fail to phone her for a couple of weeks, and would walk back into her life when it suited him, expecting everything to be the same as before, without ever mentioning the subject of their disagreement. Then she would feel hurt and rejected, but would say nothing. And that kind of emotional turmoil was no help at all when she wanted to get on with writing a book.

She thought about raising the second subject she wanted to discuss with him, but he had bent his head to his newspaper and the expression on his face was not encouraging. She was starting to think that he was a very unsatisfactory man to have a relationship with. She enjoyed his company, at least when he didn't immerse himself in the Sunday papers. It was a pity that she was so fond of him, or she would throw him out of her life. But that was something she was no good at. There was always something that made her stick with relationships, however lousy they were. Her friend Camilla put it down to the fact that she had lost her father at a young and impressionable age.

'What can I do about it?' she had asked after one particularly disastrous passage in her life.

'I doubt whether you can do anything now,' Camilla had answered. 'It's probably too late. You've been repeating the same destructive pattern in your relationships for fifteen years now. I think you're set in your ways. If you really wanted to change, you could try some expensive therapy, I suppose.'

'Have you ever known it to work?' Kate was humbled for a moment by Camilla's assessment of her.

'No. Have you?'

'Can't say I have.'

'Oh well,' Camilla had said, after a short pause. 'I suppose your lack of a good relationship with a man does mean that you're available to your women friends when they need you. You're a pretty reliable friend.'

It made her a reliable lover, too, she supposed. Or at least an undemanding one. Treat her badly, and she'd still be there when you walked back through her door, asking for forgiveness. One day she must do something about this behaviour of hers. Perhaps Camilla was right and there was no way of changing it. On the other hand, she thought as her natural optimism reasserted itself, what did Camilla know about it? She was no expert. If she, Kate, managed to be strong and assertive in all the other areas of her life – aggressive, Liam called her when he was being unfriendly – with a little practice surely she could stop behaving like an idiot in her relationships with men. If she was serious about wanting to change, that was.

This morning I have a headache. There is a bird, black and bad-tempered, living behind my eyes, beating her wings against the prison wall of my forehead. She was there yesterday, too. Doubtless she will still be there tomorrow.

They say I have a headache because I have been think-ing too much. But how can I stop?

They say that I should look out on the green of the fields and the hill, and allow my mind to come gently to rest.

But I do not want to rest. I want to grow well, and strong, and leave this place to carry out the work I have to do.

The handwriting was really dreadful. It was small, and the letters were composed entirely of slanted parallel lines of differing lengths, without distinguishing loops. Not only this, but once the writer had filled one side of the thin, nearly transparent paper, she had turned it over and written on the other side. Then, as though the paper was being rationed, she had started crossing the sheet. She crossed one side, and again she turned it over and wrote at right angles to the text on the other. It was as if she was desperate to get her thoughts down on paper and was being hindered by some outside authority.

Deciphering all these pages was going to be a long job. The words blurred on the page as Olivia stared at them, and she rubbed her eyes to try to help her tired brain. She could hardly distinguish one letter from another and had only succeeded so far in making out an occasional word.

Child, life, she

This was all she had made out so far. She turned on the powerful table lamp. That was better. She would work on through the evening. This was the work, after all, that was going to make her academic reputation.

Ant had finished his tour of the house with Biro and pad of paper. He completed his inventory, and went back downstairs to where the family were seated on the grubby yellow sofa, in front of the television.

'How long do you think we'll be stuck here in Oxford?' he asked Gren.

'Look, it's not my fault,' said Gren. 'I have to find the right part, you know.' He didn't remove his eyes from the screen. The family were watching a detective series. At least, he supposed that Angel was watching. She sat in a corner of the sofa with her face turned towards the set, but the expression on it didn't vary at all. She might have been asleep. As Ant watched, the screen filled with an image of the oversized pepperpot, so presumably it was set in Oxford. Ant preferred real life, he didn't often bother with the drama on television.

'I'm not criticizing,' said Ant. 'I'm just asking: I've seen an opening.'

'Opening?' Gren's attention was still on the screen.

'An opportunity. So, more than two days, do you reckon? Three or four, maybe?'

The black and white cue appeared in the top right-hand corner of the screen, which meant that the commercials would come up in a minute and he could claim all of Gren's attention instead of the tiny part of it that was left over from the drama series. He waited until the sexy lady had stopped trying to sell them instant coffee granules, then said:

'What do you think? How long are we going to be here?'

'Yes, three or four days, I should think,' said Gren, reluctant to admit that he couldn't deliver what the family wanted immediately.

Ant punched his shoulder approvingly. 'You meeting your mates again tomorrow?'

'I might,' said Gren, his eyes straying back to a commercial featuring pension plans.

'Well,' said Ant, 'I've got a list of things we need. Any chance of getting your hands on them?'

Gren looked at the piece of paper. 'I'll ask around,' he said. 'See what we can come up with.'

He turned back to the second part of the detective series, and watched as high-powered cars chased each other down a surprisingly empty High Street.

Ant sat back and closed his eyes. He could read Gren's responses and knew he would come up with what he had asked for. For a moment he wondered how the owner of the house would feel when he returned from his conference and saw what he had done. Then he caught sight of the cobwebs hanging from the ceiling and saw how the television gleamed where Angel had cleaned it. You just don't deserve us, he thought, and put the man out of his mind. Tomorrow he would be out looking for suitable business premises.

Ant was right about Angel. She was sitting in front of the

television because it was easier than explaining that she wanted to be on her own to think things out. She turned her face towards the screen, but the moving pictures that she watched came from within her own head.

Ever since the tour guide had told them about Leicester College she had been trying to put the pieces of the puzzle together in a way that made sense. The trouble with this was that it brought back some memories that she would prefer to forget, and was useless at bringing back the things that she really needed to remember.

First of all, there were the days before she was picked up by Ant and Dime at Leicester Square tube station. She wasn't even sure how many days there were. A week, two weeks? Maybe three. She wished she could remember *something*. Anything. The earliest memory was of walking down the street – she didn't now know what street it was – and being aware of the fact that she didn't know who she was or what she was doing.

Of all the frightening things that had happened to her at that time, this was the worst: knowing that she had lost her memory.

She didn't know what to do apart from continuing to walk down the street and trying to pick up clues that would help her. She had focused on the oddest things, she realized now. It had felt as though it was imperative to find out what the date was.

She knew now that it had been that time of year when cold wet winter gives glimpses of the spring to come, when there is still a glimmer of light in the sky at five-thirty in the afternoon. Not the best time of year for finding calendars or diaries, but at least she found a half-price display of them.

She picked one up and leafed through the empty pages, wondered how far through it the world had travelled. What had she done with all those blank days?

An assistant walked over to her at this moment and asked whether she needed any help. What could she reply? What would the assistant have done if she had answered yes, and asked for help to put her life back together? She had shaken her head and walked out of the shop. She could at least have asked what the date was, she thought afterwards.

After this, memory turned into a jumble of days that brought intense cold, and soaking wet, and constant hunger. The hunger was the only reality that stayed with her from that time. That, and the sense of fear, of being vulnerable and preyed upon by other dwellers in the streets. She had nothing that any of them wanted, she realized now, except the fact that she was female.

Perhaps it was her hunger and the savage desperation that filled the hole where her mind should have been that kept her safe from the predators. She shook her head to clear it.

'Good, innit.' Dime's voice broke into her thoughts as the television spewed out another couple of minutes' worth of expensive commercials. 'That was Oxford, Angel,' he explained kindly. 'That's where we are now.'

'Yes. I know. Thank you, Dime.' And she returned to her own thoughts. She was lucky, really. She knew the name of the place where she was staying, and the names of the four people she was staying with. All these things represented enormous stability and progress compared with the uncertainties of those early days.

After the jumble of days – weeks? – when she had learned to kick and bite, and steal food, and find a place in a doorway out of the freezing night, the next clear picture was of the day when she met Ant, Gren and Dime. She must have been in a bad way when they found her, and she still marvelled that they had bothered with her. That had been in London, they had told her later, and they had taken her back to their place in Notting Hill.

She frowned as she tried to fit the pictures of that time together again. First, darkness. Then a jumble of voices. Loud voices, shouting, angry. Gren's voice telling her not to get upset – she thought she must have been shouting and screaming herself in her distress. Gren saying that it was only the neighbours, nothing to do with them. The family never shouted.

Then there had been a period when they were on the road, travelling. They had been in the van, and she remembered the noise it made, roaring through her dreams and nightmares. The growl of the exhaust, which got louder and louder. Then stillness for a day, while Gren fixed it. They had been off again after that, but at least the van was quieter. All that came back from those days was the memory of a lot of falling asleep, and waking with a stiff neck, or when her head jolted forward on to her chest.

They must have arrived somewhere, and moved in, because at last she awoke to find that her surroundings were at rest, and she was alone.

The first thing she saw was the round-topped green hill outside her window. It rose steeply, only a few feet away, filling her uncurtained view with green. It was the green of an undisturbed pond, the green that you see in midsummer when you lie on the grass and look up into the canopy of a chestnut tree. A little higher than centre and to the right was a patch of black and brown and white. She couldn't identify what this was, unless it was some demon crouching there, waiting for her. She knew there was a demon. But she had forgotten her name.

Later, when she looked again, the patch had moved, lower, nearer in to the centre. The shapes separated so that she could make out three cows. They were chewing grass, their heads close, their tails whisking away the flies. There were darker patches of green, like mangy fur, clinging to the sides of the hill. She saw that these were some sort of low, scrubby bush. Further up, the sprouting clumps distinguished themselves as trees. Low, rounded trees, crouching against the mound as if for protection, as though height and independence would be punished by the winds.

Some time soon she would be able to get out of bed and move across to the window so that she could see more than her green rectangle with its three grazing cows. That was more than she could manage while she was in the hospital. Hospital. She stopped the thought before it could move into dangerous country. If she could walk over to the window and open it, she would be able to put the view in context.

She was in bed, some sort of bed, but where, and how, she wasn't sure. There were covers over her, and she pulled them close, and rolled on her side. If she slept, and woke, and slept again, then when she awoke it might be easier to understand.

The next memory was of waking during the night. She rolled out of bed and shuffled across to the window. The curtains were pulled open so that she could see outside. Something had caught her eye and drawn her to the window.

On the dark hillside a white object stood out from the gloom. Something white had snagged on one of the bushes, and streamers tugged against the breeze. For a moment she had thought it was a baby's bonnet. But what would such a thing be doing on a dark hillside? She drew the curtains against the night and climbed back into bed.

Outside on the hill, the plastic bag, blown from some rubbish bin and shredded by the playful wind, released its embrace of the elder bush and continued on its journey to the east, until the wind dropped just before dawn and it found a final resting place under a hedge just outside Bideford.

Kate Ivory had Dr Olivia Blacket's reply to her note lying on her desk in front of her. Two lines. Two handwritten lines in burnt-sienna ink, on a postcard with the name and address of her college at the top. Dr Blacket was sorry, but she was unable to see Miss Ivory. And this after all Kate's carefully composed and worded paragraphs, after the discussion she had had with Liam on Sunday afternoon. She had ruined the atmosphere between them and sent him home early to his rooms in college, all for nothing. And with a little help from Liam, just a couple of words from him over coffee in the Common Room perhaps, it all could have been so different.

A horrid thought came to her. Perhaps Liam *had* spoken to Olivia Blacket, and in such disparaging terms that she had changed her mind about seeing Kate. No, surely he wouldn't do that. It was much more likely that he had simply forgotten to send her an e-mail message, or leave a note in her pigeon-hole, or however it was that academics corresponded these days.

What now? But she didn't have an inventive mind and a thick skin for nothing. After her adventures in Fridesley, asking people intrusive questions about a murdered dentist, surely she could cope with an ordinary, everyday, enraged academic.

Kate went to the telephone directory. It was an unusual enough name. If she was listed, Kate would find her.

A house in North Oxford, she saw. She noted down the address. Five minutes by car. She wondered when the best time would be to catch her. She wasn't going to telephone and give her any warning. Someone who could refuse a meeting in two lines, without a word of regret, would find the telephone brush-off child's play.

Be devious, Kate, she told herself. She rang, not Dr Blacket, but Leicester College.

'I was hoping,' she fluted down the phone to the porter, in what she hoped were donnish Oxford tones, 'to catch Dr Blacket in her rooms this afternoon. I need to speak to her before the next meeting of Governing Body. Do you know whether she will be in?'

It was a well-known fact that college porters knew everything about their Fellows.

'Dr Blacket,' replied the ponderous voice. 'Let me see, now. Monday afternoon. No, madam, I'm afraid you're out of luck. Dr Blacket will be at home this afternoon, working on her research papers. And she hasn't signed in for dinner in Hall, so she won't be in this evening, either. You could try her in college tomorrow morning, though. She's giving a tutorial at ten, and she'll be in her room at least half an hour beforehand.'

'Thank you so much. I'll do that,' lied Kate, and put the phone down.

She went upstairs to consider the most appropriate

clothing to wear when gatecrashing an academic's private residence. Powerful suit, she decided, and simple shirt in a bright colour. It worked for matadors, so why not for her? Sensible shoes for escaping in a hurry. Small but solid hand-bag for use as offensive weapon in an emergency. She was glad that her policeman friend, Paul Taylor, wasn't around to watch her. He didn't approve of her fibs and her methods of getting into other people's houses. Oh well, she hadn't seen Paul for several weeks, so she needn't worry about what he thought of her. It wasn't that she missed him exactly, but now that he'd come back into her mind, maybe she'd ring him up and ask him round for lunch some time. Lunch was an unthreatening meal, and he wouldn't get the wrong idea about their relationship. She could fill him in on all she'd been doing since she last saw him, and he could have an enjoyable hour disapproving of it all. She pulled her atten-tion back to the current problem, looked at herself critically in the mirror, and added a pair of long gold earrings set with large fake rubies. Then, more optimistically, she checked the contents of her handbag and added a notebook and a couple of pencils. She was, after all, supposed to be a novelist.

Ant was out on his own, touring Oxford again. He had set the others up on their pitches, the way he had planned it. Coffin was playing his whistle on the corner of Brasenose Lane and Radcliffe Square. The sun was shining after the heavy rain, and Coffin was playing some cheerful reels and jigs and smiling at the punters as they dropped twenty-pence pieces into his black instrument box.

'Thank you kindly, sir, madam,' he was saying, in his best stage Irish. The punters loved him. Students stopped to chat when he took a breather, and he gave them gems of folk wisdom in his cod Irish voice, to take back to their college rooms.

Gren sat on the pavement on the other side of the square, in the shadow. He looked pale and thin and hungry, his natural pallor helped by the judicious application of mauve and brown eyeshadow. He managed a weak 'Help the homeless?' as people passed him, and he, too, had accumulated several pounds in his open tin box.

Angel wasn't doing badly for a beginner, either. She was sitting in the position he had chosen for her, just to one side of Blackwell's. She seemed rather more subdued than usual since they had discovered the Oxford college called Leicester. But the family couldn't see what it could have to do with their Angel: it wasn't as though she was any sort of intellectual, as Ant had pointed out. It was just another of those coincidences, he had told her, like Leicester Square tube station, where they had first met her.

Ant had been round and made the first pick-up of their takings, and given them all a few words of encouragement. What they had made so far that day would pay for their food that evening, which was good. Anything over the top could be added to his capital sum, and invested in his other business ventures. Gren had been out first thing, meeting his friends and passing on the list of Ant's requirements.

'Get them for you by the end of the day,' said Gren, before settling himself in his new pitch.

But now it was time for Ant to make arrangements for his own enterprise. He needed a place near the centre, but not in one of the four main shopping streets. Off centre. That would be a good name for it, too, he thought.

Kate drove her car to Olivia's house. This was not a thing

she often did in central Oxford, since she usually found it as quick to walk, and a lot less expensive in parking charges. Today she wasn't so much wanting to save time as to impress Dr Blacket with her status.

There was a traffic jam just past the railway station. All the traffic had stopped to allow two fire engines to come out of the fire station, and now had got itself into an impossible tangle. Just as well she hadn't got an appointment, thought Kate, because she'd be late. Nothing moved on the road ahead of her, and she put the gears into neutral, set the hand brake and sat back to watch the passing scene.

To her left was a shop front painted an acid shade of green. The windows were barred, the door fitted with a grille and with warnings of alarms. She remembered it as a rather pleasant old-fashioned jeweller's, which had recently closed down after the local council had tripled its rent. The shop had stood empty for several weeks, which seemed a bit of a waste to Kate. Surely it was better to have a live town centre with small, individual shops, even if they did pay less rent, than to have the shops empty? It would probably re-open as an estate agent or building society. Or just another shop selling souvenirs to the tourists.

But perhaps she was wrong. As she watched, a man in his early twenties, dressed in black, with long hair combed back from his face and tied in a pony tail, approached the door. He stood for a moment looking in, took something from a blue backpack, and, after a couple of moments, opened the door.

Kate blinked. What had she just seen? Was he genuine, or had he just broken into that shop? And what was the point in breaking into a jeweller's shop when all the stock had been sold off and taken away? There had been some-thing familiar about him, too, though she couldn't quite remember what.

Ahead of her, at the end of the road, the cars were starting to move. She put the car into first gear and sat with her hand on the hand brake. She had time to glance at the shop again – nothing! – before releasing the clutch and slotting into the disappearing line of traffic. Had anyone else seen what she had, or were they all too busy listening to their Barry Mani-low tapes?

The previous shopkeeper had left the place clean and clear of all rubbish, Ant saw. He was pleased, because he was getting tired of cleaning up after other people. He tried the light switch. To his surprise the ceiling light came on. Only sixty watts, but at least he could see around now. He and Gren could come up with a bogus lease agreement that would con the electricity and phone companies into switching everything on for them, but this was simpler. And for the moment they could manage without a phone.

He paced out the floor to see how large it was. Twenty feet in one direction, eighteen in the other. And through the door behind the counter he could see another room where they could store the spare stock. Then a small washroom and lavatory. A cubby-hole where they could brew up their coffee. This could be the place. He went back into the shop.

The counter was still in place, and a couple of lockable cupboards with glass fronts. There was only the centre light at the moment. They would have to bring in some portable lights, or maybe go for something moody and atmospheric. And they would need a till for the cash. That was one of the things that he had asked Gren to get hold of for him, and Gren had promised to deliver them by evening. Good old Gren: always had the right contacts, whatever town they found themselves in.

He looked out through the window. The glass was thick and reinforced, and there was wire mesh fixed across it, too. That would keep out the officious bastards from the Council. 'Don't swear, Ant. Oh, sorry, Ant.' It was becoming second nature to him. The pavement was slightly narrower than he would have liked, but there was room enough if they were careful. And he had noticed that the shop backed on to the open market. That would bring the punters in.

This place would do.

He put his blue backpack down on the floor and took out the things he needed. Hand drill. Locks. Ratchet bolts. Non-return screws. Ant was proud of the speed with which he could remove one set of locks and replace it with another.

When he had finished, he put the old locks in his backpack. Pity he hadn't got the keys so he wouldn't be able to use them again at his next stop. But they were good for practising on, anyway. Gren was getting pretty handy at opening locks himself since Ant had taken him in hand.

He swept up with the dustpan and brush that he found in the cupboard in the back room, then let himself out of the front door, locking it carefully behind him. All they needed now was the stock. It was a pity they hadn't got the van working yet. They would have to find some alternative form of transport to bring it down to the shop. He didn't like to encourage Dime in his old habits, but he was ace at finding a suitable car and hot-starting it, and this had to be one time when they used his skills.

They were going to need more than a day or two to develop the potential of this site. There was no problem, even in staying in their present home for another week. Except for Angel. Ant frowned when he thought about Angel. It was all very well going along with this obsession of hers to get to Leicester, but what were they going to do when and if they reached the place? What did Angel think she was going to find and how was it going to solve the problem of the rest of her life? He couldn't see it, himself. No, the thing to do was to go along with her current idea that it was Leicester *College* that she had wanted to get to. It couldn't do any harm, and it would keep them in Oxford until he had made his killing.

Chapter 5

Concerning Dogges:
No fellow, scholar, chaplain nor servant or any belonging to the College shall lodge any dogg except the porter to dryve oute cattell and hogges out of the College and its Chapell.

Leicester College Statutes, c. 1550

'You'll have to wait a moment while I deal with Ludo,' said Olivia Blacket, as she opened the door. She looked Kate up and down, gestured her backwards with a dismissive wave of her hand, and closed the door again.

Thank you very much, Dr Blacket, thought Kate, as she stood in front of the dark red door. Is that your typical academic? No preamble. No 'Who are you?' No 'How nice to meet you.' Just the sound of retreating footsteps and the feeling that I might wait here for an hour and never see you again. She looked at the doorbell. Should she ring it a second time, or wait for the woman to reappear? She decided to take Olivia at her word, at least for the next two or three minutes. Then she would reassess the situation.

She looked up and down the road. Very nice. Very expensive. Very North Oxford. She could imagine that academics and their families lived in each of these neat houses. Their children did their prep. in those upstairs rooms, kept their bicycles in those garages. In those front rooms television-watching was strictly rationed, and books were thrust into eager little hands. Kate's long and vulgar earrings jangled as she swung her head round again to look at the uncommunicative windows of Olivia Blacket's house.

At which point Olivia reappeared.

'I don't think I know you, do I?' she said, and stared at her until Kate was forced to answer, instead of standing there with a false and friendly smile on her face.

'My name's Kate Ivory, and I wrote to you to say that I was coming to talk to you this afternoon.'

Olivia went on staring. 'I believe I remember your letter now. I replied. In writing. I said I couldn't see you.'

'Did you? Goodness, how odd. I didn't get your letter.' And Kate stared right back at Olivia.

'And you didn't think it strange that I didn't confirm our meeting?' Kate's eyebrows shot up to her hairline as she prepared to tell another creative version of the truth, but Olivia continued, 'And if it comes to that, why have you turned up at my house instead of at college?'

Kate was working at top speed on replies to both these questions, neither of which was going to be convincing, when luckily for her there was an interruption. A tall man who looked as though he had hidden a beer barrel inside his red woolly pullover appeared behind Olivia and peered over her shoulder at Kate.

'Olivia my dear, why on earth are you standing on the

doorstep like this? Why don't you invite your nice friend inside, and then we can release Ludo from the kitchen and introduce everyone. You do like dogs, my dear, don't you?'

The correct, if not the most accurate, answer to this question had to be 'yes', so that's what Kate said. It turned out to be as effective a reply as 'open sesame'. Within seconds Kate was inside Olivia's house and, somewhat to Olivia's cool amusement, pretending to be delighted by the attentions of a mass of beige fur and muscle that failed to respond to the name of Ludo, or to any of the commands that were shouted at it by the fat man.

In the end, Olivia took pity on them and tricked Ludo into re-entering the kitchen, then shut the door on him, firmly. Kate followed her into the front room, where the huge man had already retired. She noticed that only one of her dangly earrings was swinging against her jaw. Ludo must have devoured the other during his greeting.

'It is a bit naughty of me to bring Ludo round to Olivia's house,' he said, throwing admiring looks at Kate's remaining earring. 'I don't think she's very keen on dogs, but then she doesn't like to refuse to look after Ludo for me when I ask her.'

He made Kate sit next to him on a sofa that could have engulfed and drowned a regiment. Then he leant confidentially towards her, placing on her knee a hand so massive that it covered most of her thigh as well. 'I'm her boss,' he said, and winked.

'Professor Brendan Adams,' said Olivia. 'And Brendan, this is Miss Kate Ivory, who writes books.' She managed to look down her nose and sneer simultaneously. 'Novels, I believe. Historical romances, they're called.'

'What fun!' said Brendan Adams. 'Do you make a lot of money, Miss Ivory?'

'Enough,' she said, glancing up at Olivia Blacket to show her that she had won that last point. 'Do call me Kate,' she added. Since his hand was now enveloping her whole thigh, 'Miss Ivory' would seem to be on the formal side.

'Olivia darling, why don't you go and make us all a lovely cup of tea, while I talk to this charming young friend of yours?'

One hand was still on her knee, while the other had insinuated itself round her shoulder. His face was jammed up against hers, so close that she could see the vigorous brown hairs sprouting from his nostrils.

'Now, Kate, tell me what it is you want, and I'll see what I can do to accommodate you.'

This last sentence was so full of innuendoes that Kate scarcely knew where to begin. But she thought she would get down to the meat of her enquiries before Olivia returned and turned her icy glare upon her. Yes, she was just the sort of woman who would sign her letters with ink that looked like dried blood. For a moment, she wondered what she'd done to deserve the Blacket treatment. But maybe that's the way you had to be if you wanted to succeed as a female academic.

'Maria Susanna Taylor,' she said quickly, wondering whether she could remove enough professorial hand and arm from her person to extract the notebook and pencil from her handbag and take notes.

'Ellen Ternan's sister, you mean?'

Oh good, he knew what she was talking about. 'That's the one. I'm writing a fictional account of her life. But even without the scandal of her sister's liaison with Charles Dickens, she's a fascinating character, you know.'

'I do indeed. After her spell on the stage and the ten years of marriage to the respectable Mr Taylor in Oxford, she went off to London to learn to paint, before disappearing abroad to earn her own living as a journalist in Rome. I do so admire an independent career woman, don't you?' And the trunk-like arm squeezed Kate's shoulder while the warm breath set her sole remaining earring quivering.

'I'd like to show Ellen's relationship with Dickens through Maria's eyes. And perhaps show how Ellen's experience helped to shape her own life.'

'Well, where's the problem in that? There's that excellent book by—'

'Oh yes, I know that,' said Kate, impatiently. 'I know that, and so does everybody else. What I want is a snippet of something new. Preferably, of course, something scandalous involving Dickens.'

'You mean, you'd like to be able to prove the existence of an illegitimate child?'

'Or children,' said Kate, boldly.

'In spite of the fact that no one has yet been able to show that there was any such child? Or even, if it comes to that, that there was any impropriety in the relationship between Ellen Ternan and Charles Dickens. It is only in our own age that sex has become so all-important.' Again the leer and the suggestion of male hand squeezing female thigh.

'Huh!' snorted Kate, successfully brushing away half the encroaching hand. 'If it was all so proper, why did he force his wife to leave him? Why did he burn all his letters? Why did he destroy his diaries? And you're not telling me there wasn't anything *physical* going on when they travelled to France and back, when they were involved in that awful railway accident.'

'In the company,' interrupted Brendan Adams, 'of her mother. Your problem, Kate, is that you're looking at the story through twentieth-century eyes.'

'But if you'd go along with me for the moment, just think! The most likely time for it to have happened is while Ellen disappeared from the scene, and was apparently living in France. Now at about that time, Maria married her Oxford brewer and was living in a house in the Banbury Road – less than a mile from here, incidentally. Knowing what we do about her future life, can't you imagine just how bored she must have been? She and Mr Taylor appear to have parted quite amicably in the end, so don't you think she sat in her room, just down the road here, and made her plans and shared in the excitements of her sister's life? They probably wrote to one another nearly daily. Maria must have kept a journal, at least. And since she later became a journalist and author, surely she jotted some ideas down in a notebook. I don't believe that all she wrote about was the price of bread and how enjoyable it was having tea with the vicar's wife. Nor do I believe that every single page of it has been destroyed. This is Oxford, after all. Paper, especially if covered with writing, is sacred in this city.'

'Your enthusiasm does you credit, Kate, but what makes you think there's any hard evidence?'

'There have been hints in the press. Do you know of anything in the pipeline? Anything you can give me a tiny clue about?'

'I think you'll find that it's Olivia who knows most about it. "Oxford Woman's Shock Find!"' quoted Brendan. 'How poor Olivia hated that!'

'A friend passed the paper on to me. When I saw it on the newsstand, I imagined that some defunct foot had turned up in a pizza topping,' said Kate.

'What a gruesome mind you have,' said Brendan, and his eyes twinkled like jewels from the depths of crumpled leather pouches.

'It was the article about Olivia that put me on to her.'

'Tea,' said Olivia, coming into the room empty-handed. She removed a couple of books, three folders and a broken lamp from a small table and went out again.

'Do you think she'll help me?' asked Kate, urgently.

'Probably not,' said Brendan. 'I hate to say this, but Olivia is a little strange, or even obsessive, on the subject. I have tried to extract information, not to mention the odd letter, from her, but with no success. She is deeply possessive and jealous, I am afraid. Leave it to me to quiz her about it. She seems to have taken against you. I can't think why.' This last was accompanied by another mountainous squeeze.

Olivia re-entered with a tray bearing teapot and cups and saucers and put it down on the space she had cleared. There was a small swirling of dust as she did so. She poured cups of tea and handed them round.

'Oh, does anyone take milk?' she asked, as an afterthought.

'Yes, please,' said Kate, humbly. It was just as well that she didn't want sugar, since this would evidently be beyond Olivia's housekeeping skills to provide. While Olivia was out of the room, finding lost milk, Brendan Adams inserted huge fingers into an inside pocket and brought out a very tiny visiting card.

'Ring me this evening,' he said. 'We'll arrange a meeting at my house in Garsington, where we'll be able to talk. *In private.*' This last phrase was delivered with such a horrible leer that Kate moved eighteen inches to her left and out of the orbit of the professor's arms.

'Wonderful,' she said, and smiled up at Olivia as she poured slightly curdled milk into her cup of cooling tea.

Kate stayed for a further ten uncomfortable minutes in Olivia's sitting room before making her excuses and leaving. As Olivia showed her to the front door, Kate saw through an open door what was evidently both her study and the room in which most of her living was done. Dirty coffee mugs stood on all available surfaces: on a space in her bookcase, on the floor by the chair, on her desk. The *Guardian* lay in pieces around the floor, in a way that was all too familiar to Kate. She had the impression that someone had recently been in the room: there was something about the dents in the cushions, something in the air. Not as definite as an aftershave, or a perfume, but still the air had been used, breathed in and out by some other pair of lungs, warmed by some other body. It was just a fleeting impression, then Kate was at the front door, shaking Olivia's hand, saying good-bye.

When she was halfway home to Fridesley, and approaching the railway station, Kate remembered the odd occurrence at the green-painted shop. The lights were red, and she looked over at the empty building as she waited for them to turn. There was nothing to be seen there now. The door was shut and there were no lights inside. But as the traffic lights turned green and she drew away past the station, Kate remembered where she had seen the man in the black jeans and T-shirt before. Radcliffe Square. He was the one who had bullied the young woman with the empty eyes.

In East Oxford, Angel was supervising the cleaning of the house.

'If we're going to live here for a week or more, we've got to get rid of the squalor,' she had said. Ant was pleased to notice that she no longer used the obscene word that began with a c and ended with a p. Perhaps she was getting tired of the chorus of 'No swearing, Angel!' that followed her outbursts, and of saying 'Sorry, Ant.' Or maybe she was getting the hang of the family customs and wanted to conform to them.

Once she had got over her original shock at finding that Oxford had a college called Leicester, Angel had improved no end, Ant thought. She had really got down to a bit of housework. The owner of the house would return to find his sheets washed and aired, folded and put away in the closet. His carpets were hoovered, his bathroom gleaming. Even the top of his gas stove, and the grill pan with the burned-on grease, were looking a little more respectable. The room where they watched television in the evenings was now warm, clean and cosy. Angel had spent three pounds fifty of her begging money on a bunch of flowers from the Covered Market. She had found a couple of colourful woollen rugs which she had draped over the stained velvet of the sofa and one of the chairs. She had even found some cushions at the back of one of the wardrobes upstairs. Nothing matched very well, but the effect was a lot more comfortable than it had been when they arrived.

Looking over at her face as she scrubbed the grey ring of grease from the kitchen sink, Ant thought he had never seen her so animated. Maybe she had given up at last on the idea of finding whatever it was that she had lost. Of course, she had also lost her memory of her past life, but did she really need it? She had made a new life with Ant and the family, and maybe at last she was seeing that this was the most important thing.

She's a good little housekeeper, thought Ant. She's going to make us a good little wife.

Garsington. Home of Lady Ottoline Morrell. This was where she invited all those self-obsessed bores of the Bloomsbury set for their Friday-to-Mondays. It put it in perspective to remember that Ottoline, too, had married into a wealthy Oxford brewing family, even if her husband was Member of Parliament for the county, and preferred to forget about the beer.

Kate's first impression of Garsington was of a long straight road bordered by ugly and identical between-the-wars grey houses. Not what she had imagined as a setting for the flamboyant Professor Adams. But, following his directions, she turned left and found herself in an older and much more attractive part of the village.

The Old Buttery was a long and rambling stone cottage, with an undulating tile roof and an oak door with a black lion's head knocker.

'The name Old Buttery was the invention of a previous owner,' said Professor Adams as he showed her in. 'He didn't feel that Number Six, Upper Church Lane, was quite impressive enough.'

Unlike Olivia's house, where the overcrowded rooms had made Kate feel uncomfortable, the professor's house seemed to have acquired its furniture and possessions over several generations of the same family. Chintz chair covers and faded curtains, cushions embroidered by some long-dead great aunt, sturdy old furniture smelling faintly of beeswax. And a layer of dog hair over all. The epitome of English country living. It all looked as though it had grown there. Surely no one had ever walked into a shop and ordered any of it. Unless of course there was an interior decorator so expensive that she could conjure up this amazingly harmonious mixture of patterns and styles.

'Come in, Kate,' said Brendan Adams. To her relief, now that he had her at his mercy, alone in his country cottage, the professor was behaving like a perfect gentleman. She could have worn something a little more flamboyant than her dark green trousers and shirt, and the cream linen jacket that she had considered too ladylike to provoke an attack. Even her earrings were smallish and made of real gold. She looked very much the English country lady, she thought, though perhaps the four inches of multicolour-striped socks that showed when she sat down spoiled the restrained image.

'Would you like a sherry, dear? Or a whisky, perhaps?'

She looked up towards the door, in the direction of the voice, and nearly shot to her feet in surprise. It was the professor, in drag. Tweed skirt, blue twinset, string of pearls and thick brown tights. He'd got the smudged make-up just right, and was wearing a grey, windswept wig.

'My sister, Frances,' said the professor's voice from behind her. Well, thank goodness for that. That explained his excellent behaviour, too.

'Thank you, Miss Adams. I'd really like a small whisky,' she said. She reckoned she needed it after a scare like that. 'I'm driving, but I can manage the one.'

'Doctor,' said the professor. 'Not Miss. My sister is the expert on nineteenth-century handwriting. Which is why I thought you might like to meet her.'

They sat with their whiskies – large for the professor and her sister, and small for Kate – side by side on one of the sagging but unusually comfortable sofas. Kate felt something digging into her, and retrieved a dog collar and a volume of *Martin Chuzzlewit* from under the cushion. She wondered why, if he lived with his sister, the professor found it necessary to drop his dog off on Olivia Blacket when he went away, but guessed it was simply because he enjoyed teasing the woman. It was a temptation she might have fallen for herself.

'Now, Professor, where do we start?'

'Call me Brendan,' said the professor, with just the hint of his previous leer, before he remembered the presence of his sister. 'And I know that my sister would like you to call her Frances.'

The windswept grey hair nodded from the other end of the sofa. If she got a leer from that side, Kate wasn't at all sure what she would do. The professor was speaking:

'Now, you know about Maria Ternan, or Taylor as she became when she married, coming to live in a large house in the Banbury Road.' Kate nodded. 'And it was thought that there were no diaries and letters existing from the family during the eighteen-sixties.' Kate nodded again. 'But you were right about people in Oxford not wanting to throw away paper with writing on. Bartlemas has just taken on a properly qualified archivist, and she has sorted through the boxes full of papers that were bequeathed to the college over the years. Their muniments room was full of cartons of old accounts books, letters and goodness knows what. She has indexed them and dated them and put them in order and stored them in proper conservation conditions. Really, she has done them a lovely, professional job.'

'And she's come across some of the Ternan/Taylor correspondence,' put in Kate enthusiastically. 'Some love letters from Dickens himself?' Her imagination started to run riot and Frances put in quickly:

'I have one or two pages here to show you, so that you'll understand what the problem is.'

At last, a glimpse of the outpourings of a love-torn actress, the confessions of the country's greatest novelist, the . . .

'Look at this,' said Frances, and she put a sheet of paper, slightly smaller than A5, on the table in front of Kate.

Well, it might have been all the things that Kate had thought, and more, but on the other hand it might have been a laundry list, or a note to the milkman telling him to leave three pints of semi-skimmed milk and a large pot of strawberry yoghurt.

The writing on the paper was formed by parallel strokes of the nib. The strokes had no loops, and were differentiated one from another only by their length.

'This handwriting takes some getting used to if you wish to read it,' said Frances.

'You can say that again.'

The person who wrote the letter – or whatever it was – was also apparently short of paper. She had left slight spaces between her lines, but when she had reached the bottom of the paper, she had turned it through ninety degrees and written an equal amount at right angles to the original. Then, she had turned the sheet over and done the same on the other side. The paper was no thicker than modern airmail paper, the ink was very black, the nib was old and thick. The writing from one side showed quite clearly through to the other.

'How do you even start to decipher it?'

'With an alphabet,' said Frances.

'You look through it,' explained Brendan, 'and see whether you can pick out any words you recognize. Look, here at the bottom of the page, when she crossed it, she didn't quite fill this side. It's easier to see this line.'

'We're only talking relatively easier,' said Kate, who still couldn't make out anything.

'Well, dear,' said Frances. 'Look just here. One of the first things we do is to look for the proper nouns that we would expect to find: names of friends and family, placenames. You can see that this must be a proper noun of some sort. It has a capital letter at the beginning, and is quite long, some eight letters.'

'If you say so,' said Kate, doubtfully. But as she looked at the scratches on the paper, she began to understand what Frances was talking about. 'The initial capital could be a T,' she said hesitantly.

'That's what I think, too,' said Frances. 'And I believe that the word is "Tringham".'

'I think so, too,' said Brendan, from Kate's other side, and she felt a friendly nudge from his enormous thigh against her own.

'Now, if we are right, this already gives us eight letters in our alphabet, though our correspondent does still use two different forms of the letters r and s.'

'And of course, we will have to verify them when we come across other words that we recognize,' said Frances.

'But we can make a start,' said Brendan. And in the manner of a television cook who has just said 'And here is one that I made earlier', he produced another piece of paper. 'Here, look at this. Frances made it.' And he indicated where she had very carefully copied the eight letters of Tringham, and added some others, and with admirable neatness, had written the translations beside them.

Kate nodded. At this rate it would take a month to read this one page.

'It does get easier, believe it or not,' said Frances. 'Once you have made your alphabet, you get your eye in, and you can read it comparatively easily.'

'She's right, you know,' said Brendan. 'I know at this moment you can't see that we'll ever be able to read a page like this, but we will.'

'And we have made some progress, as you see,' said Frances. On the alphabet page she had laboriously worked out some fifteen letters.

'I have a couple of questions,' said Kate, slowly, wondering how she was going to put them without antagonizing the Adamses. She started with the easier one. 'Do we know who wrote this letter – or whatever it is?'

'We can't be certain,' said Brendan. 'There's no signature, and we have nothing else to compare it with at the moment. We would like to think that it is written by Ellen, but we need to get our hands on the rest—' He stopped.

'If you're Olivia's boss, why can't you simply ask her to hand them over?' asked Kate.

'These documents have come to Dr Blacket through her

old college,' said Brendan. 'The college where she was an undergraduate. So a Fellow of Leicester has no right whatsoever to demand that she give them up. I have tried to exert just a little pressure . . .' He stopped, as though unwilling to continue this line. Kate thought of Ludo's jaws and wondered if Brendan would stop kennelling the dog at Olivia's if she agreed to share the Ternan Papers with him.

'If Dr Blacket is looking after those materials, and transcribing them and doing whatever it is scholars do to pieces of paper with writing on—'

'We call them manuscripts,' whispered Frances, in her ear.

'Well, what is this manuscript doing here? Does Olivia know that you've got it?' She waited to see whether they would throw her out of their house, but Brendan smiled a large and appreciative smile at her. The smile took in her legs, her round grey eyes and short blonde hair, but also expressed approval of her mind. Kate could get to like Professor Adams. He was wasted on Olivia Blacket, she thought.

'I may have mentioned that we are just the tiniest bit worried about Dr Blacket at the moment,' he said.

'I didn't score her very highly on basic social skills,' said Kate. 'But I didn't think that was unusual in an Oxford Senior Common Room.'

'No, no,' said the professor. 'I wasn't referring to her appalling rudeness. She's always been a complete cow, especially to other women, hasn't she, Frances?'

Frances nodded. 'I'm afraid so,' she said, and the sofa shook in sympathy.

'No, this time it's more than that. She really is getting rather *peculiar* about these letters and notes of Maria Taylor's. She has a very firm notion in her head as to what they are about, and I'm sure you appreciate that this is not a good idea when you approach a new piece of work. You should have an open mind, be prepared to find anything.'

'Even the presence of two illegitimate children?'

'Even the existence of nothing but laundry lists and an account of a teatime visit to the vicar's wife.'

'And is that why you nicked one of the papers? You wanted to see for yourself what it was about.'

'I should prefer to use the term "borrowed", but yes, you have the gist of it.'

'And can you tell me what Olivia Blacket thinks she's found?'

'Olivia at present is obsessed with the idea of babies,' said Frances. 'I suppose it's her age. Once you're over thirty and the years start ticking away, you have to make your mind up, don't you? Whether to take time off from your career to find a partner and have children, or whether to give the idea up for ever. There aren't many years left where all the options are open to you.'

Behind Frances's head glowed a high-relief in burnished golden wood of a madonna and child. The mother's head inclined tenderly towards her child. The child lifted a trusting hand towards his mother.

'How do you mean, obsessed with babies?' asked Kate. 'I thought everyone wanted to find evidence that Charles Dickens had an illegitimate baby or two with Ellen Ternan, but the canny old thing had removed all the documentary traces. I mean, why would you bother to pore through Maria's papers if you weren't looking for scandal among the literary greats?'

Frances looked her disapproval. 'Now, that is just what I

mean about keeping an open mind when reading the note-books. We are interested in them for whatever light they throw on the people involved, not just to prove that a scandal existed. But when it comes to Olivia, I have to say that for a number of months it is as though her head were filled with the thought of babies, and from a very morbid viewpoint. Everything she sees or touches speaks to her only of that. She could read a page about the price of cabbages and still find babies in there, I am afraid.'

'She didn't strike me as the strongly maternal type,' said Kate.

'But who can tell?' said Frances. 'She probably decided back in her early twenties that she wanted an academic career, and babies didn't come into her calculations. But now, well, the results of that decision are coming home to her. She hasn't got time to do anything about it at the moment, but she doesn't want to let go of the possibility entirely. The conflict of interests is affecting her judgement, I'm afraid.'

Kate wanted to point out that this was old-fashioned sexist nonsense, but didn't want to start arguing with Frances Adams. 'You think she's seeing babies everywhere?' she asked. 'In a manner of speaking, of course.'

'She seems to think that these papers are full of stories of the birth and death of children. She may well be right, of course, but Brendan and I wanted to assure ourselves that she wasn't misreading the evidence.'

'And what have you found?'

'You understand that this one leaf may well not be rep-resentative of the whole,' said Frances.

'Yes. But?'

'What we have found so far are some very sharp observations on the life of a North Oxford matron in the eighteen-sixties, with the underlying message that Maria was bored out of her mind by it. And there are indeed a couple of sentences referring to Nelly, where she seems to be saying that she is glad that her sister has not jeopardized the good name of the family by doing anything silly.'

'Oh!' Kate couldn't help sounding disappointed. Major silliness was just what she was hoping to find.

'Yes, well, I warned you that we might well be dealing with laundry lists.'

'What happens next?' Kate could see her spicy snippet disappearing out through the professor's mullioned window.

'If you look again at this leaf, you will see that it is numbered in the top right-hand corner. This means that it has been indexed and transcribed by Olivia Blacket.'

'So now you want to see what she says in her transcription, and whether it agrees with your own.'

'Of course,' said Frances, 'our own version is far from complete, and we are dealing with substantially less material than Dr Blacket, so we may well be mistaken in our conclusions—'

'Yes, yes,' interrupted Brendan. 'But Kate's right. We would love to get our hands on Olivia's version. But it looks as though we are going to have to wait until she is ready to publish, I'm afraid.'

'Haven't you tried to "borrow" the relevant page?' asked Kate, whose mind often ran in unconventional grooves.

'It doesn't appear to be in her North Oxford study,' said the professor, carefully.

Kate wondered for a moment whether the dog Ludo was

trained to sniff out interesting documents, but remembering the size and sharpness of his fangs, discarded the idea. The naughty old professor must have been rootling among Olivia's papers on one of his visits to her house.

'So if it's not in her house, can we assume that it's in her room at college?' asked Kate.

'Very likely,' said Brendan.

'So why can't you visit her there and see whether you can find it?' asked Kate.

'Oh no,' said Brendan, shocked. 'I couldn't do that.'

'Not in college,' added Frances. 'It wouldn't be at all the thing.'

Kate thought that she would never understand the Oxford academic mind. Apparently it was a bit of a giggle to con your way into someone's private house, using a combination of your superior status and the presence of your horrible dog, and then pocket a piece of their property. But to do the same thing in their college? Oh no, never. Unthinkable.

Kate, on the other hand, being a graduate of no other university than that of Life, had no such scruples.

She stood up and brushed ineffectually at the clumps of beige dog hair clinging to her trousers. She would have liked to stay and find out everything that the pair of them knew about Dickens and the Ternans, but it had got to that hour where, if you didn't leave quickly, it looked as though you were angling for an invitation to lunch. She thanked the professor and his sister for all their help.

'We thought you'd be interested in this manuscript,' said Frances. 'So I took the precaution of photocopying it before you arrived. It isn't quite as easy to work with as the original, but I'm sure you'll cope.' And she handed Kate the photocopy of page forty-three.

Kate did wonder just for a moment whether she was being given it as an inducement to lay her hands on Olivia's transcription. But no, Frances wouldn't think in so devious a manner. Would Brendan? It was one more reason for seeing whether she could borrow more of Olivia Blacket's work, though.

But as she drove home, she was wondering why it was that neither of them had mentioned the fact that 'Tringham' was the name that Charles Dickens used when he took out the lease on a house for himself and Nelly Ternan.

The road between Garsington and Cowley is long, straight and empty. Kate stood beside her car, where she had pulled on to the verge, and stared up and down it. There was no other car to be seen. In the distance, the distinctive skyline of the old Rover car works. In the middle distance, the grey bulk of a gasometer. No houses. No phone box. And her car, after handling in a strange manner for the past couple of miles, had started juddering and had worried her so much that she had pulled up off the road.

She locked the doors, took out her handbag, thanked heaven for sensible shoes, and set out to walk to the nearest garage.

She had gone about a quarter of a mile, and her car was still comfortingly visible every time she turned round to check, when she heard another car slow down behind her and draw in. She waited for the 'Give you a lift, darlin'?' that she dreaded on a lonely road.

But, 'Is that your vehicle in a stationary condition on the verge, madam?'

A nice, clean-cut policeman in a nice, clean police car. She turned to smile at him.

'Hallo, Kate.' He didn't sound surprised to see her. Paul Taylor. She stopped smiling. She hated looking a fool in front of him, and that was what always seemed to happen to her.

'I thought you might need a lift to the nearest telephone. I assume you do belong to one of the breakdown services.'

'I always meant to get round to joining,' she said. 'But somehow I never quite managed it. And how did you know it was me?'

'I can remember the number of your vehicle, and anyway, I recognized the blonde hair and the determined stride from half a mile back. Why don't you hop in?'

'Is it allowed?'

'Probably not. But if anyone asks, I can think up a reason.'

'And where are we going?'

'To find you the nearest car breakdown service.'

'One I can afford?'

'I'll do my best.'

There was something very restful about letting Paul Taylor take over the small and messy bits of her life and put them back together in a more appropriate order. The only problem was that she had the idea that, given half an ounce of encouragement, he would want to take over the large and unmanageable mess that was her emotional life, and put himself in the middle of it, and sort it out and leave it looking clean and neat and tidy. It would make her life calm and predictable, she was sure. And Liam would no longer be in evidence. What she wasn't so sure about was whether that was what she really wanted.

She looked at his pleasant and dependable profile as he drove in his usual competent way towards the city. There was plenty of time. She wasn't even as old as Olivia. She didn't have to make decisions affecting the whole of the rest of her life just yet.

Angel was sitting on the bed in her room. It was dusk, but she hadn't drawn the curtains or put the light on. It was easier to think like that, in the dark.

Long ago, when she had first met Ant and the family, she had told them that she couldn't remember her name or anything else about herself, and that had been true. She had known that she needed to get to Leicester, but she couldn't remember why.

What she hadn't told any of them was that there was one name she could remember. She hadn't known what it meant, except that it was associated in her mind with Leicester and her desperate need to get there. She also knew that it wasn't her own name.

But now, it was coming back to her. Little by little. Not all of it, by any means. Glimpses. Odd flashes and scenes on the screen of her memory.

Ant would tell her that she shouldn't keep it to herself. She should share it with the family, leave it to them to solve as a group. She wondered what Dime, for instance, would make of her story, what suggestion he would make. Or Gren, or Coffin, if it came to that. She wished that she could share the knowledge of what had happened and what she had to do about it, wished that there was someone she could talk to as a friend.

For she knew now why she had to find the person called

Blacket. And she knew what she had to do when she found her at Leicester College.

'I suppose you put that girl on to me,' said Olivia Blacket.

'Now look, Olivia, I tried to put her off. Really I did.'

'And who is she, anyway?'

'She's a writer. A novelist.'

'A writer of rubbish. Historical fiction. Romantic nonsense about things she knows nothing about.'

'I think you're being a little hard on her,' said Liam.

'And what is she to you, I'd like to know?'

There was no one who could pour venom down a telephone line quite like Olivia Blacket, thought Liam Ross. The only thing he was grateful for was that she wasn't present in person.

'She's a friend. We met at a tea party. We both liked to go for early morning runs. You don't think she's any sort of competition for you, do you?' A tiny finger of disloyalty prodded him in the back. He ignored it. 'Look, she asked me to introduce you to her.'

'Why?'

'She'd read about you. When she's looking for ideas for a new book, she goes to everyone she knows. And she'd heard that you and I were at the same college. For goodness' sake, Olivia, you're famous! *Everybody*'s heard of you.'

Had he overdone it? Would even her huge ego believe it?

'Well, I suppose I am starting to make a name for myself, even outside the confines of this university.'

Yes, she'd swallowed it. 'Of course you are, Olivia,' he said, soothingly. 'I told her that I would put the two of you in touch, although it was doubtful that you would have time to talk about the Ternan Papers on such a superficial level. But then she went behind my back and wrote to you anyway, without waiting for me to contact you. So what could I do about it?'

'And I wrote back, refusing to see her. But she turned up, *at my house*, in spite of it. How did she know where I lived?'

That was the trouble with Kate. Never took no for an answer. Especially if you gave it to her in writing. She just tore it up, threw it into the waste-paper basket and carried on regardless. Good old Kate.

'Perhaps she asked at college.'

'They wouldn't have given it to her.'

They would if she'd used her usual initiative and given them one of her best stories.

'Then maybe she looked you up in the telephone directory. You're in there, aren't you?' he said.

'And then there was the way Brendan had to invite her in, and ogle her, and tell her everything she wanted to know.'

Now he just had to make sympathetic noises. 'Oh well, you know Brendan. He'll ogle anything in a skirt. Particularly a short one.' After a few more minutes of this, he tried to extricate himself.

'Is there anything specific you want me to do about it, Olivia?'

'Yes, there is. You'll have to see the woman and talk to her.'

'It will have to wait, I'm afraid. I'm due in chapel in five minutes. And then I have a couple of students coming to see me.'

'Then I want to see you in my rooms at college tomorrow.'

The woman was quite impossible. Though that bossy voice of hers always turned him on. He would have to escape from her one day, though. It was a pity she was so good-looking. But at least she had stopped telling him what to do when they were in bed. Or wherever.

'I have a tutorial in the morning, then there's a Wine Committee meeting, and—'

'After lunch will do,' she said. He could picture her in tight, shiny black leather, with her hair drawn very severely back from her face. Boots, maybe.

'Isn't it Mourning Ale? It'll be hell trying to get in,' he said.

'Use the Fellows' Door. Surely you've got a key.'

Time to give in. It was easier than fighting. 'Yes, fine. See you, Olivia.'

'Goodbye, Liam.'

Why did he always get himself mixed up with such strong-minded women? He had seen his mistake with Olivia just a few months after they had become involved, and had tried to get out of the relationship. But that was seven years ago, and in Edinburgh, and he still jumped when she called him. And if he was honest, he still found her physically exciting.

Come to think of it, she was the only one that the dreadful dog would obey, and Ludo was much better endowed with fangs and muscle than he was, so what chance did he stand of getting free of her?

Kate was relaxing with a glass of wine and the luxury of reading a book that someone else had written, when the front doorbell rang. She was expecting no one. She was enjoying an evening on her own. She put an old index card into the book as a marker, hid the glass of wine on the mantelpiece amid a host of ornaments, and went to answer the door.

'Can I come in?'

It was Paul Taylor and he had a small parcel in his hand.

'Would you like a drink?' she asked, as they went into the sitting room. After all, the man had found her an efficient and nearly affordable breakdown service for her car, and then had run her all the way home.

'I'd prefer a coffee, but do carry on drinking your wine.'

Trust Paul to spot it there between her Staffordshire cat and the art deco scent bottle.

He followed her into the kitchen and watched her as she made the coffee, looking round with approval at the clean surfaces, the orderly arrangements of jars in the cupboard, the lack of festering objects in the fridge.

There was a short silence while she tried to put together words to thank him for coming to her rescue earlier in the day. Before she could do so, he said:

'I don't like to think of you on your own on a lonely road, with a broken-down car.'

'It doesn't happen often.'

'Unless you change that car of yours for a newer model, it's going to happen more frequently.'

'I have to wait for a royalty cheque to come in before I can do anything like that.'

'Well, in the meantime I want you to make a small monthly commitment to your personal safety.'

What on earth was the man talking about? Self-defence classes? As a matter of fact, she'd already taken a course, but it was none of his business, so she wouldn't tell him so.

'Here.' He was offering her the parcel he held in his hand. He seemed diffident, as though he was afraid that she would attack him with it.

She made an effort, and smiled, and said thank you. 'What is it?' It wasn't exactly gift-wrapping, more your common strong brown paper. At last she had it open.

'A mobile telephone.'

She didn't know what to say. She had always thought of them as the height of vulgarity. The sort of thing that people who wanted to impress used in public places.

'The phone's yours,' said Paul, quickly. 'And it's connected to one of the big networks. But you'll have to pay the modest monthly rental, and the huge bills if you actually make some calls.'

'Why should I want to call people from a mobile phone? I've got a perfectly good stationary one here.'

'Next time your car breaks down on a lonely road, or . . .' he took a deep breath as though he knew she would get angry at what he was about to say, '. . . or you find yourself in any sort of danger, you can phone me.' He hurried on, not allowing her to interrupt him. 'You see these buttons here? I've programmed them for you. You just press this one, then the Send button, and it automatically dials my number. And this one's programmed with the phone number of a reliable garage. Do you understand?'

'Oh yes, I'm not scared of technology,' she said. I'm just terrified of people who want to walk into my life and take care of me. Even kind, reliable people like Paul Taylor. Especially kind, reliable people like Paul Taylor.

'Come and drink your coffee,' she said, walking into the sitting room. And she took down her wine glass and refilled it.

It was a very generous present. In return, she would try to be pleasant and gracious to Paul for at least half an hour.

She might even tell him what she had seen happening at the door of the empty shop that afternoon. Maybe there would be Brownie points in it for a policeman.

But when he had drunk his coffee, Paul Taylor made his excuses and left, only stopping to extract a promise from her to carry her mobile phone with her at all times. So, as she explained afterwards, she didn't get the chance to tell him what she had seen.

Early that morning, Ant had left the house in East Oxford and cycled down to his shop in the centre. He was happy. He didn't play a cheerful tune on a whistle, like Coffin, or stuff down half a pizza, like Dime, but still the family would have recognized that this was one of Ant's best moods. The others were clearing up in the house, and then they would all be out working. He had found them good pitches, and – he checked his watch – in a couple of hours he would go and pick up the first lot of takings. It didn't look good to have too much money sitting in front of you when you were working the pavement. Either you got ripped off by some tearaway, or the punters thought you were doing too well to bother with you. Gren would come and sit in the shop for twenty minutes while he dealt with it.

And now he had his shop. That's what he'd always wanted. For a start, anyway. He wasn't going to stay down at the bottom of the heap, of course. He had quite a bit of capital salted away now, and he had ambitions. But meanwhile, he had his first step towards respectability. It was the natural progression after the house scam. They broke into houses, they changed the locks, they lived in them for a while, and then they moved on. So why not do the same with a shop?

Break in, change the locks, fill it with fast-moving stock, take your profit, and then move out. Gren's fake leasing agreement would fool the bureaucrats for a day or so, if they came poking their noses in. A few more days, and they were out, and away to the next place.

The location here was good, too. Two minutes' walk from the open market. On market days there should be thousands of people walking past here, looking for bargains. Anything from plastic buckets to valve radios, thought Ant. Gren's contacts had provided the fittings for the shop, minimal as they were, and some cheap, colourful tat to bring the punters in.

He had been careful how he removed the stuff from the house: he didn't want it to be obvious that they had stripped the place. The longer it took the owner to notice that stuff had gone, the longer they would have to make their way far from Oxford and start again somewhere else. Ant had made a judicious selection of the garbage lying around on every available surface and thinned it out a little. Angel would follow after him with her duster and her can of spray polish, cleaning, moving, rearranging, so that the place looked merely tidier, rather than denuded.

Ant went outside to check on his window display. On one side of the door he had put a couple of old radios, a coffee-maker, a pair of brass taps and a wooden table lamp with a silk tasselled shade. Behind them he had propped a landscape featuring a couple of cows and a small brown dog. The frame was usable, anyway. In the window on the other side of the door he had placed a few cheap household items that Gren had provided, one of the four television sets that he had found in the house, and a collection of soft toys that were sitting on the bed in one of the top-floor bedrooms. He had also found some women's clothes in the cupboard in the same room, and they were hanging at one end of a rail at the back of the shop, while three shirts, two pullovers and an old jacket, all male, occupied the other. The empty spaces in the shop were filled with piles of gaily coloured plastic buckets, courtesy of Gren's mate, two small tables packed with books (mostly belonging to their householder) and some cardboard boxes filled with the sort of small and useless objects that people loved to root through. In front of the till there were piles of jeans, complete with designer labels, priced at seven pounds each, and a few dozen navy baseball caps at two pounds fifty. He had not enquired too closely where these last items had come from.

Now he stood at the door and waited for his first customer.

Chapter 6

It is enacted that no student or other person shall by day or night carry either offensive or defensive arms, such as swords, poignards, daggers (commonly called stilettos), dirks, bows and arrows, guns or war-like weapons or implements, within the verge of the University, unless when he happens to make a journey to parts remote, or to return therefrom . . .

Laud's Code, 1636

Kate arrived at Leicester College lodge just after lunch. The narrow entry swarmed with students, most of them in T-shirts and jeans, but some wearing their caps and gowns. Three porters stood in front of them, their arms folded, their faces impassive, while the throng before them tried to crowd into the small, immaculately grassed quadrangle of Leicester College.

'I want to get inside. I need to see someone,' shouted Kate, elbowing her way forwards.

In front of her, a mass of tall, athletic students barred her way with their black-clad backs. She could see neither around nor through them. 'What's going on?' she asked the nearest one.

'Morningale,' he answered.

'What?' She must have heard him incorrectly. There was an awful lot of noise going on, with jeering and pushing and shouting all around her.

One or two students were being allowed in, though, she noticed, and she wondered how she could be among their number. She looked towards the lodge where the porters usually sat, but the door was closed and a shutter had been pulled across the window.

'Is there another way in?' she shouted at a young woman who was jammed up against her.

'There's the Broad Street door, but you need a key to get in that way.'

'Where do I get a key?' It was like conducting a long-distance conversation under water.

'Only Fellows have them.'

And she didn't think she could ask Liam to let her have his. He'd been unhelpful enough when she'd had a legitimate reason to come to his college. Goodness knows what he'd have said if he knew what she wanted to do today.

It was hopeless trying to fight her way through the mob. And even if she did, she doubted whether she could argue her way past the row of porters. They had daily practice in refusing implausible requests from beguiling and inventive students, and she wasn't even a member of their college. She turned with difficulty in the crowded space, and fought her way back into Parks Road.

There was another porter watching the students from out here. He was a tall man, and even if he was old enough to have been retired from his previous job, he was broad enough and strong enough to keep someone Kate's size out of a college.

'I've just come to see one of your Fellows,' she said to him. 'Is there any way of getting in?'

'I'm surprised anyone made an appointment for this afternoon,' he said. 'They all know that no strangers are admitted for Morningale.' He looked at her. She wasn't quite as neat and presentable as she had been when she arrived at Leicester. Someone heavy had stepped back hard on to her instep, and she thought there was probably a tear in her tights. She didn't want to draw his attention to it by looking down, though.

'No,' he answered her question, dismissively. 'You can only come in if you're from Bartlemas.'

Kate opened her mouth to declare that that was exactly where she came from, but before she could utter another untruth, he continued:

'And you'd have to be properly attired. Academic dress,' he added, sensing that she was about to argue that the hole in her tights was none of her doing, and the suit she was wearing had cost a ridiculous amount. 'Gown. Cap,' he said sternly. 'Subfusc.'

Bugger Oxford, thought Kate, and its ridiculous traditions, of which this was doubtless one of the most obscure, designed to make the uninitiated feel out of place. She had to admit that she had lost the first round. But she wasn't giving in yet. She just needed more information before she tried again.

Academic dress for a woman undergraduate, she knew, meant black skirt, white blouse, black tie, tights and shoes, and gown, with a cap that should be worn at all times.

She thought that these days it was only worn for public examinations and the fancier celebrations, when the vice-chancellor was present. This Morningale charade must be another such.

To her left stood a group of women students, pink in the face, hair escaping in strands from their black caps, but dressed in the appropriate way. They were looking pleased with themselves and drinking from glasses of a vicious-looking dark beer. She approached the nearest.

'I wonder if you could help me,' she said, at her most ingratiating. 'I need to get into Leicester to see someone rather urgently, and they tell me it's morning, or something.' She looked at her watch. 'Actually, it's half-past two in the afternoon, but I'm sure Oxford has an explanation for that. You're using some alternative calendar, perhaps?'

'It's Mourning,' said the first young woman. 'M, O, U, R . . .'

'Ah,' said Kate. 'Care to tell me what it's all about?'

A red-headed student who had just finished her tankard of beer and was feeling more cheerful than the others said: 'The Mourning – capital M – is for a student of Bartlemas College who was pursued across Magdalen Bridge, up the High and into the Turl, then through Allhallowes Street and Catte Street, as he tried to reach his college. He got as far as the gates of Leicester College, which were kept shut against him, however hard he grasped their brazen knocker and beat upon it.'

'Tough,' said Kate. 'What happened to him?'

'He was battered to death with staves and his body torn to pieces by a mob of apprentices from the town.'

'My God! When was this?'

'October the twentieth, fifteen twenty-seven,' said the girl.

'Well, time to forgive and forget,' said Kate.

'Not at all,' said the girl. 'Leicester forfeited its bronze doorknocker as a punishment. The Bishop of Lincoln nailed it to the wall of his chapterhouse, I believe. It was popularly held to provide sanctuary, which would have saved the lad if they had let him inside. And so, ever since, as an act of atonement, on the anniversary of his death, any student properly dressed and able to prove membership of Bartlemas College may demand entry to Leicester and be given a measure of Mourning Ale – specially brewed for the occasion by the college chef.'

'Oh,' said Kate, realizing at last what people had been saying to her. 'Mourning, as in black and ale, as in beer. I get it now.'

Well down their glasses of dark beer by now, the students looked at her with approval.

'And how do you prove membership of Bartlemas?' asked Kate, eyeing the caps and gowns of the group and wondering how she could acquire a set for herself.

'A letter from your tutor,' said the girl.

'And how are you off for funds at this time in the academic year?' asked Kate. 'Insolvent, anyone? Looking to earn a quick fiver, perhaps?'

'Five pounds for each of us, if you're that keen,' said the first student, pricing Kate's dark suit and white shirt. 'Five pounds for the gown, five for the cap, and another fiver for my tutor's letter. Pity about the hole in your tights, but they'll overlook it, I expect.'

'For that sum I want a scholar's gown,' growled Kate. 'None of your commoner rubbish.'

'Then you need mine,' said a rabbity-looking girl with dandruff.

'And you can have my letter,' said the redhead.

'Here's my cap,' said the first.

Kate was draped in a gown – a knee-length one with sleeves – a mortarboard was placed on her head and a letter (rather stained and crumpled) in her hand.

'And you can borrow my tie for free,' said the letter donor, placing the article around Kate's neck and tying it under her collar.

'Thanks,' said Kate. 'I'll bring you out my Mourning Ale if I manage to get my hands on some.'

'We'll be here for a while yet,' said the redhead. 'We've chipped in for a winebox from Oddbins and Mark should be back with it in a minute. We'll be sitting on the wall over there when you get out.'

'If I get in,' amended Kate. 'What's my subject?' she called to the redhead as the students crossed the road.

'*Literae Humaniores*,' said the girl.

And what the hell was that? She didn't have a clue.

Kate held the mortarboard on with one hand and clutched 'her' tutor's letter in the other as she made for the throng in Leicester lodge. In the roadway, and to one side, stood a thin, pale girl with dark shadows around her eyes and wearing a white dress. She seemed to be as desperate as Kate to get into the college, but was up against an obdurate porter.

'Sorry, miss,' he was saying. 'You have to be in academic dress before I can even speak to you today. It's Mourning Ale, you see.'

'I have to see someone,' she was saying. 'Isn't there another way in?'

Kate felt sorry for her. She wasn't showing any initiative and she'd never get in now, not dressed like that.

'There's the Fellows' Door in Broad Street,' she told her, as the porter turned away. 'But you need one of their keys to use it.'

The girl looked at her then, and as she caught the hopeless expression in the surprisingly blue eyes, Kate recognized her. The untenanted soul. The one who was being bullied by the man who later had let himself into the empty shop. And now, here she was at Leicester, apparently as keen as Kate herself to get inside. She wished she had time to find out what it was all about. 'Good luck!' she said, impulsively, and started to edge her way to the front of the crowd.

When she reached the line of porters, she gave them her best smile. Smugly she waved her letter and pointed to her gown.

The middle porter, the one with the paunch and jowls and the friendly smile, obviously didn't believe her, but let her through anyway. She would pick up her quota of Mourning Ale on her way out. For the moment she had to find Olivia Blacket's rooms.

'I'm expected by the English Tutor,' she told the porter.

'Dr Blacket? You'll find her rooms on Staircase Five. Across Clifford Quad, through the archway on your right, then second on your left in New Quad. First floor. Her name's on the door.'

Kate turned to the right, away from the people in fancy dress who were acting out some violent occurrence from the sixteenth century. The college chef was dispensing Mourning Ale in person, wearing a splendid pair of silver-buckled shoes. A small number of young people in long black

113

cassocks and lace collars looked as though they were about to sing. She hurried through into the next quad, in case someone should tell her she had a part to play in the mummery: that she had to declaim a speech in Latin, or eat a honeyed dormouse.

New Quad was empty, she was relieved to find. Now that she'd inveigled her way into the college, she had to find a way of getting into Olivia's rooms. She stopped in a quiet corner in the shadow of an archway, and reached into her handbag. The model of mobile phone that Paul had given her was quite small and light, and fitted easily inside it. She had spent some time yesterday evening finding out how it worked, and now she pulled out the aerial, punched in the number of Leicester College lodge and pressed the Send button. In spite of the pantomime taking place in Clifford Quad, there had to be someone normal there behind the shutters, living in the twentieth century, answering the phone.

There was. 'Leicester College,' said a male voice, on the third ring.

'I'd like to speak to Dr Blacket, please.' She used her fussy, academic voice.

She heard the extension ring. Six times. Ten times.

'I'm sorry, Dr Blacket is not in her office.'

Good. That's what she had hoped for.

She ended the call, pushed down the aerial and put the phone back in her bag. Seventy pence, and worth every bit of it. Perhaps not quite what Paul had in mind when he gave her the present, but he need never know about it.

Then she looked for Staircase Five.

Angel couldn't bear the noise and the crowds any more. Her

head was hurting and she was cold, in only her white cotton dress, bare feet and sandals. She didn't know how much longer these students would stand here, preventing her from getting to Leicester. It seemed stupid, after all the time and effort it had taken to get here, that she should be stopped from entering Leicester by some strange Oxford ritual. She wanted to sit down and cry, but that wouldn't help her in what she needed to do. Be strong, she told herself. You've got to be strong. Think of another way in. Don't be beaten now when you're so close to success.

Black bird beating its wings against the cage of my mind, pecking its way into the meat of my brain.

She walked back past the New Bodleian, past Blackwell's, without even glancing in their windows, and stopped at her old pitch outside the black door. The Fellows' Door, they had called it. As she had stood on the pavement, begging from the passers-by, she had sometimes noticed people going in and out. They used a key, it was true, but they didn't look too carefully behind them when they went in, and mostly they were deep in their own thoughts. Not one of them had noticed her as she stood there, and none had given her as much as twenty pence. She'd tried to get in the straight-forward way, the honest way. It was their own fault if she had to use subterfuge.

Green hill. Patches of brown and white. Green blanket. White bonnet. Splashes of scarlet.

She stood there, waiting, and eventually she was rewarded for her patience. A tall man, not very old, with dark hair, and with his thoughts far from Broad Street and Angel, unlocked the door and strode inside, leaving it to swing shut behind him.

Just before the latch caught, Angel had grasped the door. She waited for a couple of seconds to make sure that the Fellow didn't check that it had closed, then she slipped through and let the door click shut quietly after her. Her sandals made no noise on the paved path.

Behind her, a second intruder, anonymous in a black gown, followed her light-coloured figure into the grounds of the college.

She was in a narrow passage, with on the left an open-sided shed with bicycle stands along its length. Not at all her idea of an Oxford college, but she followed the passage along its length, hearing the metallic crashing sounds of a kitchen behind the wall to her right, and passing several dustbins and beer barrels. Someone came out of the kitchen door, whistling loudly, manhandling a metal barrel down the steps until it stood beside the others. Angel shrank back against the wall, wishing she was wearing a drabber-coloured dress.

Then the man returned inside, slammed the door, and she heard more loud voices and laughter. She waited for a moment to make sure that he wasn't returning, then she padded swiftly away from the door, down to the end of the passage, and didn't stop until she came out through a brick archway into a small quadrangle.

She was in.

She stood looking at the green grassy square in front of her. Her heart was thudding and she could feel sweat trickling down her back. She tried to feel braver: what could they do if they found her here, after all, except ask her to leave? She must walk round these quadrangles, through these archways, under the age-old creepers. She must read the names on the gold-lettered boards at the bottom of each staircase.

She must do what she had come for.

She had to find Olivia Blacket.

She had not noticed that, behind her, someone still followed like a shadow.

Kate, meanwhile, well ahead of her and with some idea of where to go, had found Olivia's door.

It was cream-painted, solid, had a name-plate announcing that it belonged to Dr O. R. Blacket, and was locked.

She should have expected this. At some level she had, but had somehow thought that as soon as she saw it, she would become inspired and see how to open it. She had overcome all other obstacles in the past couple of days, so that now she assumed that she could talk her way in anywhere. But not through a locked door, she conceded.

She stood and looked at it. She was not going to be beaten by a simple door. Over the past year she had solved the murder of a dentist and escaped from a psychopathic librarian. She had learned to lie and cheat her way around Oxford to help her law-abiding friends achieve their lawful aims. So now she was going to put those same skills to use to get her hands on the piece of information that was going to bring her a bestseller.

Back to the locked door. It was too late for a scout with a convenient set of keys to be cleaning rooms. The porters were all busy, even if she could think of a good enough reason to need to get into Dr Blacket's room in her absence. Perhaps she should have been choosier about her tutor's letter. Whatever *Literae Humaniores* were, she didn't think they were the same thing as English Literature.

She was standing outside the door, still dithering about

what to do next, when there were quick steps from the floor above and a young man in dark blue Lycra, with excellent biceps and handsome quads, came down the stairs. He paused when he saw Kate.

She was about to make up a story to cover why she was standing there, when she realized that her present dress provided her with an excellent reason. She opened her eyes wide, and turned them towards him.

'Is Blacket late again?' he asked, sympathetically.

Kate nodded. The less she said, the fewer mistakes in subject matter and vocabulary she was likely to make.

'She usually leaves the key up on the ledge,' he said. 'Why don't you let yourself in?' And he carried on down the narrow stone staircase, with the word Leicester gleaming in silver letters on his back.

'Thanks,' she called after him.

Thank you very much. She reached up and ran her fingers along the top of the door frame. A key. After all, it was that easy.

She unlocked the door and let herself into Olivia's room.

Two rooms. There was another door opposite her, ajar, leading into a smaller room off the main study. But she would start here in the first room. And at first glance she saw that getting in was only the beginning of her problems. She had forgotten just how untidy Olivia was. And if her house had made Kate's skin itch with its disorder, then this room was ten times worse.

Leicester College gave its tutors generously large rooms. And this one was hidden under a sea of books and papers. No, she thought, as she started to find her way round the room, not so much a sea as a volcanic landscape, with valleys and pinnacles. It was extraordinary how Olivia had managed to achieve this effect in such a short period: if asked to guess, she would have put the time needed to reach it as nearer twenty years.

Right, stop wasting time. Look for the desk. Desk: a square or rectangular object, some thirty inches off the floor. Perhaps with drawers.

She was still searching when the phone rang.

Kate jumped, and for a moment wondered whether to answer it. Then she realized that the telephone was likely to be situated on the desk and she followed the sound of ringing to its source.

The ringing stopped.

But she seemed to have reached a recent layer of chaos. There was a chair, and she sat in it and looked at the papers in front of her. She discarded what was obviously a student essay, then put aside the minutes of the last Governing Body meeting, and an invitation to Dr Blacket to read a paper at a forthcoming conference.

Then there were a couple of slate-grey cardboard boxes, fastened with ribbon ties. Sandwiched between them was a blue folder. She opened one of the grey boxes. And inside she found something that looked like the paper that Professor Adams had shown her. A whole sheaf of them in fact.

In one box the papers were numbered in their top right-hand corners, in the other they were apparently still unsorted. When she opened the folder, she found sheets, both hand and typewritten, also numbered, and apparently transcriptions of the papers in the grey box.

Well, thought Kate, since she was now well and truly committed to a life of crime, she might as well prosper from it. This was not the moment to chicken out. She shifted aside a doll that was lying on the desk, flipped through the pages in the folder and extracted number forty-three, the one that corresponded to the page that Professor Adams had 'borrowed'. Then she did a little borrowing of her own. She extracted a leaf – number sixteen – from the grey box, then quickly looked for the corresponding transcription among Olivia's notes.

At which point she heard someone at the door. A rapping, made by human knuckles on wood.

She closed the boxes, sandwiched the folder between them, strewed some random papers over the top, grabbed the two pages she had already extracted, and made for the inner room.

It was as well that she did. The knuckles rapped a second time. A voice called out 'Olivia!' and a hand tried the door. It was a pity, thought Kate, that she hadn't locked the door behind her: after all, if Olivia returned, she would not expect to find it open.

Sounds of the outer door opening, of footsteps as someone entered the room.

The room she was in held a small cupboard, which she had no intention of hiding in, a four-drawer filing cabinet, and a bentwood coatstand holding a gown, an old raincoat, a jacket and skirt on a hanger, and a green cardigan. She crouched behind the filing cabinet and very carefully pulled the coatstand in front of her. It wouldn't hide her from a proper inspection, but it would save her from a casual glance if someone came into the room.

'Are you there, Olivia?' called the same voice.

She recognized it. It belonged to Liam.

Well, that was possible. They belonged to the same college. Nothing strange about it at all. She wasn't jealous or anything stupid like that, was she? She thought about coming out of hiding and telling Liam that she was there. Then she thought that it would be a very silly idea. Liam had old-fashioned ideas about breaking and entering. Not to mention 'borrowing' a manuscript. She made herself more comfortable in her crouched position behind the filing cabinet and prepared to sit it out.

More sound effects from next door. Footsteps, door opening, second unknown person entering.

'Liam? What are you doing here?'

Olivia.

'If you remember, you asked me to come and see you after lunch.'

No, not at all friendly. Perhaps it was because they were on such bad terms that he hadn't encouraged them to meet. Perhaps he thought that a recommendation from him would put Olivia right off talking to her.

'Oh, yes. Well, I suppose you'd better come and sit down.'

A short pause, the sound of books being lifted from chairs and disposed of elsewhere, the sigh of foam cushions as bottoms sank into seats.

'You caught me on a sensitive subject, with the Ternan Papers. Everyone wants to get their hands on them, but they were given to me. They're *mine*. They're nothing to do with Leicester. They came to me because I was at Bartlemas.'

What did the professor say? Something about Olivia being obsessive about the papers? Canny old man, the professor.

'How are you getting on with them?' asked Liam in the tones that Kate recognized as soothing and placatory.

'Oh, they are *very* exciting. I know I shouldn't say this, but these notebooks and letters are *speaking* to me, Liam. I understand this woman. I *know* her. I am in touch with her feelings. We are moving through the same passages in our lives, facing the same problems, the same ambivalences and indecisions.'

The image of a high-relief madonna and child, gleaming gold in the lamplight, came back to Kate.

Then Olivia went on, 'But I am being undermined, yet again. Just because I'm a woman, and still young, there is so much jealousy. There are people who would do anything to stop me from making a reputation for myself. They are trying to get in before me. They want to sensationalize the material. Vulgarize it. Turn it into a bestseller.' She made the word sound like pornography. 'Someone is stealing my papers, I know it.'

'How can you be sure?' asked Liam.

How on earth could she tell, in this incredible mess, wondered Kate.

'I can tell, don't worry. But I think I know now who is doing it. And I shall take steps to stop them.'

'Good,' said Liam, obviously searching for something to pacify her.

'You can't build a reputation on theft,' spat Olivia. 'And when I reveal who it is—'

'It isn't always a good idea to make enemies in our business,' said Liam. 'Don't forget that there are too many of us chasing too few posts.'

'That won't be a problem much longer,' said Olivia.

'Good. Well . . .'

He was trying hard to be a New Man, and see her point

of view, but Olivia wasn't making it easy for him. She had started another diatribe and Kate heard Liam's feet moving on the carpet, the rustle of paper as he picked up a book and turned its pages. Signs that he was getting restive and wished to cop out of the conversation. She wondered whether Olivia knew how to read him yet. 'Is that it then, Olivia?' He'd be slipping out of that door any minute now.

'No of course it isn't. And I'm sure you know what I asked you here to talk about.' The same hysterical edge to her voice.

'Not again, please. I know you blame me for what happened, but really, Olivia, we did talk it over at the time. The decision was as much yours as mine.'

'Cold bastard.' Surely they weren't still speaking about the Ternan manuscripts? 'What you mean is that you talked, I listened. You made the decision. I just went along with it.'

'What do you want me to do about it? What on earth *can* I do, anyway?'

'I should have thought that was obvious.'

'Don't you think you're being a bit hasty? Have you tried talking to someone about it? Perhaps you need professional advice.'

'Who do you suggest? A counsellor? My doctor? Or how about the Warden?'

'Now you're just being ridiculous. I can see you've got a problem, but I don't see that it's got anything to do with me any longer.' She was right about his being a cold bastard, thought Kate. Or maybe Olivia was just an impossibly demanding woman.

'You're not going to get away with it, Liam.'

'You could be right, but for the moment I have to be

moving on, Olivia. I have a lecture to prepare, an essay to read . . .'

'You're just trying to wriggle out of things again, Liam. You think that once life gets a little difficult you can just walk away. Well, this time you're wrong.'

Kate heard Liam sigh. She heard his chair creak. Olivia had played it wrong, she thought. He would be out of her room within the minute. If she had something she wanted to talk about, she was on to a loser.

'Look, Olivia, we've talked this through a dozen times. I can't see that we've got anything to add to it, really.' Sounds of Liam getting to his feet and moving towards the door. 'And I really must get back to my office.' Kate imagined him standing with his hand on the doorknob. She wondered with interest what Olivia would do next. Had she reached the object-throwing stage yet?

'Oh no, you don't get out of it that easily!' Olivia's voice had risen to a shout.

She heard Liam open the door, then Olivia's angry foot-steps as she followed him out.

'Goodbye, Olivia. I really must be going.' Yes, Kate had been on the receiving end of that line in the past.

'Don't walk away from me like that!' Olivia was shrieking now, and both sets of feet were disappearing down the stairwell. Kate half hoped that she would throw something at him.

'Stop making a scene!' Liam hated scenes.

'We've got to talk about it! We've got to come to a decision.'

'You're already made your mind up. You just want me to agree with you.' Liam's voice came back faintly. Olivia's reply was too indistinct to hear, but Kate could hear that she was very angry. But this was her chance. She came out from behind the filing cabinet, ran across to the desk, opened the blue folder and extracted leaf number sixteen, and was out through the door, all within the minute.

She could no longer hear Olivia and Liam, and when her heart had stopped thudding, she started walking slowly down the staircase towards the outer door, the quadrangle and freedom.

She had walked round New Quad, was about to pass through the archway into Clifford Quad, when she stopped. Coming towards her was a familiar figure. Two familiar figures. Brendan Adams and Ludo. Kate flattened herself against the wall. She didn't trust Dog Ludo.

'Ah, my lovely young friend, Kate.'

'Hallo, Professor.'

'Brendan, please. Down, Ludo!' This last with no effect whatsoever. As Kate remembered it, Olivia was the only one who had power over Ludo. 'Have you been to visit the strong-minded Dr Blacket?' His eyes sparkled with curiosity at her costume, and a hint of malice.

This was a case for caution. 'No,' said Kate, airily. 'I've just called in for a tankard of Mourning Ale.'

'That's just as well, probably. Our Olivia is getting some very strange bees in her academic bonnet these days. It's as well to stay out of range of her venom.'

'Thanks for the advice,' said Kate, wondering how soon she could escape.

'I think you'll find the Mourning Ale is being dispensed in Clifford Quad, rather than from Staircase Five,' said the professor. 'And you must tell me about your time at

Bartlemas over a drink at the White Horse one evening. Down, Ludo!'

Kate's expensive tights were now beyond all hope. 'Are you bringing Ludo to visit Dr Blacket?' she asked, to change the subject.

'Oh, yes,' he replied, the malice now definitely to the fore. 'She does *so* love looking after him. Well, she loves any little favour she can do for me. And I use any excuse I can find to visit dear Dr Blacket.'

'You mean she'll have the dog here? Even in her college rooms?' asked Kate, with amazement.

'I'm off to London again,' said the professor. 'She'll just *have* to help me out.'

The professor was looking very dapper. The woollen pullover was no longer in evidence, but was replaced by a leather-patched tweed jacket. He nudged Kate painfully, while the dog worried at the tassel on her expensive Russell & Bromley shoes. 'I can't disappoint the lovely lady in Westbourne Terrace, can I?'

And maybe that's why he hasn't asked his sister to look after the dog, thought Kate. He's probably told her that he's spending the evening and night with colleagues in Oxford.

She watched them as they followed the path round the quad and made for Staircase Five. Kate hated to think of the chaos that the dog could wreak in that already chaotic room. Then she limped her way towards Clifford Quad. A few yards further on, Olivia, white-faced and furious, walked past her in the archway. She stared very hard at Kate in her borrowed academic dress, and frowned as though trying to remember where they had met previously. Kate gave her no opportunity to recall the occasion, but sped away in the opposite direction. Olivia would be even less happy when she found Ludo waiting for her in her room. Maybe she would assume that he had eaten the three missing papers.

Kate queued up for her tankard of Mourning Ale. She had, after all, promised to take her student friends her measure of the stuff, and she really ought to return their items of clothing, too.

She found them sitting on the wall outside, and they seemed hardly to notice that she had been gone more than five minutes. Their friend Mark had duly returned with the winebox from Oddbins, and they accepted Kate's offering of Mourning Ale and downed that, too. They insisted that she join them in a plastic beaker of Bulgarian wine. Extremely jolly by this time, they promised her that she could borrow gowns, mortarboards and anything else any time she cared to scatter her five-pound notes among them. They parted the best of friends.

As Kate turned into Broad Street with her loot, she wondered what the argument between Liam and Olivia had been about. Did Liam object to the way Olivia was interpreting the papers in her charge? Their conversation seemed to have more edge to it than a purely intellectual discussion. But then, what did she know about the workings of an Oxford college? Maybe this was the way academics carried on all the time.

She found a small shop in the Turl where they photocopied her three sheets of paper. She thought about returning the originals to Olivia immediately, but then she thought that she would like to compare originals and photocopies carefully first, in case the former were easier to read. And when she considered talking her way into Leicester College for a second time, and risking a confrontation with Olivia, she decided to fortify herself with food and strong drink and a good night's sleep before doing so. No, she would pay a quick visit to the bookshop, and then go straight home.

When she came out of Blackwell's, she stopped for a moment to get out her purse. Outside Trinity, the busker with the whistle had given way to another with a fiddle. She was all in favour of cheering up the centre of Oxford with the playing of music, and so she lobbed a twenty-pence piece into his cap and walked on. But as she slipped her purse back into her bag, she felt something large and metallic at the bottom. A key. The key to Olivia's room. She must have dropped it into her bag when she let herself in. Of course, Olivia had left the door open when she pursued Liam across the quadrangle, so she had followed her out and had forgotten all about the key.

Just for a moment she thought about going back to replace it. But the idea of borrowing all that academic gear again put her off. What would Olivia do if she found the key was missing? Then she remembered Olivia's room. The woman was presumably used to mislaying things. It could be weeks before she discovered that the key wasn't anywhere there. And at least it helped to solve one problem. She had been wondering, vaguely, how to return Olivia's documents to her when she had finished comparing them. Now it was simple. All she had to do was march past the porters as though she belonged to Leicester, walk up the staircase to Olivia's room, open the door with the key, replace the papers in their correct places in the box and folder respectively, walk out, re-locking the door, and put the key back on the ledge outside. Piece of cake. As long, that is, as no one caught her doing it, or challenged her at any point in her walk through the college.

She had halted, and was staring down at the pavement as she thought it all through. As she finally made up her mind, and turned to stride on down Broad Street, she bumped into a figure that was meandering in an indecisive way across her path. The young woman in the thin white dress and sandals. Her face was paler than ever, if possible, and the expression in her eyes more desperate. She stumbled as she walked, and Kate thought for a moment that she would fall. When she realized that Kate was looking at her, she attempted to pull her cardigan round herself. Kate had the impression that she was also attempting to hide something that she was clutching to herself underneath the cardigan.

'Are you all right? Are you hurt?'

The girl looked down at herself in terror, then up at Kate. 'Not me. No, I'm fine. Really.'

What did she expect to see? What had happened to this girl? Was this just another piece of Oxford play-acting? Over-indulgence in Mourning Ale, perhaps. But Kate didn't think so. There was real desperation in her face.

Across the road, outside the Sheldonian Theatre, an emaciated figure with a cardboard notice saying *Hungry and homeless* got to his feet with surprising vigour and started to cross the road towards them. Behind her, the fiddle player had stopped, and Kate heard the approach of the other busker, the one with the whistles.

'Can I help you?' asked Kate, urgently, as she felt the girl slipping away from her. 'I'm sure you need help,' she added.

'Yes,' said the girl, her eyes focused and intelligent now. 'I do. Please help me.'

Kate saw now what it was that she was carrying under her cardigan: a doll. A baby doll wearing a white cotton bonnet. Maybe the girl was a bit simple.

'Angel,' said a soft voice from Kate's right. The beggar had crossed the road, and stood beside them. She could feel the presence of the busker behind her, and sensed the agitation in the girl.

'She seems to be ill,' said Kate. 'I was trying to help her. Shouldn't we call an ambulance?' While she was talking, her fingers were scrabbling in her handbag, feeling for the little leather folder that she kept there. She knew the two men would refuse any official help. They were not the type to take to the likes of Paul Taylor. They had moved so that they were on either side of the girl they called Angel.

'There's no need for that. We'll look after her,' said the beggar. 'Don't worry about her. She belongs to us.' He had a hand on the girl's arm, above the elbow.

'Hey! What's wrong with Angel? What are you doing?' This last was addressed to Kate by a young man with dark curly hair, a red face and an unfortunate skin condition.

'Cool it, Dime,' said the beggar from outside the Sheldonian. 'Angel's fine. She just had a bit of a funny turn, and this lady came to her rescue.' He smiled at Kate, but the smile didn't reach his eyes.

'What's wrong with her?' asked Kate. 'Is she ill?' She would have liked to ask why she was hiding a doll under her cardigan, but didn't think anyone would tell her if she asked.

'She doesn't eat properly,' said the beggar. 'Then she comes over all faint.'

'Yeah,' said Dime, the one with the red face. 'She'll have a pizza, though. Come on, Angel, let's go and get something to eat.'

Kate was being crowded out. The four were starting to move away, the girl Angel supported by two of the others. But Kate had to try to make contact before they left. She touched her lightly on the shoulder, in a gesture of friendship. 'Are you sure you're all right?' she asked. And making certain that she had the girl's attention, she added: 'You know I'd always be of help, if I could.'

The face had its shuttered look again. She would say nothing in front of the three men. Kate didn't think she was frightened of them, or that they would hit her or anything, but she did have the impression that they were in charge of her. She stood back and let them leave without saying any more. She was glad though, that before they took her away, she had slipped her card, with her address and her phone number on it, into the pocket of the girl's green cardigan.

Did she understand? Did she know that Kate had given her the card? As the three walked off towards Catte Street, she saw that Angel had her right hand in her pocket, and she looked back over her shoulder at Kate before she disappeared round the corner. Kate wasn't sure how to read the expression on her face, but at least it hadn't been the disturbing blank stare that she had seen before. She sent her what she hoped was a reassuring smile in return, but she wasn't sure that she caught it.

Who were those men? They reminded her of something out of Dickens, thought Kate. First, the tall, thin beggar in the ragged clothes, who looked on the point of death by starvation, but who had walked vigorously across the road, and who had supported Angel well enough. Then there was the busker. He hadn't said anything, but he had been quite possessive about the girl. He had been holding the containers with their takings, and various wraps of theirs, so he hadn't

131

been able to grab hold of Angel, but he walked close to the others as though preventing her escape. And then the simple man with the red face. He had been the most concerned of all of them about the girl. And probably the most possessive. And what about the other man, the one who wore black and broke into the shop at the bottom of George Street? She was glad he hadn't been there when she gave Angel her card. She didn't think she would have fooled him the way she did the other three.

Chapter 7

These fellowships are pretty things;
We live once more like petty kings,
And dine untax'd, untroubled under
The portrait of our pious founder.
Thomas Warton, 1728–90

Kate went downstairs to her workroom. For once she would
be sensible. She would look through the papers she had
filched, and make careful notes. She had photocopies from
the shop where they took no notice of anything you gave
them. (Unlike Mrs Clack at the shop in Fridesley Road, who
charged only four pence per copy, but who would quiz Kate
unmercifully on anything she was asked to do.) And then
she would take the originals back just as soon as possible,
and preferably before Olivia knew that they had disappeared. But tomorrow morning would be quite soon enough.
Especially if Ludo was sitting in the room, ready to chew
the tassel on her other shoe and eat the papers.

Ant was sitting in the room with the french windows. The

television was murmuring and flickering in the corner, but Ant wasn't watching it. He was sitting in one of the yellow-coloured chairs, drinking a very nice single-malt whisky. The scent of woodsmoke drifted in on the autumn air from neighbouring gardens. It was a pity they couldn't stay for ever. Ant was starting to feel at home here.

'How'd we do, then?' asked Gren, walking into the room and taking in Ant's air of satisfaction with life. He poured himself a glass of whisky. 'This is good stuff.'

'I found it in the cupboard over there.'

'How'd it go?' repeated Gren. 'Business, I mean. Takings.'

'A very satisfactory start. As Dime would say, we done good,' said Ant.

'How much we make?'

'The family made over a ton. A hundred and fifteen, as a matter of fact.'

'Ace,' said Gren, and swallowed his whisky. 'And what about the gig at the new place?'

Gren had the right to know all about it, since it was his contacts that had largely set the place up.

'We made over three hundred. Well, four hundred and seventy, actually,' said Ant. 'Not bad for our first day.'

'True. What shifted?'

'The jeans went well. No one could compete with that price.'

'No way they could sell cheaper,' agreed Gren. 'They come up from London yesterday afternoon. Good gear. The real thing.'

Ant wasn't so naïve as to ask why they were so cheap and how they had turned up in Oxford. 'And the baseball caps did all right, too.'

'Not much mark-up on them,' said Gren, 'but the punters want them so we have to provide. What else?'

'The radios went, and about half the secondhand clothes. Oh, and some of the cuddly toys.'

'We only sold one of the coffee machines,' he added. 'And both the taps. Two or three of the dolls.' He was remembering the woman who came in to buy one of the dolls. Funny little doll, it was, wearing a white cotton bonnet. It had a pale face and a stringy body. Reminded him a bit of Angel. Anyway, the woman who bought it was a real weirdo. Talked to it like it was a live baby, made him wrap it up like a present, but with its face free so's it could breathe. But he didn't tell Gren about it. Or Angel, come to that.

They'd all visited him during the day. Slid into the shop, pretending they were just passing. Of course, they were taking time off their pitches, giving the competition a chance of grabbing the prime sites, but he couldn't blame them. And each of them gave him a chance of a break. It could be a bit of a strain, standing in the shop, dealing with the public without a break of any kind.

'Much shrinkage?' asked Gren.

'Not too bad. I kept my eye on the punters. The only thing I really noticed that disappeared during the morning was one of the tools.'

'The ones we took from the basement here?'

'Yeah. I wasn't sure at first which one was missing. I knew there was a set of four, and then there were only three.'

'Maybe one of the family sold it.'

'No. I asked. They didn't. Oh well, I don't suppose it matters. It wasn't valuable.'

'What was it?' There was an odd sensation in the small of

Gren's back as he asked the question.

'A hammer. A large, old-fashioned, heavy job.'

For some reason, Gren saw Angel in her white dress, having the funny turn in the street, pulling the green cardigan round herself, trying to conceal the doll.

When Kate had looked over the pages for a while, she could see that the originals were easier to work with, at least to begin with. But once her eye was in, and she had started to make herself her own alphabet, she felt she could move to the photocopies and contemplate returning the originals. She started to translate the odd word or two, and made more progress once she realized that the second s that Brendan had mentioned looked just like an f.

She was tempted once or twice to turn to the transcription, to see what Olivia had made of it, when she got stuck. But she felt that she had to see what she made of Maria's words by herself, before turning to Olivia's version. She didn't want to be affected in advance by what Olivia thought they meant.

On the other hand, she would very much like to find something useful for her own book. It was time she wrote something original, that would sell more than the modest number of copies that she had achieved so far in her career as a writer. A book about Maria Ternan containing a revelation about Charles Dickens that was proved to be true at about the time the book was published would be a real advantage.

She started with page forty-three.

Angel sat on the bed in her room and looked over at the dressing table. She had placed the baby with the light striking her from the side, so that her plastic face appeared animated, her set blue eyes in shadow.

Sitting here, watching the baby, she could allow the events of the day to slip back into the cold soup that was her memory. They sank without trace and lay there among the chopped carrots and celery of her past. But she knew that as long as she watched the baby she was safe.

She had taken off all her clothes and bathed and changed as soon as she got home. Then she had put her clothes through the hottest wash cycle giving them a prewash with the biological detergent that Coffin disliked. She knew that they were quite clean, really. But the scene with Olivia had left her feeling dirty. She was getting too fanciful. She should listen to Dime more. Eat another pizza. That would bring her down to earth.

She didn't have to run away. She didn't have to go off her head. She belonged to a family. They would look after her. They would shield her from the disaster in that room. Concentrate on the baby.

Before washing the cardigan, she had removed the card that the blonde woman had given her. Maybe she wouldn't use it, but it was comforting to have the telephone number and address. She did sometimes miss the company of another female. Not that the blonde one would ever understand all the things that had happened to her. Nobody could.

It was a pretty card: dove grey, with the initial K decorated with flowers and mythical beasts printed in a soft, deep greenish blue. Fridesley. She would have to ask where that was. But the city wasn't large, and the chances were that she could walk there in half an hour or so.

Later, when she got her clothes out of the dryer, she realized that she shouldn't have put the cardigan in with the rest. Everything was tinted green, and the cardigan was felted and shrunken after its near-boiling treatment. She held it up and looked at it again. She couldn't remember where she had got it from. It was ruined now, though. She could try giving it to Ant for the shop, but he would probably consider it past saving and throw it away. He wouldn't like it when he saw what colour her white dress was either.

She sat on the bed as dusk fell, staring into the dark at the one patch of light.

The doll sat on the dressing table, still smiling, still looking straight ahead. The baby in the white cotton bonnet.

'So how do you do it?' asked Paul.

'Do what?'

'Write a book. Do you start with the whole plot laid out in detail, then sit down and start with chapter one?'

'I start with an advance and a deadline,' replied Kate. 'Anyone can write a novel in those circumstances, can't they?'

'More coffee?' asked Paul. 'And no, I don't think they can.'

'Thanks. I start with the corner of an idea. I write it down and I go on from there. A minimum of a thousand words a day, and a lot of thinking. Mostly in the bath.'

'Here's your coffee.'

'Why can't you remember that I don't take sugar?'

'Perhaps because you haven't given me enough practice.'

The gift of a mobile phone might qualify him for a casual meal at her place, like this evening's, but she was wary of the implications in Paul's remark. 'We're both busy people,' she said, neutrally.

He wandered across to her mantelpiece in the way that

irritated her and picked up a tiny enamel box in the shape of a scarlet cherry. 'This one's new,' he said, and put it back in the correct place, so that she could release her held breath.

'Present from a friend,' she said. From Liam, on one of their good days.

He didn't comment, but sat down on the sofa.

'It's lovely to see you, Paul, but from the way you're behaving, there's something specific you want to talk to me about. So what is it?'

'Can't we just spend an hour together without wondering about ulterior motives?'

No, she thought. She could feel, like a cold current in the room, that there was something he wanted to talk about, but couldn't bring himself to broach. It must be something unpleasant. If so, she could do without it.

She picked up a paperback from the table. 'I've been reading this. The latest in crime novels, apparently. What do you think about them?'

'I don't read much fiction,' he said, predictably. 'I've tried one or two of those things, but apart from finding that they don't know much about real policemen and how they work, I notice that your modern crime novelist isn't too keen on murder.'

'But I thought that was the point of a crime novel.'

'Take a closer look next time. Mostly the murders take place off-stage. And quite often – I've read this one as it happens and it's a case in point – you get three-quarters of the way through it before there's a dead body. As though she got so fond of her characters that she didn't want to knock any of them off.'

' "She"?'

'Well, they're all written by women, aren't they?'

Kate decided to ignore this inaccurate generalization. 'And you think that's copping out?'

'It's a sign of weakness, certainly.'

They glared at each other across the half-empty coffee cups.

Paul sighed. 'Can we start again?'

'Where from?'

'I think it had better be the point where we came in here after supper, and you offered me a cup of coffee.'

'Fine.' There was still an edge to her voice.

'Because you're right. There is something I'd like to talk about.'

Kate tried to relax her jaw and stop glaring at Paul. She was only partially successful. 'What?' Not good, Kate. Try it again, without the ice crystals. This is the man who gave you the mobile phone that is such a help in ensuring that rooms are empty when you want to let yourself in without their owner's consent. 'What would you like to talk about?'

'You. Us.'

Kate's eyebrows were travelling up her forehead. 'That one's easy,' she said. 'We're friends. Sort of.'

'Don't you ever think about the future?'

'I think about the work I have to do tomorrow, about the talk I've got to give next week, the conference I'm going to attend next spring.'

'But what about the important things?'

'Those are important.'

'So are commitment, marriage, children. Having a proper home.' With an enormous effort, he said, 'I'd like your life to be different.'

Kate was about to launch herself into an explanation, involving both Liam Ross and her commitment to her writing, of why they could never be more than friends, sort of. But at that moment there was a regular bleeping sound that wasn't familiar from any of her own pieces of electronic equipment.

The bleeping stopped and Paul said, in a different tone of voice, 'I need to use your phone.'

'Help yourself.'

While Paul punched buttons, spoke, listened, Kate felt relief that they had avoided the difficult subject of their relationship. If all the ambiguities were brought out into the light, and examined, they might find that it was impossible to continue in the old, ambivalent way.

'I have to go,' he said, when he had put the receiver down.

'I thought it was your evening off.' After the relief came the disappointment.

'I have to forget about time off when there's a serious crime.'

Kate knew better than to ask him what it was about. When she had seen him out, she went back to the papers she had borrowed from Olivia Blacket, and tried not to think about the conversation that she and Paul might have had if the phone hadn't interrupted them.

. . . incident that would have interested our dear friend Mr Tringham, though perhaps these unfortunate occurrences are common in London. Here in Oxford, our criminal classes are less imaginative in their . . .

Kate worked on the manuscript for most of the next

morning. She was delighted to have deciphered so much of a continuous passage, but the following lines were again defeating her. She picked up the thread a little further on:

> ... *call it, I believe, 'skinning'. A young child, separated for a few minutes from its nursemaid, who was momentarily distracted by conversation with a friend, was seized by two evil women, divested of all its clothing, and sent naked back to its distracted family ...*

Fascinating stuff, but not exactly what Kate was looking for for her own book. And certainly rather different from the way Olivia Blacket had read it.

Olivia's problem was her obsession with babies, Kate decided. It was only natural, of course. As Frances Adams had pointed out, Olivia must be thirty-six or seven and she could hear her biological clock ticking away. Mind you, there were plenty of other women out there who were the same age and who hadn't had children, but they weren't allowing it to dominate their lives like that.

Come to think of it, she was thirty-three herself, thought Kate. And I can hear that same clock ticking away in the silent reaches of the night. Camilla had brought the subject up the last time they had talked till midnight with a bottle of wine. Camilla, who was headmistress of a posh girls' school, reckoned there were plenty more interesting things to do with your life than have children. This imperative was Nature's way of ensuring that your genes went on existing long after you didn't, she said, and should be ignored. It was all a con trick, really, Camilla reckoned. Kate wasn't quite so sure herself. Camilla's bloke was in his early twenties and was not made of conventional father material. Kate, meanwhile, had found herself peering into buggies, and she had even caught herself smiling at the horrid little toadfaced child who lived next door. But whatever had brought it to the fore, the thought was there and wouldn't go away. For, after all, it was true. If she wanted to have a child, or children, get married, in whatever order, then she had better get on with it.

What was it that Paul had been wanting to say? He had got as far as admitting that he wanted their relationship to change, but he hadn't exactly launched himself into any details.

Having babies was a nice idea, she had to admit, as long as you didn't think too hard about the practicalities. Like, how on earth did you get any writing done when you had a baby around all the time? And suppose your children turned out like the three next door? Enough, Kate.

She turned back to the manuscript. The trouble was, the beastly thing seemed to be full of observations about babies and children. It was as though there was no escape from the subject. Wherever she went in the town there were babies in carrysacks and toddlers in buggies. The good thing was that she had now transcribed the passage about Mr Tringham, and although from her personal point of view it was rather disappointing, it did also mean that Professor Adams and Frances weren't hiding anything from her.

Her eyes were tired. She leaned her face in her hands and tried to rest them for a minute. Perhaps this would be a good time to telephone the professor and tell him that she now had Olivia's transcription of the page that he and his sister had been working on.

She rang his number at Garsington. Frances answered.

'Why do you want to speak to him?' She sounded deeply suspicious and very unfriendly. What had gone wrong? Was there some old-world courtesy that she had omitted?

'It was about the Ternan Papers. I wanted a little chat about page forty-three. I may have something to add to what we were discussing, which the professor could be interested in.' There, that was delicate enough for anyone, wasn't it? Diffident to the point of extinction, she thought.

'Oh, I see.' Frances sounded marginally less frosty. Had she perhaps found out about the little friend in Westbourne Terrace, and was she suspecting Kate of being her? 'I'll get him for you, but I'm afraid you'll find he's very upset over what has happened.'

'Very upset about what?' Kate called down the phone, but Frances had already set the receiver down and her footsteps could be heard retreating across the hallway.

Was her deception at the college yesterday discovered? Or had Olivia found the pages missing and accused the professor of taking them? No, this was ridiculous. It would take Olivia years to notice that anything at all was missing from that amazing room. And even if she did, she would hardly go storming to the head of her department to accuse him of theft.

'Hallo. Kate?' The professor sounded like an old man. And an old man who had just received some terrible news. Kate forgot about the information she had to give him.

'What on earth is wrong? What's happened?'

'You haven't heard. You don't know.' Statements, not questions. They both waited while the professor thought about how to put it. 'It's Olivia. She's dead, I'm afraid.'

'How did it happen?' Tell me that it was a traffic accident. Tell me even that she went completely off her head and committed suicide. Just don't tell me that . . .

'She was murdered.'

'Oh, my God!'

'Quite. We're all devastated by the news. She was not an easy woman, but this is not what one expects in an Oxford college.'

Or anywhere. Does anyone, anywhere, ever expect it?

'How?' She could only croak out a monosyllable.

'The police are very guarded. They are giving out little information yet.'

'Do you know when it happened?'

'Yesterday afternoon, apparently.'

'Where?' asked Kate, not wanting to know the answer.

'Her room at college.'

'Was it an intruder, do you think? A thief who panicked when he was disturbed?' You could clutch at straws.

'There was the traditional Mourning Ale being dispensed, if you remember. And it was very difficult for any casual intruders to get into college.'

They were both silent for a long time, while Kate remembered talking her way into Leicester College and getting into Olivia's rooms. But Olivia was still alive, and shouting at Liam when she left. Liam. What if he had turned back to continue the row and . . .

No, not Liam. Liam only moved in one direction when a row was going on. Out. Away. And after passing Olivia, she had gone into Clifford Quad and seen the professor with Ludo. Perhaps the professor was remembering it, too.

'Would you like to come over and talk about it?' he asked.

Kate knew from experience that when a tragedy, a violent tragedy like this one, happened, the people near to it had a need to get together and talk, as though talking it out would make sense of it.

'Yes, I would. I really would.'

'I know you're driving,' said Frances. 'But you still look as if you need a drink. Here, have a whisky.'

'Thanks.' The knowledge that someone she knew had been murdered had a worse effect on her driving than a small whisky did.

'I'll leave the two of you to talk.'

The professor's ruddy face was paler and he even looked thinner and less robust.

'Yes, thank you, Frances.' But he didn't seem anxious to begin. Kate pulled her chair a little nearer to his.

'Tell me about it,' she said. 'I know from experience that it really does help.'

'I had to identify her, you know,' he said. 'Her mother died a couple of years ago and her father, who was a lot older than his wife, is old and fragile and living in a nursing home. So they asked me.'

'It must have been terrible for you.' It was appalling how all the things you could say in the circumstances were clichés.

'Yes, it was horrible. She was much too young to die. And in such a fashion.' His face screwed up, and he pressed his lips together as if to stop himself from crying. 'They prepare the ... body as best they can, to save you from the shock. But even so.'

'No. It's still an obscenity.' Kate pitied him: it might be better if he could give way to some emotion, but she knew he wouldn't, or at least not in front of her or his sister.

'When someone has been hit repeatedly on the face and head with God knows what. A rock? An iron bar? Have you any idea what it does to them? To begin with I wasn't even sure it was her. I could only think of how much blood there must have been. And not just blood.'

Kate leant over and took hold of his hand. At least he didn't object to that. She wanted to tell him to stop his description, but knew that she shouldn't. For her own sake, perhaps. Not for his.

'I suppose the police and the doctors must get hardened to it. I don't know what must be worse: to feel the full horror of it, as I did. Or to get so accustomed to sights like this one that you no longer feel anything.'

'I don't think they all lose the sense of horror, or of pity.' Paul wouldn't, she was sure.

'The other terrible thing,' he said, a little while later, still holding her hand, 'is that I didn't like the woman. I would never want this to happen to her, of course. No one deserves that. But however hard I try, I can't feel any warmth for her. Pity, yes. Horror, yes. But no affection.'

'She wasn't an easy character,' said Kate. 'I think she would have repulsed any warmth on your part, anyway. And I think perhaps there were things that happened in her life that made her the way she was. Maybe she had to grow that hard shell in order to survive. But as far as she was able, I think she was fond of you. She used to look after your dog, didn't she?'

'That was just a big tease, really. I knew she didn't want Ludo there. She felt that he interfered with her work. But she didn't like to say no, because I was her boss. She was an ambitious woman, and she wanted to keep in with me.'

'Weren't you afraid that she'd mistreat Ludo?'

'Oh no. Once Olivia said she'd do something, she was very conscientious. And Ludo was very fond of her. In his own way.'

Kate looked down at her once-beautiful shoes. The tassels hung in limp strips where they had been chewed by Ludo. The shoes would never look smart again. It reminded her of the mauling she had received at Olivia's house that first day. Perhaps Ludo and Olivia had had a lot in common.

'I haven't told the police yet, by the way. I haven't given them a very complete and coherent statement yet. I'm afraid I was too upset yesterday to tell them everything I knew.'

'What is it you haven't told them?' she asked.

'That I saw you dressed up as a scholar of Bartlemas College on the afternoon when Olivia was murdered.'

'Oh, you noticed.'

'I'm assuming that you aren't in fact a member of Bartlemas?'

'You'd be correct.'

'I'm sure it will be all right,' he said gently. 'After all, I was delivering Ludo to Olivia in her room when I met you. And Olivia was alive – though in a towering rage – when I got there. I just dropped off Ludo and escaped. I don't suppose you know why she was so angry?'

'It had nothing to do with me,' said Kate, quickly, not wanting to describe the scene between Liam and Olivia. 'And yes, you're right, I was masquerading as an undergraduate. I wanted to see Olivia and get the page of transcript from her – page forty-three, the one of which you and Frances had the original.'

'She gave it to you?' The professor spoke in tones of amazement.

'Not exactly. I'm sure she would have done, if I'd had the chance to explain the situation to her. But when I got to her room,' said Kate, conveniently forgetting her phone call from the quad, 'I found that she wasn't there.'

'But the door,' said Brendan quietly, 'would have been locked.' There was still a sharp mind at work under the emotional shock.

'On the contrary,' said Kate, not wishing to be too particular about how she got in, 'the door was open.' Well, it was once she had unlocked it, after all.

'And you conveniently found the Ternan Papers sitting in the middle of her desk?'

'Once I had located her desk, yes, she had left the papers on the top, and since she wasn't there to ask, and since I knew I was only *borrowing* a page or two . . .'

'I think I understand how it happened,' said the professor.

'That was why I phoned,' said Kate, on firmer ground at last. 'I wanted to bring you Olivia's transcription of page forty-three.'

'Have you read it?'

'Yes.'

'And what do you think?'

Kate paused. When someone died, it was very difficult to speak the truth about them. Whatever you thought of them in life, you had to soften it when they were dead.

'I think she was very concerned about babies and children. She read their presence in everything, and I think it affected her judgement of the papers.' Well, that was better than saying she thought Olivia was off her head.

Brendan was nodding. 'It's only what we thought. I wonder what sparked it off?'

'I don't suppose we'll ever know, now.' Personally, she thought that it was all part of Olivia's difficult personality.

'You must go and talk to the police, though,' he said. 'It really would be much better for you to go to them and volunteer any information you might have. They will discover, one way or another, that you were there that afternoon, and it won't look good if you don't come forward.'

He was right. She would do it. Tomorrow.

At this moment Ludo lumbered into the room. After sniffing at Kate's shoes and giving them a desultory lick, he went over to Brendan and sat with his jaw on the professor's knee and gazed up into his face.

'Stupid dog,' said Brendan, affectionately. 'Stupid bloody dog. You're all pretence, aren't you? Why couldn't you look after her for us? Why did you have to let it happen?'

Ludo wagged his tail, bringing down the contents of a small table, as Kate stood up to leave.

'Let's keep in touch,' she said.

Brendan just went on pulling at Ludo's ears and shaking his head.

Chapter 8

The duty of the Tintinnabulary is, at the death of the Master, or any of the Fellows, or Scholars, belonging to Leicester College, to put on the clothes of the deceased and to give notice of their burial by ringing eleven times that bell which is called the Mourning Bell.

Statutes of Leicester College, 1832

'You haven't forgotten the concert, have you, Kate?' It was Andrew Grove on the phone.

'Of course not.' With one thing and another, it had gone right out of her head.

'Good. For a moment there I thought you were going to tell me that you'd got yourself involved with this unsavoury business at Leicester. It's just as well that the concert is at Bartlemas, isn't it? If it had been at Leicester, I suppose they would have had to cancel it. Or substitute a requiem, perhaps.'

'Not funny, Andrew.' As a matter of fact, she was not looking forward to a concert of such determinedly cheerful

151

music. But he was the last person she wished to discuss it with. There was a dispassionate streak in Andrew that verged on the callous.

He must have read something into her voice. 'You mean you are involved? How unwise of you.'

'I'll see you at seven thirty outside Bartlemas, shall I?' Once she started talking about it she would never stop until all her scrambled emotions were winging their way down the phone line.

Back at her desk, Kate was looking again at the two pages of Olivia's neat, educated handwriting. She wanted to find out what was in Olivia's head before she was killed. And she felt she owed it to the other woman to try to understand what she had been achieving.

She hadn't noticed before, but this ink, too, was the colour of dried blood. She wrinkled up her nose. Yuck. Why couldn't she have used black?

She wished that she could confide in someone sane and dependable. Someone like Paul Taylor. But, unfortunately, a policeman was the last person she could talk to at the moment.

The phone rang. Maybe it would be Andrew, changing his mind, cancelling their concert date. She could hope.

'Kate? Liam.'

'Yes?' What on earth could she say to him?

'You've heard about Olivia Blacket?'

'Yes.' How well had he known her? Difficult to tell what their relationship had been from the flaming row that she heard that afternoon.

'Yes, you would have done. From your little policeman friend, I suppose.'

'No.' He wasn't listening to her replies. He was as bad as Olivia at hearing only the words inside his own head.

'Have you been talking to him? What have you been saying? I've had two of them round here asking questions, and now they want me to go down to the station and make a statement.'

Why on earth did he sound so distraught? This was what happened when someone was murdered. Surely he knew that? She would have to go herself and tell them that she was there and what she had seen. Tomorrow.

'We have to discuss it, Kate. You've got to put your friend straight.'

'I don't know what you're talking about, Liam.'

'Oh yes you do. Don't play your butter-wouldn't-melt games with me. I've seen you sit there with your big round eyes, making up your fictions as you talk.'

'Look, I realize that you must be upset—'

'Upset? You don't begin to understand what it's been like. I've been sitting in my room in college listening to that bloody bell. The Mourning Bell. You know they ring it eleven times when a member of college dies? Some Governing Body back in the nineteenth century sat round a table and came up with this horrible idea. Your friend dies and you have to sit and listen to the bell. You can't get away from it. It goes on and on. Eleven times. Have you any idea just how long it takes?'

'It must have been terrible for you. But what do you want me to do?'

'You have to talk to me. Listen to my side of the story. And then tell your policeman friend to lay off me.'

'I can't. I have no influence over how he does his job. And anyway, he's only a detective sergeant. I don't suppose he has any say in the decisions that are made about who is interviewed, or not.'

'You'd do something for me if you really cared. Look how you worked at hiding the truth when it was your friend Camilla in the shit. I'll come round before I go down to the police station in St Aldate's.'

'You can't. I'm going out.'

'No. Where?'

'To a concert in Bartlemas College chapel, as a matter of fact.'

'It doesn't start until seven forty-five,' he said. Trust Liam to know when a concert began. 'So I'll see you inside the chapel at seven twenty. You've got time to make it if you leave now.'

'I was just going to change.'

'That's not important. Our talk is.' And he put the phone down.

Damn these overbearing men. She should take no notice of him. On the other hand, she very much wanted to hear what he had to say. Just out of curiosity, of course.

'You're five minutes late.'

'Hallo, Liam. It's lovely to see you, too.'

Liam grabbed her arm and pushed her inside the chapel, waving his hand dismissively at the student who tried to sell him a ticket.

'In here,' he said.

The chapel was dark and the pews were high. He thrust her down on to the hard seat and stood blocking her exit. In the background, the choir was running through a few scales and exercises before the concert. Kate hardly recognized the man who stood in front of her, trapping her in her seat, as the lighthearted lover of the past few months.

Dark wooden linenfold panelling forced her to keep her back straight, while the overhanging ledge pressed the vertebrae of her neck into painful compression. They were obviously a shorter breed back in the time when they'd built the place.

'So what were you doing in Olivia's study?' asked Liam. 'I imagine that's where you'd been, when she saw you. If she had called the porter, she could have had you thrown out.'

'So why didn't she?'

'It was only after you had joined the mob for Mourning Ale that she remembered who you were, and that you had no business to be in college that day.'

'What are you accusing me of?'

'Getting yourself involved. Going round asking questions and pushing your nose into things that don't concern you. Interfering in my life. And then I suppose you'll report back to your policeman. What is it between you two, anyway?'

'Nothing. We're just friends. And I haven't done any of those things yet.' But she would, soon, and he knew it. Particularly if he pushed her too hard.

'So what were you doing in Olivia's room?' he insisted.

She could try a little fib. 'I thought I might find you there.'

'I was in a seminar. Didn't the lodge tell you?'

'Well, the lodge was shuttered and closed, so I couldn't really ask them, could I? And anyway, you weren't in a seminar.' She might as well go on the attack.

He ignored the challenge. 'And when you discovered that I wasn't in Olivia's room, what did you do next?'

He was so angry that she would have to give him an

answer. And she didn't think she could fob him off with too much flannel.

'I told you I was writing a book about Maria Susanna Taylor. And Olivia has been given the Ternan Papers to edit. As you must have known. You knew her much better than you were letting on, didn't you?'

'In your own words, we were just friends,' said Liam, with the tight-mouthed expression that meant he was not going to expand on what he was saying. 'Go on with your explanation of why you were in Olivia's room.'

'I was hoping to find a little snippet of something I could use. Just to get myself a step or two ahead of the competition.'

'I'm not sure I believe you,' Liam said. He was leaning over the pew, his face close to hers. He looked not only angry, but dangerous. She wanted to get out of the pew and away from him.

'What was the row about between you and Olivia?' she asked. Unwise to ask him this, but she wanted to know the answer.

'Absolutely not your business.' He was furious. 'And how did you know about it, anyway?'

'I think the whole college must have heard you. If you want to keep that sort of thing secret, you should do it in whispers, and behind closed doors.' She decided to go on the attack again. 'And how well did you know her? I'm not sure I go for this "just good friends" bit. I thought when we talked about the Ternan Papers the other day that you hardly knew her at all.'

'Of course I knew her,' he said. 'Why are you asking all these questions? It's bad enough having the police on my back, without you joining in as well.' He was trying out his hurt child expression. It wasn't working.

'It seems to me it's pretty important to know what you and Olivia were fighting about. It sounded as though you were about to come to blows. And it happened very shortly before she was killed, as far as I can make out.'

She thought he was angry enough to hit her. But he couldn't attack her in a college chapel. Not really, could he?

'Just keep out of my affairs. And tell your policeman friend it's none of his business, either.'

'I have this strange desire to know who has killed a woman I saw a matter of minutes before her death. Is that so odd? What are you afraid I'll find?'

The angels on the chapel ceiling laughed at her innocence, and went on playing their curious instruments. Shawm, serpent, sackbut: she'd heard the names, but had no idea what they looked like. Liam would know, but this was hardly the time to ask him.

'Excuse me, Ross, but I believe Kate is spending the next hour or two in my company.'

Andrew. Knight in shining armour.

The two men glared at one another like bristling dogs.

Liam took a step backwards. Fisticuffs in a college chapel would not help his image with the police.

'Yes, of course,' he said, stiffly. 'I'll see you soon, perhaps, Kate.'

As he walked away, Kate called, 'But when did Olivia get a chance to tell you she saw me?'

The answer was very important, but she wasn't sure that she wanted to know what it was. She had thought that Liam was in the clear. She had seen him walking away from Olivia, and Olivia was very much alive then. But he could only know of her visit to Olivia's rooms if he had spoken to her later, after she had seen Kate in the quadrangle. And there wasn't very much 'later'. Why had he gone back? And what had he done when he got there?

'Shall we find our seats?' asked Andrew. 'I've got a couple of programmes already.'

The music was easy to listen to, and from time to time during the concert Kate allowed her attention to go back to the argument with Liam. The thought that was coming to her so insistently concerned Olivia and her apparent obsession with babies. She was starting to think it was impossible for Olivia to get worked up about any subject but that one. So what did that tell her about the row she was having with Liam while Kate was hiding in her room?

Bartlemas College is not far from Magdalen Bridge. Just over the bridge lies The Plain, and the road that leads into East Oxford. Andrew Grove lived towards the north, Kate to the west of the city.

'Have you brought your car?' he asked.

'No, I walked.' She usually did.

'I've left mine in the university car park. Would you like me to give you a lift back?'

She was just about to accept, as she would be grateful for his company. She would be grateful for anyone's company at the moment, so that she didn't have to think about all the things that had happened. 'Thanks, Andrew, but I need the exercise.' Something made her refuse his offer: she had caught sight of a familiar figure, and she thought that Andrew might scare her off.

'Will you be safe on your own?'

'Don't worry,' she said, suddenly inspired to a new untruth. 'I've got my mobile phone with me in my bag, and I'll call you as soon as there's any trouble whatsoever.'

'Oh, well, fine then.' He seemed mildly relieved that she was leaving. She hadn't been very good company, she realized.

'Goodnight, and thanks, Andrew.'

She waved him goodbye as he crossed the High Street and disappeared in the direction of Parks Road. It didn't occur to him that if she did phone, he wouldn't be home to receive her call for at least fifteen minutes.

Then she turned back to see if the shadowy figure had stayed around to talk to her.

'Hallo, Angel,' she said. 'Did you want to talk to me?'

'Hallo, Kate Ivory,' said Angel. 'Yes, I do.'

'Hungry?' Kate asked, back in her kitchen in Fridesley.

'Not really,' said Angel. But she changed her mind when she saw Kate's selection of fresh vegetables and the big bowl of fruit. 'They feed me well,' she said, defensively. 'But they're not keen on green things like beans or broccoli.'

So Kate made her a stir-fry with a dozen different ingredients. They ate in the kitchen out of Kate's knobbly white china dishes, washed down with glasses of Australian Shiraz, which Kate hoped would serve as lubricant to Angel's story.

They had walked back through the dark and nearly deserted streets of Oxford, mostly in silence. Kate didn't want to frighten Angel away, but she very much wanted to know what she had been doing outside Leicester College in a state of shock, at about the time of Olivia's murder. She didn't want to land the thing on Angel, but if it let friends of hers off the hook, like Liam and the professor, not to mention herself, then she needed to hear what Angel had to say.

They drank tea after their meal, then did the washing-up and took the rest of the bottle of Shiraz into the sitting room with them.

'I'd better ring the family,' said Angel. 'Just so that they don't worry about me.'

'Help yourself,' said Kate, showing her the phone. It sounded so normal, she couldn't believe it.

'That one's a comfortable chair,' said Kate, pointing, when Angel had finished her phone call. Then she poured out two more glasses of wine and sat back in a corner of the sofa and hoped that Angel got through her story before they both fell asleep in front of the fire.

'Did you know Olivia Blacket?' asked Angel.

So she knew her name. 'Yes, but not very well. I'd met her a couple of times, both in the last week.'

'And did you know that she was dead?'

'I heard on the phone, from a colleague of hers.'

'So she wasn't a close friend or anything?'

'I went to see her the other day because I wanted some information for my new book. Olivia could provide it. That's all there was to it. I don't think we could ever have become close. She really wasn't my type.' Tall, slim, elegant. Over-educated, supercilious. Very untidy. Beautiful. No, not Kate's type. 'How about you? Is she . . . *was* she a friend of yours?'

'No. I had met her once before. In the New Year. But I couldn't remember it. I couldn't remember anything. All I knew was that I had to get to Leicester. I didn't even know it was an Oxford college until a few days ago. And I've known now for a few months that I had to see someone called Olivia Blacket. But I didn't know why.'

'Are you telling me that you'd lost your memory?'

'Yes. Parts of it have returned, but not all of it yet.' She helped herself to more wine, and sat and sipped at it for a while, not talking.

'And how did you meet up with those men?'

'They're my family. That's what they call themselves. The family. We belong to Ant. He's our leader.'

'I think I would understand it better if you started at the beginning.'

Kate worked her way slowly down her glass of wine while Angel told her story. Or at least those parts of it that she remembered. And there were still a few patches that she kept to herself, Kate reckoned. She spoke for a long time, and Kate didn't interrupt. She felt that there must be something therapeutic in this narration, and it seemed to her that what Angel needed was a touch of therapy.

'They found me at Leicester Square tube station,' said Angel. 'I don't remember it, but they've told me about it since. The only thing that's still clear about that day is the sound of the whistle playing in the background. I didn't know it then, but it was Coffin playing down in the tube station. Jigs, reels, that sort of thing. He was really good.'

Angel paused again here. Drank some more wine. Kate went to get some crackers that they could nibble between the drinks. Eventually, Angel continued with her story.

'I can remember what it felt like to be cold and hungry, and the hunted feeling of being on the streets. I don't think that went on for more than a few weeks before they found me. I don't think I'd have lasted much longer if they hadn't.

'They took me back to their place in Notting Hill, and after some time, we moved on. I don't remember much about that, either. I wasn't well after living on the streets. And my memory had gone entirely. Do you know what that is like?'

Kate shook her head. Angel was getting agitated, her eyes moving restlessly round the room.

'No, you can't imagine it unless you've been through it. It's terrifying. I walked down the street and looked in shop windows until I found one that had calendars and diaries in. That's how I found out what year it was. I felt that I had to know that. Then I'd know how old I was. Trouble was, I couldn't remember what year I was born, so I still don't know my age. Twenty-two, maybe? Twenty-three? I don't even know how many years of my life are missing.'

Her hands were clenched on her lap. Kate wondered whether she could move the story along a bit, but before she could prompt her Angel had started to talk again.

'And I don't know how long it was before I started taking notice of what was happening, but it was no longer winter, or even early spring. Late spring, maybe, or early summer. Green, anyway. Very green. With the round hill outside the window and the cows. Hangman Hill, I found out it was called. But that was later.'

So Angel had lost a couple of months of her life back in the spring.

'One morning I woke up, I mean really woke up, so that I knew that I existed, and was separate from the people around me. I've got to explain something to you,' said Angel. 'It's not just that they were kind to me, but the really surpris-

ing thing about them was that they seemed to want nothing
in return. Not that I had much to give. But on the streets
you have to look out for yourself, and you reckon that
everyone's after something. But they weren't. They just
wanted me to get better so that I could join their family.
Family is the most important thing to them. And I suppose
it is to me, now. Anyway, I was telling you about that morning
when I started to come alive.'

'Sit up,' he was saying. 'You have to sit up if you want to
eat. Aren't you hungry yet?'

A face, out of focus in its nearness. Red face, redder lips,
pouting and plump. Dark eyes, brown or dark grey maybe.
Black eyebrows. A nose that was no particular shape. Spots,
purplish against the red skin. Huge hands, with fingers like
sausages, holding a white cardboard plate near her own face
so that she breathed in the smell of hot cheese and the oil
they use in fast-food places.

'It's pizza.' A different voice. The one who spoke this time
was standing further back and she could see a section of his
face over the first one's shoulder. Pale face, long nose, dark
hair, growing unevenly, flopping over his face. He moved
sideways, and she saw a ragged white T-shirt that had been
washed with the coloureds so that it was a mauvish shade
of grey.

'We got it specially for you,' he said. 'It's good, I promise.
Eat.' His words seemed to suggest that sometimes what he
offered would not be good, might be unwholesome, or poisoned. She wished he would step out from behind the red-
and-white checked shoulder of the first man so that she could
see him properly. Nothing in her world was complete: she

had a rectangular portion of round hill, a man who was only hand, face and voice, and another who consisted of a segment of face, seen over a shoulder. She placed her hands flat down by her hips and pushed against the bed. At least there wasn't much pain now, but still she was too weak to move. There seemed to be no muscles in her arms. She braced herself against her heels, scrabbled with her feet, wriggled her torso. She succeeded in moving a few inches, and as she leaned forwards, a third person, completely invisible this one, stuffed something – pillows? cushions? – behind her back so that she was half sitting, half reclining, and could advance her chin towards the slice of pizza, open her mouth and take a bite as it was brought nearer to her. Pizza. She would have to try to remember the taste. If asked, with no prompting, she would have said cardboard, with some soft, messy topping. She chewed. She went on chewing for ever, until it turned to mush in her mouth, and she knew she would have to make the huge effort to swallow it, or else spit it out. The men, whoever they were, however many of them there were, might not like that, after all the trouble they had taken. She swallowed.

'Give her some water,' said the second man. He had moved further back into the shadows of the room so that she could just see a dark shape, with a paler top and face, in spite of the fact that she was nearly sitting now. He seemed to be in charge.

The cup was plastic, the water very cold and good tasting. Sweet. Not like the acrid stuff from the taps in the Thames Valley. She swallowed again. It was easier this time.

'Let her sleep,' said Number Two. 'We'll find out more about her next time she wakes up.' Number Three, who existed for her only as a pair of thin, pale hands emerging from dark-red sweatshirt sleeves, removed the support from behind her back and guided her down in the covers so that she was lying flat, cocooned in the rough blankets.

'What are you called?' she asked, as she felt them moving towards the door. 'What are your names?' Names would be hooks to hang the rest of experience on.

'Later,' said Number Two. 'We'll tell you later.'

She closed her eyes and heard the soft shuffling noises they made as they left the room, the click of the door as it closed behind them.

Then she lay in the dark behind her eyelids and listened to the sound of Coffin playing one of his whistles.

It might be early morning when she next wakes. Inside the room it is colourless, drab, tomblike. Outside the window the trees are springing with green leaves. It should be winter. The trees should be black sticks, the hill brown with a grey frosting of snow. The sky should be leaden. Why is there all this joyous life outside the window? Somewhere an officious bird whistles a cheerful tune. Why couldn't Nature mirror her mood instead of mocking it like this? The fat, placid cows just keep pulling at the grass.

There was a wall of fine rain between the house and the hill so that all its green colours were muted. At the top, curls of cloud, like thin white hair on an old woman's head, hid the trees from sight. If she stared at the cows on their green hillside, then closed her eyes, she could see the scene with the colours reversed. Scarlet hill, grey and white cows. She opened her eyes again quickly.

She remembered life on the streets. It was no fun sitting out in the rain, while it soaked through your thin cotton clothing and the pavement beside you shone with a thin greasy covering of mud. Every leaf, every blade of grass wept fine, saltless tears. She should be crying too, but she couldn't. If she did, she would have to remember what she was crying for, and she didn't want to do that. As she watched, the rain grew heavier, so that it streaked down her window, distorting and obscuring the view of the hill.

In the next room, Coffin was practising 'Greensleeves'.

One of them came into the room. She was starting to recognize the individuals. There were three, or perhaps four, of them. This was the one she liked the least, the one with the red face and the spots, the one who was slow to understand when she spoke to him. Yesterday he had told her his name: Dime. She had not told him hers, since it was one of the things that she did not wish to remember, but he had called her Angel. He was wearing the same red-and-white checked shirt that he wore when she first saw him. He looked as though he had had a bath, but his clothes still smelled of old food.

He sat by her bed, and smiled at her, and talked, on and on, about the family. How they had to stick together and how they were going to be great and successful and rich.

In the next room, Coffin was playing 'Bridge over Troubled Water' on his whistle.

Today she got out of bed and walked across to the window.

The window isn't large, and the glass is grey and smeared, its surface uneven, so that the view outside is distorted, as though seen through gently rippling water. The ground slopes down steeply in front of the house, and there is a row of trees – quite tall ones – at the bottom of the slope. She doesn't recognize them, except for the copper beech in the centre. She can hear water gurgling and bubbling. Maybe there is a stream down there, out of sight. One day, when she is feeling stronger, she will go and look: she feels much stronger than she did last week – or was it last year? One day soon she will be able to go outside and walk down and look at the stream. She takes her shoes off and walks through the brown water. 'Look, Daisy!' she shouts. 'Look at me walking through the stream.' Why doesn't Daisy answer?

There is a patch of mauve to the right of the copper beech: rhododendrons, growing wild. She can see more cows, too. Eleven of them. An awkward number. There should be ten, or twelve. Perhaps one is hiding behind a tree or has wandered off to the left, out of sight, like Daisy. She is too tired to work out the possibilities. She just wishes that the cow would turn up and complete the dozen, or that one of those that she can see would wander off and leave her with a round ten.

As the morning passes, the rain gets heavier, and behind the watery fence the hill appears much nearer, so that now she can see the details of the bushes and trees, the lines in the turf, like contour lines, running parallel to the line of the trees. The sky is a uniform, pearly grey, so she cannot tell which way she is facing. Water drips from every leaf.

Coffin comes into her room. He says nothing, but sits over by the window, cross-legged on the floor. He takes out one of his whistles from the velvet-lined black box, and starts to play. This morning it is 'The Green Fields of France'. When he stops playing he smiles at her. She tries to smile back.

To the right of the window stands an oak tree. A branch hangs down, well within her view, and she recognizes the leaves. *Oak* tree. A fact to hang on to. Something that she knows. She seems to know so little: and that mostly what Ant has told her. There is one thing that she hasn't told Ant, and she smiles and holds this one secret, this one little pinpoint of memory that is hers alone. It is so simple. Two words. A name. She may forget everything else, but she will always remember the name. And one day . . . But the thought of what she will have to do on that day is too much to think about yet.

Ant is the tall, pale one, with the thin, straight, dark hair, growing too long, the pale grey eyes, the long nose. He walked right into the room one day and stood next to the bed, so that she could see him completely, or at least from the knees upwards. Black T-shirt from which he had removed the sleeves, so that the shoulders stuck out and the armhole was ragged. T-shirt tucked into the waistband of black jeans. Jeans belted with black leather, a large brass buckle drawing her eye, like a winking navel; the jeans old, the material soft and creased, as though it would now hold for ever the details of the body beneath it.

He is nicer than Dime, but not as restful as Coffin. Coffin often comes in to see her these days. He hardly ever speaks, but just sits over near the window and plays his whistle. She finds it oddly comforting. The tunes he plays wrap themselves around her like warm blankets. Maybe this is how love feels.

'Remembered anything yet, Angel?' asked Ant. His mouth

was a long, thin slit, his ears pale, with very long lobes. He wore an earring, set with a shining stone, like a diamond, or a crystal bead.

'No,' she said. 'I remembered nothing. How did I get here?' Wherever *here* might be.

'This is our place,' said Ant. 'You're our guest.' He smiled at her, though it was only his mouth that moved, not his eyes. 'For the moment you're our guest. But one day you'll be one of us. One of the family. One day I'll tell you what that means.'

'Why do you call me Angel?'

'Have you remembered your old name?'

'No.' But she'd remembered the other name.

Ant said, ' "Madam Life's a piece in bloom, Death goes dogging everywhere: He's the tenant of the room, She's the ruffian on the stair." '

Angel had heard it before somewhere, but she had the impression that Ant had changed the words in some way which she couldn't grasp.

'We found you on the steps leading down to Leicester Square station,' said Ant. 'And you looked a proper little ruffian. So you're my Ruffian on the Stair. And you know who that is?'

'No.' This question was too difficult.

'She's the Angel of Death. So I called you Angel.'

Angel smiled at that. Ant didn't know just how appropriate the name was. She remembered the tune that Coffin was playing that day: it was 'She Moved through the Fair'. That was all about dying and ghosts and haunting, too.

'Just you keep getting better: we've got plans for you.'

She nodded. She was glad that someone had a plan, since

she had none and could not contemplate making any decisions.

Then he must have taken pity on her, for he said: 'We're in Devon.' And before she could comment, he said: 'Where are you from?'

'London.' It popped out. She hadn't known it before she spoke the word.

'Good,' said Ant. 'Surname?' She shook her head. She was called Angel now. She was the Ruffian on the Stair.

She didn't tell him that she had remembered the other name. Olivia Blacket. She didn't think that it had anything to do with him.

Today the sun is shining, and at nearly two o'clock in the afternoon the shadows are short, so that the hill leans away from her and the trees and bushes stand out from the grass like oddly placed ears and noses, or patches of fur. The greens are differentiated, too, from the ribbed emerald of the grass, to the rusty green of the trees higher up. Earlier, she had counted nine cows, but now they have disappeared. She is getting to recognize the cows by size and colour, and to know which ones are missing. She doesn't get so upset now when one or more of the cows are absent for a while. She knows that they will come back.

As well as daisies and buttercups, and the mauve patch of rhododendrons by the stream, she sees small pink roses cascading over a grey brick archway, and as she sniffs the air she thinks she catches their scent behind the hot-fat smell of another pizza. It must be Dime who is getting her lunch again today: a pity, since she is really getting very tired of cheese and tomato pizza. Something with olives and anchovies would be a nice change, but she doesn't think that Dime's tastes run to such sophistication.

'What are we doing in Devon?' she tried asking him.

'I dunno.' Dime looked puzzled that anyone should even ask the question. Dime, she realized now, followed Ant. Or at least, Dime was a member of the family, and the family was in Devon, so that's where Dime was. Easy. Yes, life was easier for them all if they just stuck to the main point: they belonged to Ant's family. Dime smiled at her. She knew he liked her, and it was a comforting feeling. They all liked her. Dime took her plate and the unfinished pizza slice and left the room.

'It's my turn to do the washing-up,' he said.

On the whole, she preferred being on her own, though she didn't mind listening to Coffin's music. It was peaceful with Ant and Dime, Gren and Coffin. More peaceful than . . .

She went back to the window and watched the swallows dipping low over the grass, turning so that she could see their white bellies, before skimming away to the left. She craned her neck. What was out there? Grey brick archway, pink roses, black and white swallows. Devon. She wanted to know more.

She could get out of bed on her own, now: she didn't need Dime or Ant, Gren or Coffin to help her. She looked down at herself. She was wearing an old, soft, man's shirt, and her legs stuck out, white and thin from lying down so long, shapeless with unused muscle, and covered with a fur of unshaven hair, as though, like two separate animals, they had thrived in the warmth and the darkness. Then she saw the thick purple scars on her right leg. Recent. And remembered pain came back to her. She shook her head. She was going the wrong way. Go forwards. Like the controls on the video recorder. She frowned. Video recorder. The name was there, but not the thing it belonged to. Too difficult. Concentrate on here and now.

She sniffed at herself. She smelled of unwashed body, but really, not too bad, considering. If she had a mirror she could look at herself. Strange that she couldn't remember what she looked like, or how old she was. Not so old, though, she knew.

Maybe somewhere she had a home, a family; a bathroom where she could wash and comb her hair; a life she could walk back into. If, if, if. A wave of despair threatened to engulf her again. Concentrate on what she did have, what she was lucky to have: a bed covered in blankets, a roof from the rain, a view across a sloping meadow to a rounded hill; the company of Ant, Gren, Coffin and Dime. It was better than being alone on a cold, wet pavement, that at least she did know.

Although her legs could carry her as far as the window, they still felt strange, as though someone had removed the bones and muscles, the arteries and veins, and had replaced them with smooth, pliable rubber. Maybe that was what the scars meant. She must get back to bed. She was not quite sure that when she moved a foot it would land where she intended, so she crossed the space between the window and bed in a series of ungainly lurches, her arms spread out like the feelers of a being from another planet.

Gren came in then. She hadn't had much to do with him up till then. He was just one of the people who brought her food, wiped her face, lifted her up when they made her bed.

'I could get you something to help you walk,' he said. 'I've got a friend with contacts in the trade.'

'Thanks. That would be a help.'

'No problem.'

That, she discovered later, was Gren's trademark.

He brought her a Zimmer frame, and later a walking stick, and watched proudly as she made her way with increasing confidence from the bed to the window and back again, and finally downstairs and through the front door.

She never asked where he got these things from, or who his contacts were. And Gren never told her.

Coffin sat in the corner of the room and played something fast and joyful on his whistle that she didn't recognize. In between tunes he looked up at her and smiled, encouraging her in her efforts. He was a small man, with a boy's face, and lots of curly brown hair.

'Are you really Irish, Coffin?' she asked him, wondering whether he would reply, or merely play another tune.

'On me mum's side.'

'Where's she from?'

'Kilburn,' said Coffin. 'But she's dead now.' And he chose a different whistle from the collection in his box, and played 'The Rocky Road to Dublin'.

She fell asleep again, still hearing Coffin's tunes playing in her head.

Next time Dime and Ant were there, Dime said, 'She wants to know where she is.'

'What did you tell her?' There was no expression in Ant's voice.

'I told her it were Devon,' said Dime. 'But she said she already knew.'

'And now that you're feeling better, I suppose you want to know more.'

'Yes,' said Angel.

'This is a barn, or outhouse,' said Ant. 'It adjoins a large house – Queen Anne, they tell me – whose owner is rarely here. When he is away, we live there in the main building. We take good care of it for him. He never suspects that he has us as unpaid housesitters. When he is at home, like now, we make ourselves very inconspicuous.'

Even in the room – or barn, or outhouse – she could hardly pick him out from the background.

'He has been here for five days now,' said Ant. 'We know that he never stays longer than a week, so in a couple of days we can move back in. Then we can all have a bath,' he said, looking at Dime. 'So, this time when he goes away, you can move in with us. You must promise to learn and follow the rules, to become one of the family.'

'Christ!' exclaimed Angel. 'You mean you're professional, high-class squatters?'

'No swearing,' said Dime, as though he was repeating a well-learned lesson. 'That's the first rule. No swearing.'

'And no blasphemy,' added Ant.

'Sorry,' said Angel.

'When you swear, you say, "Sorry, Ant",' said Dime.

'Sorry, Ant,' said Angel.

And this was her first lesson.

It was Gren who answered her previous question. 'Think of us as caretakers,' he said. 'We look after their houses for them when they are away, see.'

'They? Them?'

'You'll learn,' said Gren.

Coffin said nothing, but he picked up his whistle and he played to her, and she could gauge his mood, and what he thought about things, by the tune he played.

It was some time after this that Ant told her about his plans for her.

'We're not allowed casual women,' said Dime, quoting Ant. 'Women are to be respected, he says, not used.'

'Quite right, too,' said Angel.

'But one day,' said Coffin, in one of his rare speeches, 'one day we can get married.'

Angel smiled. 'All of you? At the same time?'

Gren said, 'We don't need a lot of different women. It wouldn't work, would it?'

'Four men, one wife,' said Ant. 'Think about it. It makes a lot of sense.'

'You're mine,' said Dime. 'I found you.'

'Finders keepers,' said Coffin. 'Losers weepers. She belongs to all of us.' This was the most she had ever heard Coffin say.

'The way it works,' said Ant, 'is like this. We're a family, the four of us. We've been together for a long time now. A year, maybe. And we follow the same rules. We've got discipline.' He stopped for a moment, then, as though he had judged Angel and found her capable of understanding what he was saying, he went on: 'What we've got is love. People use the word too easily. But when you've lived together, and worked together the way we have, you know what it really means. We know how to follow rules. We know how to share what we have. If we find ourselves a wife, it will work out because we'll follow the rules. We love each other, we love her. That's how it will be.'

'What about me?' asked Angel.

'We love you,' said Coffin. 'You belong to us. You can ask us for anything.'

'And then,' said Angel, 'just when I had got used to the place in Devon, just when I thought I really belonged, we were on the move again. They knew by then that I wouldn't be able to settle down with them until I had been to Leicester and found whoever it was I wanted to find, and did whatever I needed to do.'

'Olivia Blacket?' asked Kate.

'Leicester College,' said Angel.

'But why? Did you know why you had to see her?'

'Yes, I knew. I had to kill her.'

'Why?'

'Because of Daisy.'

Chapter 9

A diligent enquiry is to be instituted into the life, conduct, morals, and progress in learning, of each and all; and what requires correction then is to be corrected, and excesses are to be visited with condign punishment.

Leicester College Statutes

'But why?' asked Kate. 'Who's Daisy?'

'Daisy's mine. My kid. Was my kid.' Slow tears were leaking from Angel's eyes. Kate didn't think she was even aware of them.

This whole story is about babies and children, thought Kate, and wished that she had more experience of them. She didn't really know what to say to Angel, except to smile sympathetically and pour her another glass of wine and pass over the Kleenex. There was a big gap between gazing enviously into other people's buggies, and actually having a child yourself.

'Tell me about her,' she said, eventually.

'She was ten months and three weeks old. The last time I

saw her she was sitting in her buggy, wearing her white cotton bonnet, the one she always insisted on wearing when we went out to the shops. Even in winter. It was winter then. Cold. Not as cold as here. London isn't, you know.'

'You lived in London?'

'Yes,' said Angel.

'When? When was this?'

'At the beginning of the year.'

'Are you sure you want to tell me about it?' She wasn't sure she could bear to hear the story. It had been bad enough listening to Brendan Adams describe how Olivia died. At least Olivia had lived over thirty years of her life before dying. But ten months and three weeks weren't nearly long enough.

'We were on our way to the rec,' said Angel, slowly. 'I remember that. Funny, isn't it, what you remember and what you forget?'

'Must be odd,' said Kate, drinking her own wine to the bottom of the glass.

'This car came out of nowhere,' said Angel. 'One minute we were crossing the road, and everything was normal. I was talking to Daisy, telling her that I would give her a push on the swing, and the next, it was all over. Everything changed. Nothing was ever the same again. In just the one instant. You can't believe it, afterwards. You think there must have been a mistake. If only you could rerun the tape, you could wind time backwards and play it again and it would be different. It happens every night when I try to sleep. I see the same thing happening, and each time I think I can change it.' She reached into the box of tissues, took a handful and scrubbed at her cheeks. 'Sometimes I try really hard, and I believe that if I go into the next room I'll find Daisy there.

But it's not Daisy. It's just a doll. And the crying I hear is Coffin playing his whistle.'

They both sat in silence for a while. Then Angel carried on, as though she had to get to the end of her story. An exercise in punishment.

'The car came round the corner too fast and caught us as we were crossing the road. She hit me on the right leg, below the knee. Daisy was hit full on, in her buggy, and thrown over the top of the car and . . .'

Some time later she added, 'Well, she killed Daisy straight away.'

There was another silence while they both thought about it. Kate reached out a hand and took hold of Angel's.

'I don't remember much about the hospital,' said Angel. 'But I remember the pain. And that there was something I didn't want to think about, but had to. And the way they wouldn't meet my eyes, and were so kind and cheerful that I knew something dreadful had happened.'

'What about your husband? Partner? Couldn't he help?'

'I've never been married. My boyfriend walked soon after Daisy was born. I didn't care. It was only Daisy I loved.'

'Parents?'

'They didn't want to know. They were quite old when I was born and they didn't understand my generation. As far as they were concerned, Daisy was a bastard. Can you imagine it? She was a baby, a child. And they put a name on her like that. And now she's dead. They call me an immoral woman, and they don't want to know me. After Daisy died, my mother tore up all the photographs she had of her, and said I should learn to forget her. It was best, she said.'

'What did you do?'

Angel was more fluent now they had left the pictures of Daisy's death behind.

'Went off my head. Left the house to go to Tesco's for a few bits of food, and came to five months later in Devon. I still can't really remember all of it. There are great blank patches. I can't remember the accident very well. Just the pain afterwards.'

'So you went back to live with your parents after you came out of hospital?'

'Yes. It was a great mistake. Then came the trial. I thought that this woman who was driving too fast, who didn't see the crossing and the kid in the buggy, whose attention had been caught by something in a shop window, would get put away for years.'

Yes, that's what people did think.

'You'd think they'd give you some justice, wouldn't you? Don't they ever think about the victims? I wanted to show them the photos of her. I wanted to shout out that she was alive and happy and wanted to go to the rec and play on the swings. And now it was all over. She'd never sit on a swing, and laugh, and ask me to push her higher, not ever again. I wanted them to put that woman away in prison until she was old and ugly and could never have children of her own. I wanted her to cry the way I had cried. It wouldn't have made up for Daisy's death, but it would have been something. Something to show that she had lived. But they let her off. She had an expensive lawyer who stood up and argued that none of it was her fault.'

Angel had tears running down her face now, and her breathing came in sobs. She wiped her face with her hands, as though pushing memories behind her.

'So if it wasn't her fault, whose fault was it?' she cried. 'Daisy's, maybe? Mine? Some man came up with these clever arguments. No one listened to me and Daisy. We had nothing to do with it. She walked. She was fined two hundred pounds and she walked. I swore I'd find her and kill her.'

'And so that's what you did?'

Angel pressed tissues to her eyes. Wiped the mess from her face. At last, when she had her breathing under control, she looked straight at Kate.

'Oh no,' she said. 'I didn't kill her. I wanted to. When I got there and saw her, and remembered what she had done, I really wanted to. But then I realized at the end that it would be wrong. I found her all right. But I found that she had been through hell, too. There had been enough dying. She hadn't had it easy after all. She was still alive when I left her in her room.'

Kate sat and stared at her. There were too many questions that still needed to be answered, but the time was after two in the morning, the bottle of wine was nearly empty, and Angel was about to fall asleep on her pink sofa.

'So if you didn't kill her, who did?' asked Kate.

'I don't know. I can't think about it any more. Leave me alone, will you? I've had it. I just want to lie down and go to sleep.'

'OK. You'd better have the spare bed,' said Kate. 'I'll show you where it is.'

Angel fell asleep a few minutes after she had put her head down on the pillow. Kate, looking in on her and putting out the light, wondered whether it was possible to kill someone and then sleep so soundly. She doubted it.

Kate was roused by the sound of urgent ringing at her front door. Was it really morning so soon? Her head was still hurting from the previous night's wine, and she grabbed her dressing gown and rubbed at her eyes as she went downstairs to open the door.

Paul Taylor.

'What do you want?'

It was less than gracious, but it was also the best she could manage at that moment. She was too aware of Angel, lying upstairs asleep in her spare room, to be welcoming. She pushed back the lock of hair that was hanging in front of her eyes.

'To save your life, probably. But don't worry, I don't expect any thanks for it.'

'Just because you once, or perhaps twice, turned up in time – in the nick, as you might say – to rescue me from a murderer who was about to lose his final marble, doesn't mean you can pretend to save my life every week, you know.'

'I don't know why I bother,' said Paul, following her into the kitchen. 'You're so brittle, you'll break yourself one of these days. Here, let me make the coffee. You go and splash some water on your face and clean your teeth or something. Anything that will make you behave more like a human being. What on earth were you doing last night? You look awful.'

'Thanks a lot. But I drank less than half a bottle of wine,' she said, defensively.

'Then who drank the other half?' asked Paul, holding up the empty bottle.

'None of your business,' said Kate, briskly, hoping that Angel wouldn't suddenly appear from upstairs. She didn't want her to meet Paul Taylor until she had extracted the rest of the story from her. Paul would have her down at the police station and in custody so fast that Angel wouldn't know what was happening to her. 'I'll go and clean my teeth.'

Five minutes later they both had a mug of coffee and Kate could see out of her bleary eyes. Her mouth tasted less of an old parrot cage, more like fresh minty fluoride. It was probably an improvement, but she wasn't going to tell Paul that.

'So what do you want to tell me?'

Paul looked awkward. Unsure of himself. Quite unlike the Paul Taylor who usually irritated the hell out of her. She took a deep breath and made a conscious effort to relax. She tried a smile. It nearly worked. She tried to empathize, to see his point of view (whatever that might be this morning).

'Start at the beginning,' she said. 'I promise not to interrupt and not to lose my temper, at least until you've got to the end. I'll even make you another cup of coffee. Have you eaten? Would you like some cereal or something?' Perhaps she should become a professional listener. She was getting a lot of practice, and it might be easier than writing for a living.

'No, thanks. More coffee would be fine.'

'So?'

'You've got to promise, really promise, that you won't tell anyone – and that includes all your close friends – what I'm going to tell you.'

'You'll arrest me if I do?' She could have bitten her tongue. Pity she hadn't. It was absolutely the wrong tone to take with Paul if she wanted to learn anything from him.

'No. You'll just lose me my job.'

'Right.' She looked solemn. Hell, she *felt* solemn. 'I promise. I really do promise. I won't go out and tell any of my friends, or anyone else, anything that you tell me. OK?'

'It's about Liam Ross.' He kept his voice level, free of nasty emotions like jealousy. Kate tried to keep calm and match his neutral tone.

'Yes? What about Liam?'

'Look, Kate, I don't want to tell you this. You're going to think it's because I'm . . .'

'Paul, I think I know you well enough now to be sure that if you come round here when you know I'll be in a filthy mood, to tell me something about Liam, then it's because you honestly believe I need to know it.'

'Yes. Thanks.' He drank some more of his coffee. 'It's about Olivia Blacket. The woman who taught at Leicester College. The college where Liam Ross is also employed.'

'The woman who has just been murdered.'

'Who told you?'

'Hasn't it been on the news?'

'Yesterday evening. But you were drinking with a friend, not watching television. So how do you know?'

'Brendan Adams, Olivia's boss, told me. I rang him about something unrelated to the murder, and he told me all about it. Well, all that he knew, anyway. Poor old boy was very upset.' Kate had learnt that when Paul wanted the answer to a question she might as well give it, because he wouldn't carry on talking until she had.

Paul looked relieved at her answer. Maybe he thought that Liam had been round, giving her all the gory details, and getting her drunk so that he could have his wicked way with her. He said:

'Poor old boy was also upset because we dragged him away from the flat of a Miss Lexie Domino—'

'You've got to be joking! And what does she do for a living, then?'

Paul unbent a little and grinned. 'We didn't get a list of her specialities, but I'm sure she would have provided one if we had asked, together with her prices.'

'Just out of interest, how did you find Miss Domino's address?' She couldn't see Frances copying it down into her Filofax and then passing it on to the police.

'I didn't deal with it personally, but I believe that after we had failed to locate the professor at the home of the colleague whom his sister believed him to be dining with, one of the porters at Leicester College gave Miss Domino's address to our officer.'

Of course, college porters knew everything about their senior members, and about most of the rest of the staff, too.

For a moment, Kate and Paul had relaxed, laughing together at the foibles of human nature, but now they both remembered that Paul had come to tell her something unpleasant. Kate thought it was probably time they got it over with.

'But there was something you wanted to tell me about Olivia. And about Liam Ross.'

'Yes. Do you know that for the past seven years, off and on, Olivia Blacket and Liam Ross have been lovers?'

Her face felt numb. She didn't believe him. She couldn't believe him. She didn't want to integrate this thought into her memories of the last year. He had paused and was watching her anxiously as she went through the events of the past few months and re-interpreted them in accordance with this new idea.

'No, I didn't. I don't believe it. Are you sure?' It was only to buy a little time. It was, of course, an idea that had been playing just under the surface of her consciousness. An idea that she did not want to believe, and therefore never examined. But Paul would never come round to her house and tell her something like that unless he was absolutely sure. And he wouldn't tell her at all unless he had a good reason for it.

'Oh yes, we're quite sure.'

Of course, it wasn't only Paul who knew about Liam's betrayal and her own stupidity. The whole of the Thames Valley Police must know about it by now and were laughing at her gullibility.

'Why are you telling me about it?'

She could tell by his face that this bit was going to be even more difficult. Poor old Paul. How much of his job was spent telling people unpalatable facts?

'This is the bit that you're really going to hate,' he said. 'But don't just deny what I say. Think about it.'

'What?'

'Don't you see that Ross is the most likely person to have killed her?'

No. No. No.

'I had to tell you about it. If he did do it, you're at risk, too.'

No.

'Why? Why on earth should he kill her?'

'Because he wanted out of the relationship. He'd met you. Olivia wouldn't let him go. She was a very jealous and possessive woman. She could make big dents in his career.'

'And because the first suspect in a case like this is the woman's lover.'

'I can see that you don't want to believe me. But please, Kate. Think about it. Remember what you promised and forget about rushing round to confront him with it. In fact, please don't rush round to his place at all. And don't invite him back here. Don't let yourself be alone with him. Ever. Not until this thing is cleared up. One way or the other.'

Through the horrible confusion and pain she could see Paul's face, just a couple of feet away from her. Ordinary. Safe. Nice blue eyes. At this moment the whole covered with a look that was a mixture of embarrassment and concern. Poor man was hating every minute of this. But he had come round and had this conversation with her because he felt it was his duty. Or because he cared about her. At any rate, for some unselfish reason. She could surely make a small effort in return, even if every square inch of her was hurting and all she wanted to do at this moment was to shout and rage at him, deny every single thing he had just said, and then rush upstairs, get back into bed and cover her face with the duvet.

Upstairs. The spare room. Angel. She could tell Paul about Angel. He ought to be told, surely. Angel was far more likely to have killed Olivia than Liam was. Then she recalled the expression on Angel's face when she had said that she didn't kill her, that she no longer wanted to and Kate believed her. The girl had looked too exhausted to lie. But then, she had believed Liam, too.

As soon as Paul had left she would get the truth out of Angel. All of it.

Then if she had any doubts about her she would shop her to the police and Liam would be free. Now she must get rid of Paul.

'Thanks, Paul,' she said. 'I appreciate what you're saying.' Her voice came out dry and cracked. Insincere. She tried again. 'It can't have been easy for you.' Better. 'And don't worry, I won't breathe a word of it to anyone.'

'Especially to Liam Ross,' he said.

'I imagine that if he's been down at the police station answering questions all night, he might have got the idea by now that you suspect him of murdering Olivia,' she said. Bitter, Kate.

'I'd better go now.'

'Yes.'

'You've still got the mobile phone?'

'Yes.'

'And you'll use it if you need me.'

'I'll call the police if I think I'm in any danger, yes.'

They were at the door. She felt cold and dead inside and she just wished he would go so that she could look at what she was feeling without a critical audience.

Eventually, when she could face it, she made another pot of coffee and went upstairs to call Angel. It was time Angel braved the daylight and explained what she was doing at Leicester College on the afternoon of the murder. In Olivia's room with, by her own admission, the intention of murdering her.

She knocked on the door of the spare room. No reply. She opened it and called out, 'Angel!'

But Angel had left.

It was easier if you had something to do. She had found this before. You could forget about it, whatever the pain was, for whole minutes at a time if you made sure that you were busy.

Liam on Sunday afternoons, strewing the newspapers all over her neat sitting room. Liam in the mornings, his long body taking over her bed, his dark hair on her pillow. His toothbrush in her bathroom. Liam on the telephone, telling her he was too busy to see her any evening that week. Liam disappearing off for the weekend and saying that he was going to a concert at the other end of the country. Liam and Olivia. Seven years. *Seven years.* No wonder Olivia had been so unpleasant to her.

Find something to do, remember. Concentrate on the other side of the problem.

She picked up the pages of transcription. She didn't know what significance they had or whether they even had anything at all to do with her murder, but what they did do was give an insight into Olivia's state of mind just before it happened. If she was feeling so awful about Liam and Olivia, what had Olivia felt? Had she known that she and Liam were lovers, too? If a man treated one woman badly, the chances were that he treated the others in his life the same way. He had probably been lying to both of them. She had known Liam only since the early spring. Olivia had had seven years of his off-hand treatment. And in her eyes, it was Kate who was the other woman. What had she been thinking about in the days before she died?

She turned to the pages of the Ternan Papers.

Perhaps these unfortunate occurrences are common in London. Here in Oxford the death of a child would be headline news in the local paper.

She looked again at her own version of the same passage.

Yes, the original was difficult to make out, but surely Olivia was mistaken. Her own version started off the same, but then diverged radically from Olivia's. It was as though Olivia started reading the words as they were written, and then was led into her own world of children and death. Further down, she had written:

They call it, I believe, 'skinning'. A young child, separated for a few minutes from its mother, who was momentarily distracted by conversation with a friend, ran out into the road. No, the child was too young. She couldn't have run.

Daisy. Olivia was writing about Daisy. Angel was right about her. She had cared about killing the child. She had found herself a good solicitor and paid a small fine, but then, who wouldn't try to get out of a jail sentence? It didn't mean that she wasn't gutted at the thought of what she had done.

She had wondered before what Olivia was on about. Now that she knew about Daisy, it fell into place. Olivia stopped seeing what was on the paper and started putting down the words from inside her head.

Kate sat and thought about it for a while. But there was surely more to it than that. If you had a child and then it died, you would never forget it, would you? It was true of Angel. Could it also be true of Olivia? But if so, then she would have to think about who the father was. And that was something she didn't want to think about.

Oh hell, what did she know about motherhood, and having and losing children? She could only imagine it, she knew nothing first-hand. On the other hand, she was a novelist, and she made her living by imagining herself inside other people's heads and convincing the readers that she had got it right.

But then she reminded herself, uncomfortably, that in real life she had got her reading of people tragically and dangerously wrong. Twice.

Put it to one side. Forget about it. Forget about him. Find a pad and a pencil. Make a list. Think about the possibilities. Work out what happened. Get it all in order and *under control*. The pencil point went through the paper and broke off. She clicked up another few millimetres of lead and started on her list again.

1. Find Angel.
   How?
2. Speak to Liam. Find out how he knew that she, Kate, had been seen by Olivia that afternoon. Ask him what Olivia meant to him, what he meant to Olivia. Find out how long he has been deceiving you. *Kill him*. Not funny, Kate.
3. See Brendan Adams. What or whom did he see when he dropped off Ludo at Olivia's room? And how far would he go to get his hands on the Ternan Papers?
4. FIND ANGEL. She must know more than anyone else.
5. Ant, Gren, Dime, Coffin. Three of them were there, outside Leicester, yesterday afternoon. They probably wouldn't talk to her, but they might lead her to Angel. Dime and Coffin didn't sound much use, but Gren and Ant lived in the real world at least part of the time.

She read through the list. It was full of imperatives, but she didn't feel like obeying many of them. 'Find Angel' sounded simple enough, but where could she start?

Had Angel given any clue as to where she lived? No, except that she lived in a squat somewhere. When the family had taken her away yesterday afternoon from Broad Street they had been moving east. So, probably somewhere off the Cowley Road. Kate sighed. It was a large area.

Ant, Gren, Dime, Coffin. She could walk around the centre of Oxford looking at all the buskers and beggars. What did she do if she found one of them? Play it by ear, the way she had everything else.

Ant. She could go back and look for the shop in George Street. If he was still there, it could well be her best lead.

Brendan Adams. She would ring him up, ask if she could come over to Garsington to talk to him. Take him a bottle of whisky, perhaps. If she spoke to him on his home ground, taking plenty of time over it, he might well remember some important small detail that would make everything clear. Or he might say something that gave him away.

Clear. Liam. She was back to where she started. He held some of the facts, but he was the last person she wanted to speak to. She would have to. What was it Paul had said? She was to be very careful. She was in danger. Paul was over-cautious. And anyway, she had his mobile phone, she could call for help any time she needed it.

Forget Liam for the moment. Put him right out of your mind. Find the tissues. Splash your face with cold water. Pull yourself together. Back to the pad and pencil. Another list.

1. Phone Brendan Adams and fix a time to go over to Garsington to talk to him.

2. Walk around the centre of Oxford looking for any members of the family. Try to persuade one of them to tell you where Angel is.
3. Look for the shop where you saw Ant.
4. Ring up Liam and ask him about Olivia.

She stared at the list and then crossed out the fourth item. While she was doing it, she broke the point off her pencil again.

Stop thinking about it, she told herself. There's nothing you can do to change the past. Walk away from it. But she couldn't walk away until she had solved the mystery of who had killed Olivia.

She went to the phone and was about to dial, when something occurred to her. The last person to use this phone had been Angel. She had rung the family and told them that she was fine, all right, really she was, and they weren't to worry about her. She was staying the night with a girl friend, and would be back in the morning. Kate pressed the button that redialled the last number.

She heard it ring. She imagined Angel, and Dime perhaps, standing watching it, listening to it, wondering whether or not to answer. It rang six times, seven.

'Hallo.' A man's voice, slow, deliberate. From Angel's description, this had to be Dime.

'Dime?'

'Yeah.' He sounded puzzled, as well he might.

'This is a friend of Angel's. Can I speak to her?' She made herself sound bright, confident, authoritative but non-threatening. A masterpiece of acting.

'No. She's not here.'

'Do you know where she is?'

193

'She's at a friend's house. She'll be back this morning.' Damn, she could have told Dime that.

'Maybe I'll call round,' said Kate. 'Can you give me the address?' She held her breath.

'I dunno,' said Dime. 'I dunno the address.'

'Where are you at the moment?' asked Kate, patiently.

'Standing by the telephone,' said Dime, helpfully.

Kate tried again. 'Are you in the hall, Dime?'

'Yeah.'

'Good. Well, why don't you put the telephone receiver down on the hall table, open the front door and take a look outside. The name of the street will be written in black letters on a white board somewhere near the corner. And the house number should be on your front door.'

'I'm not stupid,' said Dime, affronted. 'I know all that.'

'Well, do you think you could look, and come back and tell me?'

There was a long wait, while Kate hoped that no other member of the family would walk through the hall and replace the receiver. But eventually she heard heavy footsteps approaching at the other end, and Dime picked up the receiver and said, 'Hallo?'

'Hallo, Dime. Well?'

'It's number two-and-five,' he said.

'And the street?'

'It begins with a Dime.'

'It does what?'

'D is for Dime,' said Dime.

'And the rest of it?'

She could hear Dime thinking about it. 'I dunno.'

Oh bother it. She might have guessed that Dime wouldn't

194

be any good at reading. There wasn't much use in asking him the other question either, in that case. But she gave it a try. 'Can you look at the telephone dial and tell me what the number is?' It might not occur to him to wonder how she had rung if she didn't know the number.

'No,' said Dime. 'There's too many.' He sounded uncomfortable. 'Who are you?' he asked belatedly. 'Are you the one who gave her the doll?'

'No, I'm not. What doll? Do you mean the one she was carrying with her yesterday afternoon in Oxford?'

'I've got to go now,' said Dime. 'Goodbye.'

She pulled a face at the receiver, then replaced it.

What had she got? Angel lived at number twenty-five – or possibly number fifty-two – in some street that might be in East Oxford and started with the letter D, or had the letter D somewhere in the name, or if Dime was dyslexic, maybe ended with a D. And even if she managed to find the house, there was nothing to guarantee that Angel would ever return there.

She turned back to her list. If she phoned Brendan Adams now, she wouldn't be able to phone back Angel's house. Then she remembered her neat little mobile phone. Keeping Angel's phone number on her machine had to be worth another minute or two of air time.

'Hallo, Brendan? I wondered whether I could come over and talk to you?'

'About Olivia?'

'Yes, if you feel you can face it. I seem to need to talk about her to someone else who knew her.'

'Violent death seems so far outside our experience that we need to make sense of it, somehow.'

'That's how I feel.'

'How about this afternoon?' said the professor.

'Fine. What time?'

'Make it two o'clock. Oh, and Kate—'

'Yes?'

'Could you bring any pages of the Ternan Papers that you might have? And Olivia's transcriptions, of course.'

'Sure. See you then.'

The machine bleeped gently at her as she cut the connection.

It sounded as though Brendan was starting to get over Olivia's death. He wasn't as distraught as he was yesterday, at least. And his first thoughts had been for the Ternan Papers.

Now, into Oxford to find the family. She went to put on some jeans and a pair of comfortable walking shoes. She felt that she was going to need them.

And she had another question to ask Angel. Who gave her the doll? She didn't even know if the answer was important, but it was one more piece of the puzzle to slot into place, and it stopped her thinking about Liam.

It was cold and drizzling in Oxford, and uncongenial to buskers. There were beggars on the street, but the passers-by were hurrying along in their anoraks, their hoods up, their faces down, not stopping to put anything in the out-stretched hands.

Where were they when she saw them before? Around Radcliffe Square, in front of the Sheldonian, in Broad Street. She walked all round the centre of the town, looked up Catte Street and along Brasenose Lane, but she couldn't see Gren's emaciated form or Dime's red-and-white checked shirt. She stood and listened for Coffin's whistle, but all she could hear was a fiddle player outside Brasenose College. Not up to Coffin's standard, she thought.

She walked back down Broad Street and then turned towards the station.

She found them in Gloucester Green. They didn't look as though they were doing very well, though they were working the crowds who were coming off the long-distance coaches. Coffin was playing a desperately cheerful tune, his hair beaded with raindrops. A brown-and-white dog was sniffing at his legs. Coffin looked down at it, without interrupting his playing, and smiled. The dog settled itself contentedly at his feet, its head resting on Coffin's trainers, and closed its eyes. Three people, passing and seeing the dog, threw coins into his hat. Angel had said he had a gift with dogs, and she was right. Maybe he even talked to them the way he didn't to people.

She hunkered down next to Gren, who was sitting on the wet pavement with his stick-like legs straight out in front of him, and his *Hungry and homeless* notice balanced on his knees.

'How're you doing?' she asked, and tossed a twenty-pence piece into his nearly empty tin.

Gren sneered at the coin, so she quickly added fifty pence.

'Who're you?' he asked. 'Do I know you?'

'I'm a friend of Angel's,' she said.

'Oh yeah?'

A pound coin joined the others in his tin. This was getting to be expensive for no return at all.

'I'm looking for her,' she said.

'What do you want with Angel?' he asked.

'Just wondering how she was doing. I was a bit worried about her.'

'You're the one who was with her on Wednesday afternoon, aren't you?' said Gren.

'Yes, like I said, I'm a friend of hers.' She tried the open and amiable smile. Guileless. Stupid, even.

There was no corresponding smile from Gren. 'There's no need to worry about Angel. She's well looked after. She belongs to us, I told you before.'

'I'd still like to talk to her.'

'They're all interested in our Angel.' It was the red-faced one. Dime. 'There was a phone call just before I came out,' he said. 'They was asking for Angel, too. She weren't there, though.'

'Was that you?' asked Gren, glaring at Kate. 'How did you get our phone number?'

Behind her, she heard the sound of the whistle, playing 'Easy and Free'. The sound was coming closer.

'I just want to talk to her,' repeated Kate. 'I want to make sure that she's all right. That's all. I'm her friend.'

To her own ears she was sounding desperate, not very credible.

'Well now,' said a new voice, to her left, 'if you're her friend, you can prove it, easy. You'll know what her real name is, won't you?'

It was the one in the black jeans and T-shirt. No jacket, even in this cold weather. This must be Ant.

'We'll trade with you,' said Ant. 'You tell us her name. We'll let you talk to Angel.'

Could she bluff? She thought somehow Ant was more

experienced at the game than she was, and would find her out immediately. Then she had an idea and she said:

'I do know who she is.' She stared at them, defiantly.

'Go ahead then,' said Ant, softly. 'Tell us.'

'She's Daisy's mother.'

She had the advantage at last.

'What's that supposed to mean?' asked Ant.

'Let me talk to Angel, and I'll tell you.'

'We come too,' said Gren. 'She's not seeing Angel on her own.'

'Do we agree she can talk to her, then?' asked Ant.

'You'll have to let me if you want to know about Daisy,' said Kate, boldly.

'You tell terrible lies,' said Ant. 'But remember that you're no match for us. What's your name?'

'Kate. Kate Ivory.'

'You can come to the shop, Kate Ivory. Dime, you fetch Angel.'

Dime disappeared down a narrow lane. Kate couldn't see which way he turned when he got to the bottom.

Gren stood up, handed his coins over to Ant, closed his tin and tucked his cardboard notice away somewhere inside his shirt. Coffin woke the dog, which had followed him across the square, pulled its ears and told it to go home. He, too, gave his money to Ant before gathering up his hat, sticking his whistle in his back pocket and coming to stand close to Kate, as though forming part of her guard. They marched her round by the back of the cinema and down an alleyway, then in through the back door to the shop.

The back room was neat, as she might have imagined. Items were stored in clean cardboard cartons, and there were no dirty coffee mugs or old sandwich wrappings. A man after her own heart.

'Come through into the shop,' said Ant. 'I don't want to miss out on any more business.'

He propped the door open, and the rest of them took what seats they could find at the back of the shop, sat in a semi-circle and stared at Kate.

'How long will she be?' asked Kate. 'Has she got far to come?'

'Not far,' said Ant, neutrally, and turned round to serve a couple of women who had entered the shop behind him.

'This is a clever game,' she said, when they had left. 'A new variation on squatting.'

'Not so new,' said Ant. 'There's a few of us at it. The Council'll catch on to what we're doing eventually. But it takes a few days to get us out. We'll have moved by then. You need to be quick to play, though. Get in, move in your stock, make your money and get out again. That's how it works.'

She could see him in a few years' time, wearing a sharp suit, driving an expensive car, indistinguishable from the other successful men who made money from buying and selling.

'You're fond of Angel, then?' she asked Coffin, who had taken out his whistle and was turning it round in his hands as though unable to make up his mind what to play. 'She told me you played for her every day when she was ill.'

'Music be the food of love,' said Coffin, and started to play 'The Lark in the Clear Air'.

'What about you?' she asked Gren. 'Do you love her, too?'

'What sort of question is that?'

'I was wondering how she felt about all of you,' said Kate. 'It could be a bit overpowering, all this loving and caring.'

'You know nothing about it,' said Gren.

Well, he could be right, at that, thought Kate, given my track record, and she shut up until Dime returned with Angel.

When she arrived, the men ranged themselves on her side, and Kate felt she must ask her questions very carefully indeed, or Angel would be whisked away and hidden from her again.

'Hallo, Angel,' she started. They couldn't quarrel with that.

'Hallo, Kate. I'm sorry I left without saying thanks this morning, but I heard that man in the kitchen, and I thought it was time I moved out.'

'That's all right. He was nothing to do with you,' she said. 'Just a friend, warning me I might be in danger.' She looked around at the faces in front of her. She was probably in more danger here, at least if the family thought she was a threat to their Angel.

'I suppose you want to ask me what happened the day before yesterday?' said Angel.

'A friend of mine is mixed up in it, and may be accused of Olivia Blacket's murder. I would like to know what you saw, so that I can be clearer about his part in it.'

'Georgie Porgie pudding and pie,' said Coffin.

'Kissed the girls and made them cry,' agreed Kate. 'Yes, that's the man, Coffin.' It was restful talking to Coffin, since you didn't have to think up your own words. You just found a rhyme that fitted the situation, and quoted it. Here we go round the mulberry bush.

'I tried to get in through the main door of the college, but

201

it was crowded with people and I couldn't. So I got in through the other door,' said Angel. 'I waited until someone went through in front of me, then I slipped in behind him before the door closed.'

It occurred to Kate that anyone could have got into the college like that. The Fellows wouldn't have attempted to push their way through the crowd fighting for the Mourning Ale. They would all have used their own door, in Broad Street. There must have been many more people than usual going in and out through that door on the afternoon when Olivia was killed. Who was to notice if the occasional stranger slipped in in the wake of a member of college?

'Go on,' said Ant. 'Tell us what happened after you got inside.'

'It took me some time to find Olivia Blacket's room,' said Angel, pushing a hand through her hair so that they could see her face. Its expression was strained. 'I didn't dare ask anyone the way, in case they wanted to know who I was and what I was doing there.'

'In my experience,' said Kate, 'they would have taken you by the hand, led you right to her door, and shown you how to open the door if it happened to be locked. They're a trusting lot, once you get inside the gates of one of these colleges.' But she could imagine Angel creeping round the quadrangles, hiding in archways, melting into corridors, waiting until no one was there before she looked to see which was Staircase Five.

'But you found it in the end?'

'I found the staircase and her door with the name on it, Dr O. R. Blacket. The door was open, but I couldn't see anyone inside, so I went in.' Angel's eyes opened wide. 'Then I saw the dog.'

'Ludo,' said Kate. 'The Hound from Hell.'

'He growled at me, and started barking. I went to the opposite side of the room and stood behind a big table thing covered in papers.'

'Her desk,' said Kate, softly.

'Her desk,' repeated Angel. 'I felt safer there. The place was full of books, and papers, and there was a doll sitting on the desk, in the middle of it all. She was wearing a white bonnet, like Daisy's. Then the woman came into the room. Olivia Blacket must have been downstairs, maybe in the other quadrangle. She started shouting at me, asking what I was doing in her room, and all the while the dog was barking. There was a terrible racket going on. I wanted to leave, but I thought about Daisy and I stayed where I was. I shouted back at her. I said that she had killed Daisy and that I had come to kill her. She listened to me then.'

'I bet she did,' said Kate. 'Even Olivia would listen to you if you said something like that.'

' "You," she said. "You're the child's mother. I should have known you'd come." And she sat down, as though her legs had given up. "That made two dead children," she said. And I think she must have been talking about a child of her own, as well as Daisy. We sat staring at each other. She looked terrible. As though it had just come home to her about Daisy dying, and the other one, whoever it was, too. I nearly felt sorry for her. I put the hammer down then.'

'Is that how you were going to kill her?' asked Kate.

'I'd taken a hammer from the shop that morning, when Ant wasn't looking.'

'That was naughty, Angel,' said Ant. 'You should have asked me before taking something from the shop.'

'Sorry, Ant,' said Angel, meekly.

Oh great, thought Kate. She has to apologize for taking a hammer that has probably fallen off the back of a lorry, but he doesn't say anything about her intention to kill Olivia.

'I wrapped the hammer in a plastic carrier bag, and no one noticed I was carrying it. I had put it down on the desk in front of me. When she first came into the room and started shouting at me, I took the hammer out of the bag. Anyway, there we were, just staring at each other, and the dog barking all the while. Then she told the dog to shut up. Ludo, she called it. The dog sat down by the window and stopped barking. She told me she would explain about Daisy and how it wasn't really her fault. And I was going to listen to what she had to say, when the telephone rang. We both sat and looked at it. In the end she picked it up and said "Hallo." It was a man at the other end, I could hear him across the room. She called him some funny name.'

'Liam,' said Kate.

'Pudding and pie,' said Coffin.

'That's right,' said Angel. 'Liam. I sat there and listened to them. Already I suppose I knew really that I wouldn't kill her. I could have done it if I'd done it at once, without thinking. It's not that I wasn't still angry with her, but I couldn't just walk across the room and hit her with the hammer. And then there was the dog: I don't like dogs. It was no good, I couldn't do it. You need such a lot of anger if you're going to kill someone, don't you?'

'You need a lot of something,' said Kate. 'Anger. Fear. Love. Greed. One of them at least, I suppose.'

'I started listening to what she was saying. She was screaming at him, down the phone, that he had to come and help her. She needed him, she said. That there was this mad woman in her office who was going to kill her. But I wasn't, not then. I lifted up my hands to show her that I wasn't going to use the hammer. I think she understood me. She was telling him that he really had to come. She was going on about this woman who had come to see her, and who had got into her room while she was out. I think that was you,' she said to Kate.

Kate nodded. 'I bumped into her in Clifford Quad on my way out. She must have remembered who I was a few minutes later.'

'She called you a crap novelist and said you were trying to steal her work. She said what happened was all his fault. If it hadn't been for the baby, she would never have lost concentration like that. And what was Liam doing fooling around with someone like you? Sorry, Kate, but that's what she said. And now she was being followed by these women who kept threatening her.'

'Lizzie Borden,' said Coffin.

'Quite,' said Kate. 'And did he come running to her rescue?'

'No. He must have said he'd ring the lodge and get a porter to come up, because she was shrieking that he was an unfeeling bastard and she didn't want a porter, she wanted him.'

'Then what?'

'She slammed the phone down. She said she was sorry about Daisy, she really was, and she wasn't trying to excuse what she'd done, but it wasn't her fault. He'd made her do it. And if anyone deserved to be murdered, it was the man on the phone. But I'd better leave, because he'd sent for a porter to throw me out.'

'She'd be lucky if one turned up within fifteen minutes,' said Kate. 'They were all busy with that Mourning Ale nonsense.'

'Then she shouted at me again,' said Angel. 'Asked me what I was doing with her papers. Her voice was cold and angry. Well, I hadn't even noticed what was on her desk. I'd got my hand on this old letter or something. I suppose it was the one she thought you wanted to steal.'

'Did you see what it said?' asked Kate, her curiosity taking over.

'No. I wasn't interested in it, but she'd bugged me by then. I didn't want to kill her any more, but she was such a cow that I picked up the paper and ran out of the room. I ran really fast, because I was scared she'd send the dog after me. I went out through the door, down the stairs and along the passage that runs by the kitchens.'

'Did you see anyone who might have come into her room after her?' asked Kate.

'No,' said Angel. 'There were lots of people around. But no one I knew. I just wanted to get out. I'd had enough of that woman and her college.'

'I don't suppose you've still got the paper you took from her desk?' asked Kate.

'No, I threw it away. It was written in dark red ink, like dried blood.'

'Damn,' said Kate, and ignored Dime's disapproving look.

'But I did read it before I threw it away,' said Angel. 'And it was really weird. Because if she, that Olivia woman, did write it, she wasn't as evil as I thought.'

'I don't suppose you can remember what it said?'

'Yeah. Not exactly. But it was something like this: "The

child has died and it is all my fault. The child was so beautiful, with her fair hair and skin. She wore a white dress and bonnet, with lace ties, and I stood by the tiny white coffin and wept. Would she have died if I had not spoken as I did?" '

Silence, while they all tried to fit this in with the Olivia they had known or heard about.

'That was Daisy, wasn't it? She'd written those words about her. You see,' said Angel, 'when I thought about it, she must have seen a photo of her. She must have seen her to have written that. I didn't see her again. I couldn't, I was stuffed full of painkillers and I didn't know what was happening. They took photos for me, and gave them to me afterwards so that I should know what the funeral was like, and where she was buried. But Olivia must have been there, or maybe she asked about it. Maybe she wasn't as bad as I thought.'

'Maybe,' said Kate. Maybe Angel was right. But she wasn't convinced, herself.

Ant said, 'What did you do with the hammer?'

'I left it there.'

She was biting her lip, looking as though she was going to start crying again.

'That's enough now,' said Ant. 'You can stop, Angel.'

'I think you can guess who Daisy is,' said Kate.

'Was she yours, this Daisy?' asked Dime, his red face drawn down into a lozenge of unhappiness.

'My kid,' said Angel. 'My little girl.'

'We'll give you another one,' said Dime.

Angel turned her face away.

'I'd better go now, hadn't I?' said Kate.

'Yes,' said Ant. 'Gren will show you out through the back way.'

Gren marched her back up the alley and out into Cornmarket Street. She knew that behind her the family would be hurrying Angel away through the front of the shop and back to wherever it was that they lived.

Number two and five. In the street that began with a Dime.

As soon as Gren and Kate had left, Ant went across to the door and closed it.

'We've got to get out of here,' he said. 'Fast.'

Angel said, 'Why? We were making good money.'

'We'll make more,' said Ant. 'But not here. When Kate Ivory gets home, she'll start turning over what she's heard in her mind. She may be your friend while things are going well for her, but it's her bloke who's caught up in this murder. If it's a choice between him and you, you'll lose. She'll consider the options, worry about them, for maybe twenty minutes. Then she'll phone the police and they'll be round here.'

'But why? I haven't done anything wrong,' said Angel.

'You were there,' said Ant. 'She saw all of you there at about the time that woman was killed.'

'The place was crawling with people,' said Coffin. 'It could of been any of them. Why pick on us?'

'Because we're strangers. We don't belong to their world. And when something like this happens, they like to think that it's one of us, not one of them, that did it. We're different, so we're guilty. And there's another thing. Where did you get that green cardigan from, Angel? You didn't have it before you went to the college, did you?'

Angel stood there with the tears rolling down her face.

'And I've seen the doll. It was hers, was it?'

'It's mine.' Angel closed her lips in a pout.

Ant gave up. He went into the back room and fetched some empty cartons.

'Dime, Coffin and I pack up and take the stuff out to the back alley. Angel cleans and dusts. We want no sign that we've been here. Soon as Gren gets back, he brings the van round, we load up, and we're off. I want us out of here in thirty minutes.'

When he saw what they were doing, Gren said, 'Torching the place would get rid of any evidence.'

'I don't like destroying things,' said Ant. 'This will be good enough. They won't find us in a hurry. We don't even know where we're going ourselves.'

Chapter 10

Women (that season) in Oxforde were busye
                    Will Forrest, *The Second Gresyld*

Kate was on her way to Garsington when she heard the local news on her car radio.

'In the case of the murdered Oxford woman academic, police say that a man is helping them with their enquiries, and they hope for an early conclusion to the case. It is understood that the man in question is a colleague of the murdered woman's.'

Liam. They were questioning Liam and they were expecting to arrest him for Olivia's murder. That's what the news bulletin meant. She had to stop them. The family knew more about what had happened that afternoon than anyone else. But the police wouldn't know about the family and Angel unless she told them.

She thought of Angel's white strained face, and Angel's agony at Daisy's death. Angel had trusted her, and now she was going to phone the police and tell them where to find her. She thought about it. On the one hand, Liam, with his infidelities and lies. On the other, Angel, with her tragedy and her loss of memory. But Angel knew what happened that afternoon. Kate had seen it in her face, and in the faces of the others. At least one of them knew exactly who had killed Olivia. Liam could have prevented it, if he had come to her room when Olivia had called for help. But that wasn't the same as hitting her over the head with a hammer. She pulled in at the side of the road, and closed her eyes for a moment.

It came down to a choice between Liam and Angel. She made her decision.

The mobile phone was still in her handbag. Paul's phone number was programmed into it. She pressed the Send button and heard the ringing tone.

'Paul Taylor.'

'It's Kate.' She couldn't help the sharp note that crept into her voice. She could never let him know what she really felt. Often he irritated the hell out of her, but still he was one of the few people in the world that she really trusted. But she could never tell him that. 'And since this is costing me seventy pence a minute, you'd better listen carefully and take notes. I've just heard on the radio that you've got Liam there at the police station. I'm sure that you and your friends think that the bastard did it, and really, I'd like to agree with you, but I can't. And I think I know who really killed her. Well, not precisely who, but it must be one of four. Or five.'

'Which group of four – or five – are you talking about?'

'They're a family. Not a real family, not a biological family, but a group of five people who live together and look out for each other.' She wasn't doing well at this explanation, she could hear Paul's exasperation coming over the airwaves.

'I've come across this group of people, and it's got to be one of them.' The line crackled. Could he still hear her? Hell, how did you explain about Angel and the family to a supercilious policeman? 'They're sort of street people.' Try again. 'No, not street people, more squatters. House-squatters. Shop-squatters. Business men from the other side of the street.'

'Yes, I understand the sort of people you're talking about.'

Thank goodness for that; it was more than she did. 'Well, one of them, Angel, came to Oxford to murder Olivia Blacket.' Oh dear, that did sound melodramatic. Paul wouldn't like that at all. 'But then she got to see Olivia, and changed her mind. She didn't kill her. But I believe that one of the others did, and Angel knows which one it was.'

'I see.' She must have been more coherent than she thought. 'So you'd better give me an address for this Angel and her friends, and I'll send a nice, gentle woman police officer round to talk to her.'

'Yes, well, I don't know exactly where she lives. I know it's in East Oxford. And the house is number twenty-five. Or fifty-two. And the street name starts with a D. Or maybe ends with it. And the house probably belongs to someone who is away from home for a couple of weeks.'

There was a sigh at the other end of the line, but Paul didn't argue with her. 'I'll get on with finding it. I don't suppose you know any of their names? Their real names, I mean.'

'No. Except that Angel had a daughter called Daisy who was killed in a road accident at the beginning of the year. I'm not sure where, but it could have been in London.'

'Right. That's better than nothing. And do you know which shop they were trading from?'

'I don't know its name, but it was just past the cinema in George Street.'

'They've probably moved on by now, especially if they think you're going to report them to the police, but I'll get down there and check it out. And you'd better disconnect now, while you can still afford to pay the bill.'

'One more thing.'

'Yes?'

'What was the murder weapon?'

'Why do you want to know?' She might have guessed that he wouldn't tell her.

'Well, was it a hammer?' she asked. If it wasn't, then Angel and her friends were out of it.

'A hammer would be consistent with the pattern of injuries sustained by the victim.' No, they were still in the frame.

'And did you find a hammer in Olivia's rooms?'

'No.'

'Or anything else that could have been used to kill her?'

'No. Although I believe a detailed inventory of the items in her room is still being taken.' Well, that should keep the Thames Valley Police out of mischief until Christmas. And beyond.

'What about a plastic carrier bag?'

'It's difficult to say how many plastic carrier bags are among the multiple layers of Dr Blacket's effects in those two rooms.'

'This one would have been on the desk. The topmost layer.'

'Yes. There was one there.'

'Thanks.'

'Oh, Kate, before you go. Where are you at the moment? You're not off to do anything risky, are you?' So he was still

214

a human being. He'd had her wondering for a bit.

'You know my motto, Paul: Take a risk a day.'

She couldn't help teasing. It would be so dull to tell him that she was off to see an academic, and the greatest risk she ran in the next hour or so was of having her thigh groped. She pressed the red symbol, the machine beeped at her, and she put it back in her handbag.

She was grateful to him for not probing her reasons for asking those particular questions. She didn't want to look too closely at her feelings for Liam Ross. If she admitted, even to herself, that she had been at all serious about him, she might start feeling hurt and rejected. Pain. Anger. Despair. No, she would stay with the present moment. She would go and talk to the professor and find out if he had seen anything that might help prove that Liam was innocent.

She felt very much alone. While she had been talking to Paul she had had the lovely warm feeling that someone else was going to shoulder her responsibilities for her. Just another of life's rotten illusions, she realized. If Angel was telling the truth when she said she left the hammer behind in Olivia's room, then someone else had used it and removed it from the scene. Which of them had done it, how had he got it out without anyone remarking on it, since he hadn't taken the carrier bag to put it in? And where was it now? And, finally, who had taken the doll and given it to Angel?

She heard Dime saying, 'We'll give you another one.' But Dime wasn't bright enough to get into Leicester College, find Olivia's room and murder her and escape undetected, surely?

She would ring Paul again in the evening: perhaps he would have found Angel and the family for her by then.

Whoever had killed Olivia, it wasn't Liam. Definitely.

Unless of course, he had changed his mind about telephoning for a porter and had gone over to her room himself. And then had picked up Angel's hammer and . . . come to think of it, Oxford must be full of people who would want Olivia dead. She must have got up a whole lot of noses with that impossible manner of hers.

The long straight road to Garsington stretched in front of her, and she got back into her car, started the engine and drove to Professor Brendan Adams's house.

'Come in,' he said, opening the door.

The house had an empty feel to it.

'Is your sister not in?'

'She's gone to the supermarket. For some reason she likes to go to one ten miles away. She'll be away for quite a time.' A finger of anxiety touched Kate's spine.

A dog barked. Ludo. So she wasn't quite alone with the professor.

'It's a little early for tea,' he said. 'Would you like coffee?'

'No, thanks.'

'Before we go in, perhaps you would let me have the items from the Ternan Papers that are still in your possession.'

She handed over the three sheets. How important to him were these papers? As he snatched them out of her hand, she wondered whether they were important enough to kill for. She wasn't keen to see them go, but she had no right to them whatsoever. And anyway, she had taken photocopies, so she could refresh her memory of their contents when she needed to. She watched Brendan walk into a room that was obviously his study, and place the three sheets inside a fat folder on his desk. For a moment, she wondered what right the professor had to the papers, since they had come to Olivia through her old college, Bartlemas, but he seemed very sure of himself, and it was hardly her place to argue about things like that. On the other hand, the Ternan Papers surely had a value outside the academic world, and could lead to fame and fortune for the person who had charge of them.

Brendan had brought her into a room full of beautiful objects. Paintings filled every available space on the walls. Sculptures, small and not so small, stood on pretty fruitwood tables. All the rugs were oriental. Bookshelves overflowed with hardback editions. Brendan Adams and his sister had certainly inherited a taste for expensive things. How far did an Oxford academic's salary go towards satisfying such taste?

He had seated her in a deep armchair on the side of the room furthest from the door, while he sank into the depths of the sofa opposite her. She had read somewhere that when you were uncertain of the person you were with, you should make sure that you placed yourself between them and the door. She had got it wrong today, and, said a voice inside her head, with a man who had been seen going into the victim's room shortly before she was found murdered.

Why hadn't she thought of that before getting herself into this situation? The low, deep armchair held her fast. There was no way she could leap to her feet and out through the door in a single bound if she found herself in danger. No, she was being ridiculous. It was time to get to the matter that brought her here. Angel. The family. Liam. All suspects. And she was on her own with another of them: the professor.

'I can't help thinking about Olivia,' she began carefully. 'Perhaps it was because I was there, in Leicester College, at about the time it must have happened.'

'Have you been questioned by the police yet?'

'Not yet. I have to admit that my presence there was—'

'A little unorthodox, I thought.'

'Yes. Did you tell the police that?'

'The fact that you were there slipped my mind until you rang me this morning. And I haven't had the chance to speak to the police since then. Perhaps, Kate, it would look better if you volunteered to make a statement before I passed the information on, don't you think?'

'I expect you're right. I'll get on to them when I leave here.' Another argument with Paul. Why hadn't she told him before? Well, she would have done, but she would have had to explain so much, about Mourning Ale, and the gown, and cap, and the tutor's letter . . . Not to mention the way she had let herself into Olivia's room and listened to the conversation with Liam. Perhaps she would put it off until tomorrow. She had a vague memory of promising herself the same thing yesterday. But Paul wasn't good at seeing her point of view when it came to these amusing little deceptions of hers. That was the problem with the police, no sense of humour.

The professor was saying, 'Did you want to talk to me about something specific, or just about Olivia in general?'

She decided to be truthful. 'I expect you've heard that Liam Ross is being questioned by the police. And I suppose he must be their main suspect at the moment.'

'He had known Olivia for a number of years, since they met in Edinburgh, I believe, and they were very close, on and off. So yes, I suppose that does make him a suspect. It seems that the most likely people to kill us are our nearest and dearest.' And he smiled at Kate. A wolfish smile, she thought. But luckily she was no Little Red Riding Hood.

'You may be right, but even if he really was her nearest and dearest, in Liam's case I don't believe that he killed her.'

'There really is no doubt of the nearest and dearest part, I am afraid. And is it possible that you're a little biased in his favour?'

'If you mean that he deceived me, double-crossed me, and behaved like a toad, yes, you could say that I'm biased,' replied Kate. 'But I still don't think that he killed Olivia. It isn't in his nature to confront people and batter them over the head with a heavy object. He's much more likely to agree with everything they say, then slide out of the room and go his own way. It's almost impossible to have a row with him. You look up after making a particularly telling point to find that he's not there. You might get a telephone call a week later, making no reference to your argument, but inviting you to a concert. Any attempt to bring up the subject again, whatever it was, would be met with the same blank incomprehension.'

'Yes, I see. An impossible man. And what do you think I can do to help him?' He leant forward with one of his old, lecherous, smiles. 'And to help *you*, of course, Kate.'

Kate said: 'You were there, seeing Olivia, dropping off Ludo, after I had left. I just wondered whether there was anything you saw or heard, anything at all, that might be helpful.' Suddenly there was the electric charge of danger between them again.

'What are you suggesting?' He spoke very softly.

Kate hurried on: 'Nothing. I just hoped that you had seen something that would help clear Liam. I wasn't trying to . . .' But then she thought it was unwise to say that she was not trying to implicate Brendan himself, for he might think just the opposite.

He sat back in his seat and watched her carefully as he spoke, as though trying to read the thoughts behind her words. 'Well, just before I met you, I did see your Dr Ross, striding across the quadrangle in the direction of his own staircase. He looked a little upset, I thought. Not quite his usual smug self. I assumed that Olivia had fired off a few shots and scored direct hits in the centre of his self-esteem.'

She ignored the insults to Liam and said: 'So, unless he turned round and went back again, he's in the clear. Presumably Olivia was still alive when you saw her.' She stopped. What was she saying? Electricity crackled again between them.

'She was certainly alive when I got there,' said Brendan, drily. 'You're wondering, I suppose, whether she was equally alive when I left?' The pouched eyes glittered at her.

'I don't think I'd be sitting here with you, alone in the house, if I had any doubts about it,' said Kate, hoping that he believed her. He stared back at her, and she wondered what he was really thinking. 'Did you see anyone else, other than me and Liam?'

'There were a lot of people in college that day. Clifford Quad was full of undergraduates. Our own, and those of Bartlemas College, of course. But it is considered a bit of a joke to get yourself into Leicester for Mourning Ale, even if you aren't a member of either college. So there were all sorts of young people milling about, in various stages of intoxication, none of whom I recognized.' For a few moments she was back on safe ground.

Kate thought of describing the members of the family, but

it was hopeless. One long and thin, with dark hair drawn back into a pony tail; one even thinner, with pale skin and light-coloured hair; one small and wiry with lots of curly brown hair and a green knitted hat; or Dime, maybe. 'You didn't see one young man with dark hair, a red face and bad acne?'

'Several,' said Brendan, unhelpfully.

'A young woman in a white dress?'

'Was she pretty?'

'Not very.'

'I doubt that I noticed her, then.'

'Oh dear. We're not being much help to Liam, are we? I was hoping that we could come up with something that would take the attention of the police away from him.'

'And what possible reason could any of these people have for killing Olivia?'

'Well, there were the Ternan Papers,' said Kate. 'Weren't they worth stealing? And Olivia's involvement with them had been reported in the newspapers.'

'But nobody has stolen them.' His voice was silky, but there were spots of colour in his cheeks. Kate thought of the bulging file on his desk, the glitter of acquisitiveness in his eyes when he saw the pages she had brought. There was the hint of a threat in his expression. It was time to change the subject. She remembered the doll. It was probably unimportant, but it would get them away from the dangerous matter of the Ternan Papers. 'There's just one more thing,' she said brightly. 'This is a bit tricky, but did you notice something that wasn't usually in her room?' She didn't want to prompt him with the idea of a doll unless she had to. 'Or, and this is even trickier, was anything missing, do you think?'

'Something missing? What do you mean? You keep hinting

that I went to Olivia's room to remove something. What are you accusing me of?' Damn, he hadn't realized that she had changed the subject. He thought she was still talking about the Ternan Papers.

'Nothing, nothing, Brendan. I was wondering whether you saw a doll on her desk, that's all.'

'A doll? That childish doll on her desk, do you mean? Don't be ridiculous! We both know what you're really talking about. You've come here with an accusation, haven't you? What do you want? A share in the proceeds?'

'Oh no! No! Not at all!' There was no way she could get out of this chair in a hurry. The seat was nearly on the floor, and her knees were stuck up by her chin.

'They're always accusing me of stealing! And now you're doing it, too. "Did you notice if anything was missing?" You think you're being so subtle!'

'I'm sure you're mistaken. Goodness! No one could ever imagine—'

Brendan had hold of her arm, was heaving her up out of the chair.

'How dare you accuse me of any such thing! It's what the young ones do, you know, all the time. They learn everything you can teach them, and then they come up with their paltry little theses, claiming they're original. But the work in this department is all mine, so if I want to put my name to a paper, I have every right to do so. If you don't publish in this business, you're finished.'

'I do understand,' said Kate. 'My own profession is tough on that, too. If you don't publish, you can't call yourself a writer, can you?'

She was talking garbage because Brendan had propelled

her out of her chair and was dragging her across the room, and she wasn't at all sure what was going to happen to her next.

'Ludo!' he was bellowing. What did he intend doing with her? Was he going to feed her to the Hound?

'I won't have it!' said Brendan. 'First of all that fool Olivia, with her obsession over babies, and now you. All these wild accusations! I haven't stolen anything. The papers should have come to me, not to her, anyway.'

'No, really!' Kate was saying. 'I'm not accusing you of anything. I mean, who would imagine that you would possibly want to take something from Olivia?'

'So why did you ask me about it? We both know you're after the Ternan Papers. You want to beat me to it. Publish before I do. Sensationalize the whole thing. Distort the story. You're all at it. All of you.' He was so close that she saw that his eyes were veined with scarlet. His huge hand encircled her arm.

'I have as much right to those papers as she had! More! I am senior to her. Senior to them all! Just because they were found at Bartlemas rather than Leicester didn't mean that she could take them away from me. She thought the papers were all about children and childbirth. Do you think like that? Is that what you're interested in?'

'No, no,' Kate assured him. 'I've absolutely no interest in babies whatsoever.'

'Because that's not what the notebooks and letters are about at all. You know that, don't you?' Kate nodded, vigorously. 'Sex,' he said.

Kate said, 'No, thanks all the same,' but he carried on without listening to her:

'Sex, that's what they're about. The erotic masturbatory fantasies of a bored North Oxford tradesman's wife. Her notebooks are full of them. Marvellous. Dark, labyrinthine. Singular. That's what we have here. And the intimate sexual details of the relationship between Charles Dickens and his mistress, Nelly Ternan. I'll have a bestseller at last! I shall transcribe, I shall annotate, I shall comment, I shall publish. I shall choose something suitable, rich with rosy naked flesh, for the dust jacket. The public will love it. Smut with a moral face. I shall clean up!'

'It's a lovely thought,' agreed Kate. 'I had something similar in mind, myself.'

'Well, you'll just have to forget all about it,' said Brendan, viciously. 'Because I'm going to make quite sure you can't get into the market before me.'

'What do you mean? What are you going to do?'

'I can tell the police how I saw you, in disguise, in Leicester College, just before Olivia was murdered. I shall tell them how Liam Ross cruelly deceived you with Olivia Blacket, and how you cried upon my shoulder in the bitterness of your jealousy and rage. And then you tried to steal the Ternan Papers which were in my possession, and attacked me. I, of course, had to defend myself. And I shall restrain you until the police arrive.'

'You should take up fiction writing.'

'Perhaps I will. Erotic fiction, naturally.'

'You're mad! You can't do this to me!'

'I just wish to keep you out of circulation for long enough to get the proposal for my own book accepted. It will be an unfortunate misunderstanding. I'm sure the police will sort it out, eventually. Come on!'

He jerked her along the passage by her left arm.

She thought he was quite right: the police would love to lock her up for a day or two and question her about her involvement in Olivia's death. She was an interfering amateur, in their eyes, and very far from popular. She had to get away before the police came screaming up with their blue lights flashing.

Ahead of her was the kitchen, where presumably Ludo was incarcerated, and longing for his next meal. To her left was the front door, but Brendan stood between her and that route to freedom. To her right was a short passage with a door at the end of it. She relaxed the arm that Brendan was holding, so that he let it fall a little, then she jerked it rapidly up and outwards, freeing herself in the way she had learnt in her self-defence classes. She stamped down hard on his instep, jabbed her thumb in his eye then started to sprint, and hoped that she had guessed right about what lay behind the door. Behind her, Brendan was howling with pain and rage. She threw the door open.

Yes. Dustbins. A small yard with a clothes line. A path that circled the house and led back to the front drive where she had parked her car.

She still had her handbag with her, and she extracted her car keys as she ran, and hurled herself into the driver's seat. The engine was still warm and started immediately, and she was down the drive, with the gravel spurting behind her, as Brendan came blundering out of the house after her.

She drove for about a mile before she pulled up on the side of the road. Time to phone for help, she thought. She looked at her phone and thought about telling Paul Taylor about what had nearly happened to her at Brendan Adams's house. Then she sighed, put it back in her handbag, and drove slowly back to Oxford.

Angel sat on a chair at the dressing table in her bedroom. The doll sat in front of her and slightly to one side, so that when she looked up from her work and out of the window to think of a word or phrase, she caught its eye.

Really, it was nothing at all like Daisy, but she had seen it so often now that its features were starting to take over from her daughter's, so that now when she tried to visualize her own child, she saw the doll. Only the white bonnet was similar, really. Daisy's favourite white bonnet. She refused to go out without it, even when winter arrived.

She was wearing it that day.

She was wearing it when they put her in her small white coffin. Or one very much like it. Angel knew about it because she had a photograph. She had been lying in a hospital bed, with metal pins in her leg, and her head full of painkillers so that she didn't know what was going on. But they didn't take your child away and bury her in the cold earth without taking a Polaroid photograph for you to remember her by. Maybe they thought she wouldn't accept the fact that she was dead without it. But the one thing that Angel remembered was the sight of Daisy, flung over the bonnet of the car, disappearing over the roof, coming to rest in the road behind the car. No one could survive that. Certainly not a ten-month-old child.

After that she only remembered the pain.

She was glad that she had got rid of the green cardigan. Ant was right of course. She hadn't told quite all the truth that day in the shop with that Kate woman asking all the questions. Someone had wrapped the green cardigan round her because she was cold. And had given her the doll. She had held it to her, underneath the cardigan. Kate Ivory had seen it and wondered about it, but she hadn't found out who had taken it from Olivia Blacket's room and given it to her. And she had no intention of ever telling anyone now. Kate Ivory wasn't quite as clever as she thought she was. She didn't know it all.

Angel had her notebook open, her pencil in her hand.

Her face is so white, even against the white lining of the coffin. They bury babies in white. Did you know that? Tiny white coffin. It only takes one man to lift it and carry it. And white flowers. Lilies with yellow tongues. They wrote a card for Daisy, to go with the white lilies, and they signed it with my name. I knew nothing about it, but I'm glad now that they did that for me. And for her.

They used to believe, long ago, that dead children went to heaven and turned into angels. Angel Daisy. How ridiculous that sounds.

Angel of Death.

Kate had given in to her need for company, and had rung Paul. Now they were both in her kitchen while she prepared comforting food.

She filled the kettle, placed slices of bread under the grill. 'You can make the slices much thicker than you can in the toaster,' she told him, as she found butter, jam, honey, biscuits and a section of the carrot cake that her friend Camilla had brought over a few days ago. 'Milk? Sugar?' and she put them all on the kitchen table, together with a couple of plates. If Paul wondered why she needed all this comfort food, he didn't ask her about it.

'Help yourself to toast and stuff,' she said, pouring the tea. 'Have you had any luck finding the house I told you about?'

'Your friend Dime didn't do very well at giving you his address. I'm still looking for the house. I haven't found it yet.'

'Why aren't there hundreds of men in blue out searching for it?'

'Because I'm the only one who thinks it may be important.'

'Oh. Well, here's something else for you. When I was talking to the whole group of them, and I mentioned the doll, I could tell by their faces that they knew what I was talking about, but they wouldn't answer my question.'

'Don't tell me,' said Paul. 'You confronted a group of outlaws, one of whom is probably a murderer, and you asked them all a lot of impertinent questions. And you did this in a confined space, presumably, with no outsiders present?'

'Something like that,' said Kate airily. 'And I survived, so where's the harm? But to get back to the important part. I think Olivia had a baby doll, wearing a white bonnet, sitting on her desk. She must have bought it that day, as she would surely not have left it sitting there for very long before taking it home. She may even have bought it from Ant's shop. It was there when I was in her room.'

'You what?'

'Didn't I tell you how I went to visit her in her room?'

'You know you didn't.'

'Oh dear, it must have slipped my mind.'

'Kate!'

'Yes, all right, it was on the day of the murder.'

'I think you'd better explain.'

'Later. Have some more tea and stop looking distraught.

The carrot cake in particular brings comfort to the troubled soul. Right, where was I?'

'The doll.'

'The doll. I saw it when I arrived. Then Liam came and went, and it was still there. I asked Brendan Adams whether he saw it, and after becoming enraged about being accused of thieving, he admitted that he had seen the doll, too. But when I asked you, you said no, it wasn't there. And I think that whoever murdered Olivia took the doll away with them – and later gave it to Angel. I'm sure it's the same doll that she was trying to hide under her cardigan when I met her outside the college.'

'It sounds highly unlikely.'

'Yes. But now it's my turn to eat carrot cake while we do our information swap.'

'When we searched Olivia's house, we found a cupboard in her bedroom, one of those massive old pieces of furniture in some dark wood that you don't often see nowadays, and in the top half there was a shelf packed with dolls. Eleven of them.'

'That's weird.'

'As you say. They were sitting there in a row, all facing towards the front. They were all baby dolls. None of your walking, talking, crying numbers. No Barbies or Cindies. And they all wore white cotton bonnets.'

'She was obsessed with babies,' said Kate. 'Everyone noticed it. Even the professor. Whatever she was doing, she twisted it round so that it had to do with infants.'

'Women!' said Paul. 'You're all the same!' But he looked at her sideways, so she knew that this time he wasn't serious, he was only winding her up.

'I agree that women of her age – what was she? Thirty-six or so? – do have to consider seriously whether or not they want to have children, but this is a bit over the top, isn't it? I mean, I'm in my thirties, but you won't find cupboards full of dolls, or even fluffy toys, in my house.'

'Books,' said Paul. 'Your place is full of books. No toys, only books in your house. That's weird, too.'

'I shan't offer you the last chocolate biscuit after that. No, what I'm trying to say is that there must be more to it than biology. Either she felt so guilty about killing Daisy that she kept trying to replace the dead child with a doll, or there was something more personal behind it. And, knowing Olivia even as little as I did, I should think that it was her own loss she was concerned with, not Angel's.'

They sat and polished off the remains of the food in silence. Kate was trying to recall the conversation she had overheard between Liam and Olivia. She had the feeling that Liam could tell her what this corner of the puzzle was all about.

'Have you arrested Liam Ross yet?' she asked Paul.

'No. He's got himself a solicitor, and he's free.' He relented, and added, 'There was no good reason to hold him. He seemed the obvious candidate at first: unwilling lover trying to free himself from a long-running affair with a jealous and possessive older woman who was making threats to his career. But none of it held up when you looked into it. And although they were heard having a row on the afternoon of her death, he was also seen leaving her rooms, pursued by a furious Olivia. If there was any battering to be done in that relationship, it looked as though Ross would have been the victim.'

'You're telling me it would be safe for me to go and ask

him some questions? I wouldn't be confronting a murderer?'

'If you must.' He hated the idea, she could see. But he knew better than to try to stop her.

'And we're still left with the question of who killed Olivia,' said Kate. Not only that, she thought. I still haven't got any new information for my book, either.

'You still think it was one of this elusive family of yours?' asked Paul.

'What other suspects have you got?' she countered.

'You,' he said. 'But I wasn't going to tell you that.'

'So why aren't your most senior colleagues sitting here in my kitchen, spurning my apricot jam and asking me questions?'

'They don't yet know who you are. They know that a woman conned her way into Leicester and probably let herself into Olivia's room. I think it would be a very good idea if you went down to the station and made a statement as soon as possible. Try to be helpful for a change.'

'That could have been Angel, not me,' said Kate, ignoring the unpleasant part of his speech.

'But they don't know anything about Angel, do they? They don't even know that she exists.'

'You don't believe in them either, do you?' She was going to lose her temper in a moment. She could feel her face getting hot, which was always a bad sign. Her hands were cold and tingling, which meant that the countdown to the explosion had already started.

'Yes I do.' He spoke very calmly, as though he knew how close she was to throwing a serious tantrum. 'If I didn't believe in them, I wouldn't be spending half my spare time poring over a map of Oxford and walking up every street east of Magdalen Bridge that had a D in it.'

'Oh, thanks. I don't suppose you've had much time off since I rang you.'

'And do you realize that I've had to look at everything called "Road", since that, too, ends in a D? And from your description of Dime, he's quite simple enough not to recognize the word.'

'Would you like some more toast?'

'No, thanks. I don't suppose you've seen what vehicle they drive, have you?'

'No. They've always been on foot. I imagine they have one of those beat-up old vans.'

'Probably. But that isn't a lot to go on, is it?'

She had to agree with him. She could see that if they were going to find the family, it was down to her. And time must be running out. They could be on their way out of Oxford at this very moment.

'There's one more thing.'

'Yes?'

'You have to get down to St Aldate's and make a statement. I promise not to be around to hear the more creative sections, but you've got to tell the important facts. Apart from any considerations of justice, and civic duty, you could be in trouble if you don't.'

'Yes, of course.' That had to be the first time she'd agreed to anything he said without arguing.

She would even get on to it straight away. But once she'd done it, she had to talk to Liam, whatever Paul Taylor thought about it.

She was glad that Paul wasn't there when she made her

statement to a serious young constable at the police station. She had passed Leicester College on her way to St Aldate's, and the place was swarming with blue uniforms. They must have taken dozens of statements by now, and had several reports of a woman with short blonde hair who was seen on the premises at the relevant time.

'Yes, I'm afraid I thought it was a bit of a joke to con my way into the college while they were dispensing the Mourning Ale,' she said. 'But I did have an appointment with Dr Blacket. She was working on the notebooks and letters of a woman that I'm very interested in. I'm a writer, you see,' she simpered. The police constable ignored both the simper and the eyelash work that went with it.

'When I got to her room, there was no one there, but she had given me the key, in case she was late, so that I could let myself in.'

And with the air of a conjuror, she produced Olivia's key from her handbag.

'I waited in her room for just a few minutes before she arrived. She handed me the two pages of the Ternan Papers that I had requested, and I left. I'm afraid I didn't see or hear anything that could be of help to you.'

The constable made a note of the time that Kate was in Olivia's room, took the key from her, and told her that she could expect a visit from a more senior officer to confirm her statement later.

'And we would like to take your fingerprints, please, madam.'

'Why?'

'So that we can identify them among those that we found in Dr Blacket's room. We wouldn't want to get your prints mixed up with those of any criminals,' he said.

Kate's fingerprints were taken, her statement was typed up and signed, and then she was free to leave the police station.

Chapter 11

Then the devil taketh him up into the holy city, and
setteth him on a pinnacle of the temple.

Matthew IV, 5

Kate went home and scrubbed the black ink from her fingers.
Then she made up her mind. There was no point in waiting,
or telephoning, or putting it off. If she was going to see Liam,
she might as well walk back into Oxford, and catch him in
his room in college, right away.

She made sure she looked the way she would want him
to remember her, with regret, in the coming months, then
she set off.

She walked through the gateway at Leicester College without asking the porter to phone ahead. She didn't want him
to have notice of her arrival so that he could discover a
meeting he should attend, or arrange for someone to call in
and interrupt them.

She knocked on his door and walked straight in.

He was sitting at his desk, as she always imagined him,
one hand keeping his place in a book. He had long, sensitive

hands, with well-shaped fingers. She suspected that he knew this very well, and even practised displaying them to advantage against the pages of a book. His computer sat on the desk to the right of him, a pile of papers on his left.

'Kate!' He might well look startled. She had never walked in on him unannounced before. She watched him think up three reasons why she couldn't stay, or he had to leave, but before he had time to say any of them aloud she had sat down on the comfortable chair he kept for favoured undergraduates, and said:

'This won't take long, but it is a conversation we have to have. So don't tell me you should be somewhere else, or are expecting someone to arrive. You can put your telephone answering machine on, and you can close your outer door.'

He looked at her and decided that she meant what she said.

'Sherry?' he asked. She might, even now, meeting him for the first time, be taken in by that face, with its gentle, caring expression. I bet that the women undergraduates all sit in this chair thinking how marvellous you are, and you sit over there, in yours, drinking it in and loving every moment of it.

'No sherry, thanks. I hate the stuff. Don't you want to know what this is about?'

He raised a well-shaped eyebrow. Everything he did now seemed to her as though it was calculated, practised.

'I imagine you've heard about Olivia and want to ask me about her. Then you can lose your temper and storm out, shouting that you never want to see me again in your life. Are you sure you wouldn't like a drink first?'

Kate shook her head. He got up from the desk and went and poured himself a whisky, then returned to one of the other armchairs, facing Kate.

'You are close,' she said. 'Except that I've got past the stage of losing my temper. And as for seeing you again, I really don't care about it. Though on the whole I would prefer not to.'

'So what is the point of this meeting?'

'I'd like to get a few things straight. I'd quite like to know who killed Olivia.'

'Since you're sitting here on your own, with the door closed, I assume you don't think I did it. Or is your little policeman friend lurking outside the door, waiting for me to confess everything to you?'

She held on to her temper. It was the only advantage she had in this situation. 'I'm trying to find out about the doll,' she said.

She could see from his expression that he knew what she was talking about. But it would take another jolt to get the truth out of him. She was starting to recognize the signs of Liam preparing to tell a lie. She wondered whether she was quite that transparent herself.

'I know about the one that was on her desk that afternoon, and about the ten or so that she had in a cupboard in her bedroom,' she said. 'They were all baby dolls, bought over a range of time, apparently. Each of them wearing a white cotton bonnet trimmed with lace. What I don't know is why she needed them. She was obsessed with babies, I know that, too. It affected her academic judgement, and distorted her reading of the Ternan Papers, but I don't know why. And I know that she killed Daisy, even if it was an accident.'

Liam didn't meet her eyes. He stared down at the pattern on the rug as though he had never seen it before and was determined to commit its every detail to memory.

'It started in Edinburgh,' he said, finally, still staring at the rug. 'I was doing my Ph.D., she had her first academic post. She is, as you probably noticed, three or four years older than me. I fell for her, but then everybody did. She really had style: tall, blonde, slim, beautifully dressed. She always looked as though she had just walked out of a very expensive dress shop.'

'Yes, all right, I get the idea,' said Kate, sitting up as straight as possible to make the best of her five feet and five inches.

'I was flattered when she took notice of me. And then we had this thing going all the time I was there.' His high, intellectual forehead was attractively furrowed with the intensity of his thoughts.

'You mean, you were lovers.'

'Yes, I suppose so. Don't interrupt, or I won't be able to get through it. For me, this isn't easy to talk about, Kate. I'm not an insensitive man, you know. Where was I? Oh yes. I completed my doctorate and applied for this job in Oxford. She was upset when I got it: Edinburgh and Oxford really are a long way apart. So, it ended. We stopped being lovers, if that's how you want to put it. We wrote, occasionally. Phoned from time to time. Met up a couple of times in London. But it fizzled out, inevitably.' He stopped. He would like to think that that was all there was to it, thought Kate.

'Then, a couple of years ago, she applied for a Clifford Fellowship at Leicester and was successful. She took it up in September last year. She moved to Oxford, and we started seeing one another again. You know how it is.'

Olivia was, after all, still tall, slim, blonde and extremely stylish. Yes, Kate knew how it must be. She hadn't thought she could ever be this dispassionate about Liam Ross, though.

'What I hadn't realized was that she had got it fixed in her mind that she had to have a child. Well, she wasn't exactly old, but I suppose she was in her mid-thirties and women need to make their minds up about having children, don't they?'

'I suppose so,' said Kate, through slightly gritted teeth.

'Only she made this decision unilaterally, as it were, and just presented me with the result.'

'You mean she got pregnant without talking over her decision with you first?'

'Yes.'

'And you were the father?'

'So she said. I had to believe her.'

'That's unnecessarily insulting.'

'OK, I was definitely the father. Satisfied? She said that we had to get married. That she wanted it, had always wanted it, and I must see that it was the best thing for all three of us.'

'And what did you respond to that?' No wonder Liam was a bit distracted when she first met him, last February. He probably started going out with her as a relief from all this pressure from Olivia. And she, fool that she was, imagined that it was something to do with love. She tried not to think about Liam and Olivia, and their child.

'I said that it wasn't on. That I didn't want to get married. That I didn't want to marry *her*. That I didn't want children.'

'I bet you didn't have that conversation at all,' said Kate, sharply. 'I bet that what actually happened was that you looked guilty and disappeared for a couple of weeks, and hoped that it would all go away. You wouldn't be having *this* conversation if I hadn't trapped you in your room, would you?'

'Well, perhaps we didn't exactly have a row about it,' said Liam. 'Maybe we didn't have a conversation, as such. But she must have known that I wasn't keen on the idea of getting married. She should have known how I felt. I'd never said that I wanted to get married. And I've never expressed any interest in children, have I?'

'None,' said Kate. Poor Olivia. Poor deluded Olivia. 'What did she do?'

'She got into rather an emotional state,' said Liam, awkwardly.

'I bet she did,' said Kate. 'Any woman would. I expect she shouted and screamed a lot, knowing Olivia. And I bet you, Liam, ran away from it. Nasty, messy things, emotions.'

'Well, they're not my sort of thing, are they?' he said, reasonably.

'What happened after that?'

'She had an abortion. She fixed it all up herself without telling me about it. Well, if she had, I'd have offered to pay for at least half of it.'

'You are a complete bastard.'

He looked hurt. 'What else could I do?'

'Go on with the story.'

'In between fixing the abortion and actually going through with the thing, she was staying up in London.'

'You weren't there with her?'

'I was busy. I had an opera to produce. It was during the Christmas vacation. There wasn't anything I could have done to help. She didn't need me to sit and hold her hand. And, like I say, she was in a very emotional state all the time.

And that's when she had the accident in the car, and the child – Daisy, did you say her name was? – was killed. I believe the mother was hurt, too, but she recovered all right.'

'Not particularly all right. She made her mind up to come to Leicester and kill Olivia.'

'My God! You mean she's the one who did it? Have you told the police? I rang Olivia that afternoon and she shrieked at me about some mad woman who had broken into her room and was threatening her. She asked me to call the porters to have her thrown out.'

'Why didn't you?'

'I thought she was talking about you.'

'Well, it was Angel. Though that isn't her real name. She's forgotten what that is, as a result of Daisy's death. She did go to Olivia's rooms to kill her, but when it came to it, she couldn't bring herself to. And what would you like me to tell the police? I don't even know the woman's name, and I don't know where she's living.' She wasn't going to tell Liam that Paul was probably at this very moment walking the streets of East Oxford, searching for Angel.

'Now, to get back to the dolls,' said Kate.

'Fuck the dolls! What the hell do they matter? If we can find this woman, the police will be off my back. I mean, with someone like that at large, they couldn't still suspect me of killing Olivia, could they?'

She really couldn't stay in the room with this man any longer. She had learnt enough about what happened between him and Olivia to explain the presence of those sad, dead, baby dolls in her cupboard. She could leave.

She had to get out of here and find Angel and the family. She was only sorry that if she did so, it might well get Liam off the hook. She would like to leave him hanging on it for as long as possible.

'I'm going now,' she said, getting up from the chair.

He stood up and walked with her to the door. He had lovely manners. 'I'll give you a ring in a week or so, when all this has blown over. Maybe we could go to a concert or something.'

'No, thank you. Goodbye, Liam.'

He had a beautiful voice, too. The sort that could murmur in your ear and convince you that he was a sweet, sensitive man. She knew at last that she never wanted to hear it again.

Kate came out through the gateway and turned into Broad Street. She felt a mixture of elation at having got through the scene with Liam without giving in and agreeing to see him again, and damp depression because what she had thought was the great relationship of her life was finally over.

That's it, she thought. Over. Never again. Just stick with your work.

But first find Angel and the family.

She crossed Broad Street and walked down Catte Street and into Radcliffe Square. Ahead of her she saw a tall man, his clothes nearly invisible in the dark night, his hair long and worn in a pony tail. It was difficult to recognize anyone in that light, but still, there was something familiar in his walk. She was almost sure that it was Ant.

He was moving fast towards the High Street, and she increased her own speed to catch up with him. His legs were a lot longer than hers, and for once she was wearing impractical boots with narrow lacing and high heels. She tried to run, but all she could manage in her short, tight skirt and silly boots was a knock-kneed scamper. She longed for jeans and a pair of trainers. She would take on anyone if she had a decent pair of running shoes on her feet.

She might have lost him completely, for he would soon reach the High Street and be out of sight, if at that moment a group of undergraduates hadn't turned from the High Street and blocked the narrow passageway into the square. They were dressed in dinner jackets and were very pleased with themselves. Their voices were loud, and the group stretched from one side of the path to the other. They weren't going to let any outsider through their ranks. The man stopped and turned. Saw Kate scampering towards him. Recognized her at the same moment that she recognized him. It was certainly Ant.

He veered abruptly to his right to cross in front of the church of St Mary's. There was another exit into the High Street by Brasenose, and he made for it. Then he saw the policeman standing there.

Kate didn't know why the policeman was there. Probably he was waiting to catch some driver taking an illicit shortcut through the square, but Ant must have thought that he was pursued by the law. He would have to pass the policeman if he wanted to sprint round to Brasenose Lane and escape through the Turl. The gate at the far side of the Schools Quadrangle of the Bodleian would be locked, so there was only one alternative: he raced back towards the Radcliffe Camera, and vaulted lightly over the railings on to the grass then made for the steps and the main entrance to the building. Watching him, Kate wondered whether he knew that there was only nine inches of turf between his feet and the bookstack below the square. He had a fair turn of speed, she noticed admiringly as he sprinted for the Camera. The oversized pepperpot. A college, or maybe a church. In fact, as Kate could have told him, it was a circular, three-storeyed library.

Kate changed direction and made for the Camera, too. There was no way she could climb over the fence in her tight skirt. She had to scurry as quickly as she could round its perimeter, up the only path and in through the main door. She scrabbled in her bag for her Bodleian card, but there were no porters on duty at that time of evening. Once inside the building, she paused, and listened. Had Ant gone into the reading room they called the Lower Camera? She walked down the steps.

She stood by the door of the reading room and looked inside. This was the only exit for readers, so if he was inside, he could not get out again without passing her.

In front of her was a small central island with card catalogues and two or three computer terminals. On her left was the Reserve where she could see an assistant groping for a book on a dimly lit bookshelf. Desks radiated out from the centre like spokes from a bicycle wheel, each one crowded with students, and lit with table lamps with cream, drum-shaped shades. Civilized lighting, but not brilliant. Puddles of amber light in an ocean of darkness. She looked all around. No movement. Perhaps he was sitting at a desk, pretending to read. She studied each person there as closely as she could. There were few as tall as Ant, though quite a few dressed all in black. Hair, male and female, was being worn convict-short this term, apparently, which was a help. She tried hard to penetrate the shadows, but could make out nothing that looked like Ant. Not here. He must be upstairs.

She backed out of the room, watching all the time for a movement from him. Nothing, except for one or two curious glances from readers. The wide staircase with its intricate iron banisters curved up to the next floor, and Kate climbed up it and went into the Upper Camera. She arrived, panting, in the reading room.

There was an area in the centre, shaped like an exclamation mark, where the assistant on evening duty would sit. The lighting up here was more modern, but she still couldn't see Ant anywhere. She went up to the desk and gasped:

'Have you seen a man?'

'Kate, my dear, I thought you had at least two. Are you as desperate as all that?'

It was Andrew Grove, looking up from his book and peering at her in amazement.

'Don't be facetious, Andrew.'

'Well, are you looking for a particular man, or would anyone do?' He was getting his own back for her tease about Isabel and Swervedriver, but this had gone far enough.

'Stop buggering about, Andrew.' A couple of heads raised themselves from books and stared at her, but not necessarily in disapproval, she thought. She lowered her voice a decibel or two, however, in deference to her surroundings. She had the continuing existence of her Bodleian reader's card to consider. 'Did a young man, dressed in black, with long dark hair in a pony tail, come in a few minutes ago?'

'My goodness. So many of them fit that description. And I have to say that I was sitting here, so engrossed in the new Dick Francis, that really I haven't looked to see who has come in. Or who hasn't.'

Kate turned her back on him and started walking round

the reading room. There were a couple of spiral staircases leading to the gallery, but she ignored these for the moment while she completed the circuit of the main floor. She very soon lost track of where she was, since the room was circular, and her sense of direction was not brilliant at the best of times. But she ended up next to another computer terminal, fell over a kickstep, and saw in front of her an open door, leading into a tiny room, with a sink, a shelf and a kettle. On the shelf stood several jars of instant coffee, some powdered milk and a tin of powdered chocolate.

'So you've found our staff cubby-hole. Would you like a cup of cocoa? I was just making myself one.' Andrew had followed her.

Beyond the cocoa-making cupboard rose another spiral staircase. Less ornamental, this one, with plain stone steps.

'No thanks. Where does this staircase go to?' Ant didn't seem to be anywhere in the room, so she might as well try higher up.

'To the superintendent's office. I hope you're not going up there. He likes to eat his sandwiches in peace. He doesn't take kindly to being disturbed by readers when he's in the middle of the latest Ruth Rendell.'

Kate pretended she hadn't heard and walked straight past the antique notice that said *Private. Staff Only* and went up the stairs.

Luckily, the crime-fiction fan was not sitting at his desk, so Kate dodged round a partition and found herself on a balcony, looking down into the reading room. Above her soared the dome of the Camera, its plasterwork as decorative as a wedding cake, while opposite her were pillared archways and a balcony that was a continuation of the one on which she stood.

A movement. She stared across. A dark shadow moving from right to left and disappearing behind more pillars. A tall figure, hair in a pony tail. It had to be Ant.

There was a puffing sound behind her.

'Kate, I must insist that you come downstairs again. I will happily accompany you on a tour of the building on some other occasion. But at the moment I really must stay down at the desk. I shouldn't have left it unattended like this, as it is.'

Kate didn't have time to argue. She pointed across at the clump of pillars where she had last seen Ant. 'What's behind there?'

'A staircase up to the roof.'

'Is it locked?'

'It should be, but I have just been fetching some fresh milk from my private cold store on the stairs, and it is just possible that I've left—'

'It's open, then, and Ant could have gone through. Is there another way up? What are those stairs there?' She indicated the door behind her.

'They lead up to the roof as well. It is a wonderful view, but we only allow people to go there by appointment, and when accompanied by— Kate! what are you doing? Come back here!'

But Kate had started climbing up the stairs. She could still hear Andrew's dismayed voice behind her as she stepped through a door like the visor on a helmet, and out on to the roof.

Beneath and all around her swung the city of Oxford. Above her soared lighted golden windows that pointed the way through the centre of the Camera and right down to the floor. Kate took a deep breath and closed her eyes. Why does this happen to me? she wondered. Do they all know that I'm frightened of heights? Do they do it on purpose? Now, water, that would be different. I'm not at all nervous of anything to do with water. I can dive into it and swim underneath the stuff quite happily. I can swim on top of it for miles. She opened her eyes, warily, and concentrated on the things close to her. To her right, a window with graffiti. People had scratched their names on the glass at about the time of the French Revolution. *All bad lots*, someone had written. Quite so. In France, heads rolled from the guillotine. In Oxford, people scratched their names on windows.

In front of her, a buttress, a narrow pathway, and to her left, a balustrade, decorated with giant smooth stone pineapples set on fluted saucers.

So far, so good. Her head wasn't spinning too badly yet. She could chance a look over the top at the view.

The sky had cleared after the earlier rain, and the moon was nearly full. Around her, floodlights picked out the most appealing items of architecture for her inspection. The roof of the Bodleian, a bright apple green, lay to her left, surrounded by sharpened sticks of celery, carved from white stone. Ninety degrees further round and she was eyeball to eyeball with the twin towers of All Souls.

She wanted to sit on the lead roof and hug her knees, preferably with her eyes closed again, but she still had something to do. Where was Ant?

There was a slight noise from the balustrade, just out of sight, behind her.

'Ant? Are you there?'

The thin black figure moved out from behind a buttress and stepped up on to the flat top of the balustrade. Yes, he did know that she hated heights. Up there, with nothing between him and the hard flagstones of Radcliffe Square but a lot of empty space, he was quite safe from Kate Ivory.

'You wanted to talk to me?' He put a casual arm around a stone pineapple, and looked down into the square.

'Yes.' Then she couldn't help herself from adding, 'Please don't do that!'

'Does it worry you? It shouldn't. There's a ledge just below here. Look. Three feet down. Two feet wide.' And he leant over the edge to see it better.

Kate closed her eyes. When she opened them a moment later the whole black and gold world swung round in an arc about her head. When it had steadied again she saw the glint of his teeth against the dusk of his face.

'You want to know about the woman who was killed?' he said.

'Yes. I think I know the reason why she was murdered.'

'What would that be?'

'She was killed for love.'

'And what do you know of love, Kate Ivory?'

'Very little, Ant.'

'We do, you see.'

'I know. I think it has all been about Angel's love for Daisy. And Olivia's love for her unborn child. And the way a woman goes mad when a child dies, whether the child is born or not.'

'Mother love,' said Ant. 'It's not the only kind.'

'No,' said Kate. 'There's the love between the members of the family.'

'It's what we're about,' said Ant. 'We all got there by

different roads, but we found each other, and now we stick together.'

'Love as cement,' said Kate. 'It's one definition.'

'Defining it isn't important,' said Ant. 'Living it is.'

'So are you going to tell me how it happened?'

'I thought you knew. You said you understood it.'

'I know that Angel wanted to kill Olivia, but when she got there in the same room with her, face to face, she couldn't do it.'

'It might have been better if she had. Only she'd never have got away with it. That took some organizing.'

'So one of the family followed her, and killed Olivia for Angel's sake. And Daisy's.'

'If he did, he did it for love. For love of Angel.'

'I know. I understand. I do. He knew what Daisy's death had done to Angel. It had robbed her of her whole life, and of her memory as well. It nearly cost her her life. Perhaps he thought that if Angel were free of Olivia, then she would be able to start afresh.'

'It's what's wrong with your world,' said Ant. 'People don't listen. They hear each other, but somehow the words twist and change their shape as they move through the air from lips to ears. And so they change their meaning. Angel shouted at Olivia, but Olivia didn't hear what she said. Angel wrote in her notebook, and the words meant something different every time, depending on who read them.'

'I tried to listen to her,' said Kate. 'I tried to understand what she was saying. Doesn't that count?'

'People hear what they expect to hear, read what they expect to see. Those pages that Angel saw on Olivia's desk, who knows what they really said, and what the woman intended who set the words down on the paper?'

'Which of you did it?' cried Kate. 'I want to know!'

'It doesn't matter,' said Ant. 'And it's better that you shouldn't know.'

'What happens to Angel now?' asked Kate.

'We want to marry her,' said Ant. 'Four men, one wife. I don't suppose you like that idea, but it suits us. It suits our Angel. Four men to look after her and love her. It's what she needs. And she can have more children. We know that they won't take the place of Daisy, but it will be the beginning of a new life for her.'

'And I'll never know the answer.'

'Why do you need to know?'

'Only because I like neat endings, all the odd strands sewn in. This is untidy.'

'You'll have to learn to live in a world with untidy endings, threads hanging out of the seams.'

'I like order,' said Kate. 'I like to be in control.'

'And does your passion for tidiness include shopping us to the police?'

'Not necessarily.' If she stayed down on the lead roof, the balustrade was comfortingly high. Ant was the one in danger, balanced up there against the void. 'Do you think you'll get away with it?'

'We're leaving Oxford tonight. I don't think you'll catch us, you and your policeman friend.'

Behind Ant's head she could see the hills of Wytham and Cumnor, and the string of flashing yellow diamonds that were headlights moving along the bypass. She imagined Ant and the family joining it and disappearing into new lives and names, beyond the reach of Paul and his colleagues.

'I could shout for help from up here. There's a policeman standing down by Brasenose.'

'No,' said Ant. 'He's already gone.'

'Well?'

'I could throw you over the edge,' said Ant, without emotion.

'But you don't want to kill anyone else, do you? Olivia's death may have been necessary. Mine isn't.'

'You tell good stories,' said Ant. 'I wouldn't want to rob the world of that. So, I'll tell you what we'll do.'

Why was she standing on top of a giant pepperpot bargaining with a probable murderer? Why wasn't she getting out her mobile phone and ringing for the police? They could be here in minutes. They could surround the Camera and trap Ant. Then what? He would simply deny everything she said. And there was something else.

She liked Ant.

She thought his family had a lot going for it. It beat what had happened between Liam and Olivia any day. Let alone what had happened between Liam and herself.

'Tell me,' she said. 'Give me an alternative.'

'Give me a two-minute start. Then you can go back through that door, and down that spiral staircase. When you get to the main door, at the bottom, you're free. You can make your own decision. What you do when you get into the square is up to you.'

'You'll trust me?' she asked.

'I have to.'

She had to trust him, as well. If he jumped down on to the roof beside her, then pulled her up on to the balustrade, she would be at his mercy. No one had seen him come up on to the roof. She could fall into the square and die, and no one would ever know that it was anything but an accident. Not even Andrew had seen Ant. On the other hand, if she shouted for help, Andrew could summon porters and the police. She made her decision.

'All right,' she said. 'I agree.'

For a moment he was silhouetted in the light from the doorway. Then he was gone.

Over the balustrade and on to the narrow ledge. Running light-footed round to the other side, where the second staircase emerged through another door like a visor. She hoped he wasn't afraid of heights, at least.

'Goodbye, Ant.' She said it quietly. She didn't think he could hear her.

'What on earth were you doing up on the roof, Kate?'

It was Andrew, looking worried.

'And who was that young man who came down the other staircase just before you? I tried to tell him that I wished to examine his reader's card, but he laughed at me and walked out of the reading room. Was he a friend of yours?'

'No. But I shouldn't worry about it, Andrew. I don't think he stole any books, and I don't think he'll be back. Why don't you make us both a cup of cocoa, and we can forget all about it.'

A little later, Kate, too, left the Camera.

When she got outside, she stood on the steps and looked around her. There was no sign of Ant anywhere. But then, she hadn't expected it.

Chapter 12

Why shouldst thou fear the beautiful angel, Death?
Adelaide Ann Procter, 1825–64

When she got home to Fridesley, Kate unlaced her boots and kicked them off, left them just where they lay in the hall, and went into the kitchen to see what she had to eat. All she could find, after her session with Paul, were healthy green vegetables, fresh fruit and some low-fat cheese. What she needed was ice cream, preferably Belgian-chocolate flavour, with chocolate chips, added dark chocolate sauce and a topping of whipped cream.

Failing that, she took out a bottle of red wine and opened it. You could always rely on red wine to get you into a seriously depressed state and leave you with a filthy headache in the morning.

And why should she care whether she was fit to work in the morning or not? Her book was going nowhere. She knew no more now about Maria Taylor than she had a couple of weeks ago. All she could write was a competent, predictable story, rehashing the facts that everyone knew.

And as for men. She was through with them. For ever.

She switched on the television and looked for a really trashy programme. All she found was the news. At least that wouldn't attempt to be cheerful and jolt her out of her lousy mood.

She drank a glass of wine and poured herself another immediately.

The family had eaten their supper, cleared the dishes away, and were watching television when Ant returned. Dime had tuned it to Central, but switched channels quickly to BBC1 when Ant came into the living room to join them. Ant sat down with his sandwich in front of the screen. When he had finished eating it, he would tell them it was time to pack up and leave.

The item that interested them came towards the end of the news. Ant had been paying no attention up till then, just sitting facing the screen and making plans for when they left Oxford. The van was mended and parked a hundred yards away, where no one would take any notice of it. They could be on the road within the hour. At least now they needn't head for Leicester. They could go wherever they wanted.

Ant tuned in to what the woman on the television was saying.

'. . . in connection with the murder of high-flying academic, Dr Olivia Blacket, the police wish to interview a woman called Julia Paley. It is understood that Miss Paley was involved in a road-traffic accident in January this year, in which her ten-month-old baby died. Miss Paley herself was also injured in the same accident, but discharged herself from hospital and has not been seen by her family or friends since she left home some months ago. Dr Blacket was driving the car involved in the accident, and was convicted of driving without due care and attention, and fined two hundred pounds. The police spokesperson emphasized that if Miss Paley presented herself at the police station to answer certain questions, she would be treated with every sympathy . . .'

Ant walked across to the television and turned it off.

'That was you, wasn't it?' he said to Angel. 'That Julia Paley person.'

'I suppose so,' she answered. 'I can't remember. But it doesn't matter now. That was the old life and it's over now.'

'Right,' said Ant. 'If you're sure?'

'None of it matters any more,' said Angel.

'Time to go,' said Ant, speaking to all the family. 'We can't stay in Oxford after that.'

'Where to?' asked Gren.

'North,' said Ant. 'Now let's get this place ready to leave.'

Dime collected their bed linen and put it through the wash, ready to put back, clean, on the beds. Angel went through the house dusting, hoovering, polishing the bits of old furniture she had taken a fancy to. Ant and Green adjusted objects on shelves and in cupboards to fill in the empty spaces. When they had finished, the place looked much as it had when they came in, only a lot cleaner and tidier. The houseplants were thriving.

'What about the shop?' asked Gren. 'How much did we clear?'

'Enough,' said Ant. 'It'll give us working capital when we get to the new place. And we've still got the remains of the stock in the back of the van. We can find suitable premises and set up in business straight away. We'll be there by morning.'

Gren nodded. Ant was right, as usual.

Finally they put their own possessions back into supermarket carrier bags and stowed them in the van.

'Where's Angel?' asked Coffin.

Angel was nowhere to be found. She had quietly packed her own possessions and left. In her room, on the dressing table by the window, they found only the doll in the white cotton bonnet.

'She's left the doll I gave her,' said Coffin.

'Maybe she doesn't need it any more,' said Ant. 'It's best if she can leave all that behind.'

'But I took it specially for her, to make up for Daisy,' said Coffin. 'She was cold, so I gave her the cardigan, and she was sad, so I gave her the doll.'

'It looks like one of the dolls we sold in the shop,' said Ant. 'The day that woman was murdered.'

'The Blacket woman shouldn't have killed Daisy,' said Coffin. 'Whatever excuses she made, she deserved to die. I did it for Angel.'

'Come on,' said Ant, after a pause. 'Let's get in the van.'

They stowed the rest of their gear in the back. Coffin brought the doll along and put it with his pack and the bundle of whistles tied with a length of soft cord.

'What happened to that black box of yours?' asked Gren. 'I haven't seen you use it for a while.'

'I had to get rid of it,' said Coffin.

'But it was special. Lined with velvet,' said Gren.

'I put the hammer inside. Afterwards. Carried it home. Cleaned the hammer. Put it back in the drawer downstairs.

But the box was spoiled. There was a bonfire at the bottom of the garden next door,' said Coffin. 'So I put the box on it. And the black gown thing.'

'What gown was that?' asked Ant.

'The one I took to get into the college. It had blood on it, afterwards. I rolled it up and brought it home and burnt it, too. Gren said that burning would get rid of any evidence.'

'Gren was right,' said Ant. 'Time to get on the road.'

'We can't go without Angel,' said Dime.

Gren and Coffin stood close to him and faced Ant.

'All right,' he said. 'We'll give her an hour. Then we have to go. We don't want them to find us in this house. That would put Coffin in danger. We've got to get out of the place. We'll find Angel somehow, but we can't stay around here.'

Angel had walked back into the centre of Oxford. It was dark, and a cold drizzle was falling once more. She hadn't eaten much supper, and was hungry again already. She didn't know where her next meal was going to come from. She had got used to having practical problems like that solved for her by the family. When you were hungry, there was food on the table. Ant organized all that.

She thought about going to see Kate Ivory again. She still remembered where the house was. But what advice could Kate give her? She might let her stay there for a night or two, but after that she would have to move on, make her own decisions.

She found herself in the square with the giant pepperpot and the abundance of architecture. There were lights on in all the windows. The buildings were full of people who knew what they were doing with their lives.

They were all reading books. They were only a year or two younger than she was and yet they knew nothing of the life she had led so far. She saw them at their desks, each one lit by a pool of light. They might be aliens from another planet.

This city was not for her. She had come here to kill Olivia. She hadn't done it, but she had caused her death. Now it was time to leave. She would never return to Oxford.

She couldn't go back to the family, either. She had gone along with them while she was recovering, but she had found their closeness overwhelming. All the time she had been with them, she had promised herself that she would leave as soon as she had done what she had to. And she had brought terrible things to them. Death. Danger. Love. She hadn't wanted anyone to kill Olivia for her, and she knew that he had only done it for love of her. He used to sit there, in her room, before she even knew who he was, and play to her on his whistle. She'd realized then, really. But she wasn't ready for anyone to love her while she was still recovering, and she wasn't sure that she ever would be, now. Coffin had given her the devotion he'd have lavished on a dog, if Ant had allowed him to have one.

But the radio had said that the police knew who she was. Julia Paley. The name didn't sound any more real to her than Angel did. But it was only a matter of time before they found her. She'd seen all the blue uniforms when she'd glanced into Leicester College, and now they were looking for her. The least she could do for the family was to lead them away.

She started to walk north, up St Giles, then the Banbury Road. When she got to the bypass, she would hitch a lift.

Maybe she'd go back to London. Or on to Birmingham.

As she walked, the exercise made her feel warmer. For a while she forgot that she was hungry.

'Time to go,' said Ant. 'We can't wait here any longer.'

'We got to look for her,' said Dime. 'I'll find her.'

'Yeah, sure,' said Ant. 'I said we'd look for her. We'll take the van.'

'Which way?' asked Gren, when the van reached the end of the road. Left to the bypass. Right into central Oxford.

'Right,' said Coffin.

'Maybe she wanted one last look,' said Gren. 'I'll drive all round the centre. You watch out for Angel.'

'OK,' said Ant. 'We can get to the motorway the long way round.'

Magdalen tower rose like a pale finger in front of them.

'Pretty,' said Dime. Then, remembering Ant's lesson, 'But no good for business.' And there was no sign of Angel on the bridge.

Buildings rose through the drizzle on either side, warm golden light shining out on to the pavement through their huge, ancient windows. The van's heater blasted out warmth to protect them from the raw cold outside.

'Nice,' said Dime. But he sounded worried.

They turned down St Aldate's, past Christ Church, then branched off to the right, towards the station. The streets were nearly empty, and they had the town to themselves. If Angel were anywhere around, they would see her.

'That's the police station,' said Gren, pointing left, as they passed the portico of the college.

'Ice rink,' said Ant, as they took the road to the right of

them. 'Multi-storey car park.' No Angel.

They circled round the one-way system, searching the streets for a glimpse of the once-white dress, the pale hair, before heading up St Giles.

'Good little retail outlet, that,' said Gren, as they passed the green shop.

'We'll do it again,' said Ant. 'Only better. Open a chain of them, maybe.'

'It won't be the same without Angel,' said Coffin. 'I'm not leaving without her.'

'More old colleges,' said Ant, pointing across St Giles, as they turned left past the Ashmolean. 'The place is full of the things.' But still not a sign of their Angel.

Coffin found one of his whistles and started to play 'The Leaving of Liverpool'.

By the time the van reached the last roundabout, no one had spoken for ten minutes. The signboards informed them that they were headed for the M40. It had been hopeless, looking for one person in that city. They knew, really, that she hadn't wanted them to find her.

'Which way?' asked Gren, who was driving. 'London or Birmingham?'

Ant knew he would have to say something, break the silence. 'Birmingham,' he said.

Gren moved into the left-hand lane.

At least that was one decision made. Perhaps it would become gradually easier. People said there were good opportunities for business in Birmingham. And maybe one day they'd meet another woman. Not like Angel, but someone. It was time they got married.

Gren was swinging the van round the roundabout, taking the Birmingham exit, when they saw the swirl of a pale skirt, the lifted thumb.

'Hitchhiker,' said Dime. 'Girl.'

Gren was already stopping the van. The girl came running up to the passenger side of the cab. She was wet, and her hair fell in rats' tails over her eyes. Ant rolled down the window.

Angel.

'Want a lift to Birmingham?' asked Ant.

'Sounds good,' said Angel.

'Hop in the back, then.'

'I've got your doll for you,' said Coffin.

'Thanks, Coffin,' said Angel. 'I don't think I need it any more.'

'Keep it,' said Ant. 'It might come in handy for one of the children.'

'Are you sure?' asked Angel. 'Do you really want me to go with you? I could bring trouble.'

'No way,' said Gren.

'They won't find us,' said Ant. 'They're looking for someone called Julia Paley, and she doesn't exist any more.'

She was glad, really. She'd forgotten what it was like, being on your own. There was plenty of room for her, between Coffin and Dime. And it was warm and dry there, too. Not like out on the road.

Gren pulled away and accelerated on to the motorway.

'How're you doing?' Angel said to Dime.

'All right now,' said Dime. 'Are you hungry?'

'A bit,' said Angel.

'We'll stop off at the next services for you,' said Dime.

'I'd like a nice pizza,' said Angel. 'Tomato and cheese. With chips.'

Dime smiled happily in the darkness. Everything was back to normal.

'It's good to be back,' said Angel. 'I feel like I've come home.'

'Yeah,' said Coffin. 'Family's best. You know we'd do anything for you, don't you, Angel?'

'Would you?'

'I would, anyway. Anything,' said Coffin.

The noise of the doorbell entered Kate's dream and woke her up. She opened an unwilling eye and looked at her bedside clock. Nine forty-five. Sunlight streamed across her bed. Her head hurt. She didn't want to get out of bed. After all, why should she? She could write her next chapter any time she wanted to. And really it didn't matter whether the thing got written or not.

The doorbell shrilled again.

Go away, she thought. She would have said it out loud, she would have shouted it, even. But that would have taken too much effort. If writing was too much for her this morning, so was getting out of bed. Camilla would look at her accusingly and tell her that she had writer's block but did not wish to face the fact. Writer's block? Her? That was strictly for amateurs. Professionals just got on with the job. No such self-indulgences for them.

The doorbell screamed, twice. A heavy fist pounded on the door. Someone lifted the flap of her letterbox and shouted, 'Come down and open the door. Kate! I know you're in there, Kate. So come down. Now.'

Shut up and go away, said the voice inside her head. But both her eyes were open now, and her feet swung, by themselves as it were, out from under the creased, sweaty duvet, and hit the floor.

'I'm coming,' she croaked. 'Just stop shouting at me, OK?'

Dressing gown. She ought to put on a dressing down. She gripped it somewhere around her waist, since it took more coordination than she could muster to tie the belt, and went downstairs. Her ankles felt as stiff as an old woman's and she thought her breath would probably repel the most persistent doorstep salesman.

There was a familiar form visible through the frosted glass of her front door.

'Hallo,' she said, sticking her nose and a portion of chin out through the gap in the door. 'What do you want? Why don't you go away?'

'Charming. Even for you, Kate, this is a bit much.'

Somehow he was inside and she was standing defensively outside the sitting-room door. He had a large cardboard box in his hands.

'I've brought you a present,' he said.

'What is it?' she asked, eyeing the box with suspicion. 'It's too big for my mantelpiece.'

'I hope so,' said Paul. 'If you promise not to turn the contents to stone with one look, you can open the box.'

She opened the sitting-room door, went in, and took the box from him. She opened it, slowly. Then stood looking at the contents in disbelief.

It was a kitten. Not a small, fluffy, cute kitten, but one with long, gawky legs, short marmalade fur and large ears. It flattened its ears at her and yowled.

'But I don't want a cat.'

'Yes you do. You need it.'

'What will I do when I want to go away? Who'll look after it? Young Toadface? He'd start doing cruel and unusual experiments on the poor animal.'

'You hardly ever go away. And when you do, I'll look after it for you.'

Kate looked at him through bleary eyes. 'What makes you say I need a cat?'

'It's obvious. You need someone else to care about.'

'Someone else?'

'Something. Anything other than yourself. Something that will disorganize your house and interrupt your predictable routine. Carry on like this and you'll get stuck like it, Kate.'

'Stop talking at me like an Enid Blyton book.'

'Someone's got to tell you.'

They glared at each other for a moment. Then Kate said, 'Does it need feeding?'

'Not yet, but it will soon.'

'I suppose it has a whole list of requirements,' she said, pushing her hair out of her eyes and squinting at the kitten, who was crawling round the room on its belly, examining the undersides of her furniture.

'I've brought you some of its food, its litter tray, the stuff to go in it . . .'

'I'll go and warm some milk,' said Kate. 'And find that chipped blue bowl that I was going to chuck out.'

The kitten emerged from under the pink sofa and yowled at them.

'Poor little thing's hungry,' said Kate, accusingly.

'Poor little thing tells lies,' said Paul, unsympathetically.

'We might get on together after all,' said Kate. 'What's its name? Well, what's its gender, if it comes to that?'

'Female,' said Paul. 'I wouldn't risk a male in this house. And she hasn't got a name yet. I thought I'd leave that to you.'

'What happens to her if I refuse to accept your present?'

'She goes back down the pound. I expect she'll be quite happy there, once she gets used to the place and the feline riff-raff element you meet there.'

Kate looked at him: he was getting to use much longer words since she first met him. She tried rubbing her forefinger between the cat's ears. It pushed its head towards her as though it enjoyed the experience.

'There, she likes you,' said Paul.

'I think I'll call her Susanna.'

'Right then, Susie, I think you've got a new home.' And Paul placed her without ceremony on Kate's shoulder, where she pushed her claws into Kate's ratty dressing gown and rubbed her chin against Kate's ear.

'I'll just bring her things in from the car for you, then I'll be going,' he said.

Kate wasn't listening. She and Susanna were moving into the kitchen and having a conversation about food.

'I wondered if you'd like to come out to dinner tonight,' said Paul. He was speaking to Kate on her ordinary phone, so she had time to prevaricate.

'I know it's an odd sort of evening for dinner, and short notice, but my social life has to fit in with my shifts,' he said, since she didn't reply.

The trouble was, she wasn't sure whether she could cope

with him in her life. What would her friends think? They wouldn't blink at something masculine in black leather and steel studs, shiny hair taken back in a pony tail. Or even something female, ditto, but crew-cut. Someone who put aitches in the wrong places, someone too old, or much too young – all would be acceptable to her friends. But a policeman? They wouldn't know how to talk to him.

The silence had gone on for too long.

'Unless you don't fancy the idea,' said Paul, unusually humble, though she knew that he couldn't really accept it. 'How about it?'

If she didn't answer quickly, the offer would be withdrawn.

'Thanks, it's a nice idea. But why don't you come round to my place?' she said. 'I'm not a bad cook, and you can meet your friend Susanna again. Check that I'm looking after her properly.'

'Yes, if you like. Thanks.' He sounded surprised.

'Well, if we decide to talk about Angel and company, it will be easier at my place than in public, won't it?'

It was certainly easier than meeting one of her friends and explaining that she was having dinner with a policeman.

'Which one do you think did it, then?' asked Paul.

They had eaten three courses of Kate's dinner, had drunk their way through the first bottle of wine, and were just starting on the second. Paul had put a new CD on the player and now came to sit next to Kate on the sofa.

'I've thought it out. It had to be Coffin.'

'What makes you think it was him?' asked Paul, helping them both to more wine.

'Are you going to be able to drive home after that glass?'

'Probably not. We'll have to think of an alternative. If you drink yours up, a convenient solution might come to you.'

He picked the kitten up from the end of the sofa, where it was sharpening its claws, and put it out in the kitchen, where it curled up in its basket.

'I knew that kitten needed some discipline,' said Kate watching him.

'Why don't you think it was one of the others?' he asked, when he was sitting down again. 'I think Ant was the most likely. He had the brains and the initiative.'

'He was scared of dogs. Even quite small, friendly ones. He'd never had gone into a room with Ludo.'

'Dime?'

'Dime couldn't have got himself into the college. Someone would have asked him who he was and thrown him out within thirty seconds.'

'What about Gren?'

'Gren had another half to his life. Wherever they went, he had contacts. He and Ant were the traders, the entrepreneurs. He wouldn't have got so wrapped up in Angel's affairs that he would actually go out and murder for her.'

'So you think it was Coffin.'

'I think he was capable of it. And then, "Because of the curious incident of the dog in the night-time," ' said Kate.

'What dog? Which night-time?' asked Paul.

' " 'The dog did nothing in the night-time. That was the curious incident,' remarked Sherlock Holmes." A quotation,' explained Kate. 'I thought at the time there was something I should have noticed about Brendan's dog, Ludo. There was only one person it would obey: Olivia. It took no notice of the professor even. Liam sneezed whenever he saw a dog.

269

As for me, it chewed my shoes to pieces and ate one of my favourite earrings.'

'But you think Coffin could bring it under control?'

'Coffin could if anyone could. He had an affinity with dogs. He was always talking to them, and going on at Ant about getting one. Angel told me about him. Ant wouldn't because, like I said, I think it was the one thing he was afraid of.'

'How did he get into the college?'

'The same way I did, probably. By borrowing or nicking a gown and either following Angel through the Fellows' door, or sneaking through the crowd at the lodge. Once he was inside, no one would have looked at him twice. He had a boy's face and an innocent expression.'

'We didn't find the weapon. You're probably right that it was a hammer. But how did he get out, carrying a bloody hammer in his hand? Even an Oxford college might think that was a bit much and ask him what he was doing.'

'When I first saw Coffin around the city, playing his whistle, he put out one of those squarish black boxes to collect the money in. It had probably been a clarinet or a flute case, I suppose. He used it for keeping his collection of whistles in, usually. He could have hidden a hammer in it and walked out of the college without anyone taking any notice.'

'Like a Chicago gangster with a violin case. What about his penny whistles?'

'He stuck them in his back pocket.'

'Whoever killed Olivia would have been splashed with blood.'

Kate pulled a face. She was squeamish about blood. 'I expect the gown was, so he took it off and rolled it up. There was a tap and basin in the small room, so he could have washed his hands and whatever else needed it. It would still only have taken a few minutes.'

'What did he do with the gown, afterwards?'

'At the end of October there are bonfires all over Oxford. I should think he added it to someone's bonfire. Likewise the black case.'

'The hammer's not so easy to dispose of.'

'After he cleaned it, he could have sold it in that shop of theirs. Or left it in the house where they were squatting. Maybe he's still got it with him.'

'That leaves the doll.'

'I think he took the doll for Angel. Shoved it inside his sweatshirt and walked out with it. He was only a few minutes behind her. I think he gave her the doll before I saw them in Broad Street. She had a doll clutched underneath her cardigan, and it could have been the same one.'

'You could be right. But there's no evidence.'

'We could change the subject, then, couldn't we?' asked Kate.

'Good idea. Have you come up with an alternative to pushing me out of that door to face a possible drink-driving charge?' asked Paul.

'Let me show you the way to the spare bedroom.'

In the back of the van, Coffin took out his penny whistle and started to play. The girl they called Angel, whose name had once been Julia Paley, hummed along with the tune. After a while, they all joined in and sang their way up the motorway.

Soon they would be in Birmingham and could start all over again. They might get married in Birmingham, if Angel agreed. If she wasn't ready for that yet, they could wait. She was on the mend now, and it wouldn't be long.

Dr Rory Williams arrived at Heathrow Airport at 18.05 hours on the first of November. An hour and ten minutes later he picked up his car from the long-term car park and drove back to his house in East Oxford. He never slept properly on a transatlantic flight, and he was looking forward to an early night and a good long sleep in his own bed.

The time away had been good for him. It had allowed him to come to terms with the fact that Lynne had walked out on him just before he went away. His mind quickly arranged the thought. The fact that he had allowed Lynne to go. That was better. Less brutal than the other way round.

He wouldn't miss Lynne. She had only been with him for two or three weeks, then she had made a big production number of it when she walked out, telling him that he lived in a tip and unless he got himself civilized, no woman would ever stay with him. She was being ridiculous. He would see just what sort of a tip he had left behind him when he got home.

He let himself into the house and dropped his flight bag and case in the hall. He would unpack later. For the moment he needed only toothbrush and pyjamas to take upstairs. He threw shirts, jeans and grubby underwear out of his case to find what he wanted. Then he went into the kitchen to make himself a mug of tea, leaving the top of the packet open. The kitchen was immaculate. There, he had known that women made too much fuss. He opened a tin and helped himself to unfamiliar biscuits that Lynne must have left behind. He took the teabag out of the mug by its tag and left it lying on the draining board like a dead mouse. He swiped at a puddle of spilled tea with a cloth that smelled faintly of bleach, but ignored the crumbs he had left on the floor. He would tidy up tomorrow when he was feeling better. He wondered where Lynne had put the Hoover. He would have to find it some time, he supposed. Eventually. The top of the cooker twinkled at him, but he didn't notice.

Really, the place didn't look at all bad, he thought, as he stood under the shower. The taps gleamed, the bath and basin were clean. He took the soft, folded towel from the towel rail and wrapped it round himself before going back into the bedroom. If you left the house alone, it would look after itself.

Next morning, by the time he had taken another shower, and left the damp towel on the bathroom floor, and then scrabbled through his luggage to find a clean shirt, the place didn't look quite as tidy as he remembered it. When he opened the kitchen cupboard to look for cereal, the door fell off. Stupid people had used too short a screw. He went downstairs to the basement to find a longer screw, and his screwdriver. He found the screws all right, but when he opened the drawer where he thought he kept his tools, he found it tidy, but surprisingly empty. There were no screwdrivers, just a pair of wirecutters and a large hammer. This last looked familiar, but very clean, as though someone had taken it out and scrubbed it recently.

He went back upstairs and put the door on one side. He would deal with it later. Meanwhile he removed the milk from the fridge, splashed it liberally over his bowl of Rice Crispies, dribbled it across the work top, and sat down at the table to eat his breakfast.

The bowl left a white ring of milk on the polished surface of the table.

The doorbell rang. When he opened the door there was a medium-sized, clean-looking man of around thirty standing there. He had light red hair and very blue eyes, that looked straight at Rory.

'Detective Sergeant Paul Taylor,' he said.

'Identification,' replied Rory, and examined it, carefully.

'Dr Rory Williams?'

'That's right.'

'I need to see some identification, too, I'm afraid.'

Rory's passport was still lying on the floor where he had left it the previous evening, and he fetched it for Paul Taylor, who also examined it carefully.

'Can I come in? The matter is a little difficult to explain on the doorstep,' said Paul.

'Sure,' and Rory led the way into the sitting room. They sat at right angles on the two sofas. 'Now, what's it about?'

'I gather you've been away, sir.'

'That's right, for about three weeks.'

'And was the house just the same when you returned? Did you notice anything amiss?'

'What on earth are you talking about?'

Paul took a deep breath. Apart from the signs of an untidy man arriving from foreign parts, there was nothing untoward about the house that he had seen so far. 'It is possible, sir, that your house was taken over by squatters while you were away.'

'Don't be ridiculous. Take a look around you. Does it look as though squatters have just moved out? And if there were squatters, incidentally, that is exactly what they wouldn't have done.'

'They were very unusual squatters, I admit.'

'Well, since that answers your question, I imagine, that must be all you want to know.'

'If you're sure that everything is as you left it, sir.' Really, he couldn't insist any more without appearing ridiculous.

There was a funny smell coming from the kitchen.

'Did you by any chance leave some toast under the grill, sir?'

'Oh dear, I do believe you're right.' And Rory leapt off into the kitchen to rescue the toast. Paul heard sounds of scraping, then the lid of the rubbish bin opening and the clunk as it closed again. He imagined the trail of black crumbs that now led across the kitchen.

There was nothing more he could do here. If the householder had noticed nothing wrong, he couldn't insist that they search the place, looking for Ant, and Gren, Coffin, Dime and Angel. He was willing to bet that the family had polished away all its fingerprints, anyway.

'Have you had a bonfire in the garden recently, sir?'

'No, I haven't got round to tidying up, yet.'

'But many of the neighbours have, I take it.'

'Probably. I really haven't noticed.'

Paul got up to leave. Outside the house, he wondered for a moment whether he had found the right place. Number twenty-five. The road was short and only went up as far as forty-eight, so it couldn't be fifty-two. And there, on the corner by the Leicester Arms, it said Denton Road. D for Dime. Well, he could have got it wrong, he supposed. But somehow he didn't think so. That was the house where Ant and Dime, Gren, Coffin and Angel had been living. But he'd never be able to prove it now, let alone find enough evidence to pin the murder on one of them.

Oh well, he thought. That would leave a big question mark hanging over the head of Dr Liam Ross.

And serve the bastard right.

Kate had fed the kitten and scrunched up a piece of paper and played with it for far too long on a working morning. The kitten was lying exhausted in a corner of the pink velvet sofa, and Kate went down to her workroom.

It was too long since she had looked at her book. She read through a previous chapter. Now she remembered: it had been quite good, but predictable, and after a couple of weeks away from it it still looked the same. And her adventures had given her no new information to use. All that breaking and entering and 'borrowing' had left her with nothing she couldn't have found in one of the standard reference works.

The pages of the Ternan Papers that she had photocopied were in a folder on top of her notebook. She took them out and looked at them again. There was page sixteen, with its account of the child who had its clothes stolen and was sent home naked and weeping. But what about page forty-three? She started painfully making her way through the first paragraph.

It is very difficult to find congenial company in this city. Members of the university want nothing to do with those of us who are in trade, though they are content to avail themselves of our products. The wives of the other trades- men know nothing of life outside this provincial town. I am starved of company of my own kind.

Kate could sympathize, but it wasn't telling her anything

that she didn't already know. If only dear Maria Susanna would be less discreet. Perhaps she had taken the only two dull pages in the entire set of papers. Perhaps the rest were crammed full with indiscretions about Nelly Ternan and Charles Dickens.

It would be months, if not years, before the papers were sorted out again, and a new scholar chosen to study them. Far too late for Kate and her book. But what about the passage that Angel had quoted in the shop. She couldn't remember it exactly. But it was something about a dead baby. Concentrate, Kate. Listen to Angel's voice in your head.

The child had died and it is all my fault. The child was so beautiful, with her fair hair and skin. She wore a white dress and bonnet, with lace ties, and I stood by the tiny white coffin and wept. Would she have died if I had not spoken as I did?

How much of it was written by Maria Susanna, or her correspondent, and how much of it was twisted by Olivia and made to fit her own preoccupation? Just suppose for a moment that it was all written by Maria. How would she interpret it? . . . And a new and wicked thought came to Kate as she sat at her word processor.

If it was to take so long before anything was published about the Ternan Papers, who was to know what was in them? It might, as her imagination insisted on telling her, be scandal and indiscretion. No one would be able to argue with her for years, and her book would be long remaindered by then.

She set to work with renewed interest.

Nelly Ternan looked at the infant that the nurse had passed to her. The labour had been long and painful, but all that was forgotten as she held the new life in her arms. She gazed adoringly at the puckered red face. Surely the baby looked just like her father. She looked across to the photograph of Charles Dickens that stood by her bedside. Oh yes, there was no mistake. The baby certainly favoured her father . . .

Kate typed on while the kitten chewed through ten pages of her latest printout that she had left on the table.

Maria Susanna bent her face down towards her sister, her expression concerned.

'It would be better not to grow too attached to the infant,' she murmured. 'She has an air about her of not being long for this world.'

The kitten, meanwhile, went to sharpen her claws on the seat of Kate's pink velvet sofa, before using the bookcase as a ladder to reach the mantelpiece. There were all sorts of exciting toys to play with there, including a small red enamel cherry, which she batted off the mantelpiece, to lie forgotten under a distant chair.

'She must lie in a white coffin,' said Nelly, her voice breaking with grief. 'She shall wear her white bonnet with the lace ribbons, and have only lilies to go with her on her long journey.'

'I see her there in heaven,' wept Maria. 'A little angel, dressed in spotless white, the radiance of the skies creating a halo around her sweet head. She is praying for us, waiting for us . . .'

The kitten played quite contentedly as Kate typed on, until it got hungry and demanded another meal and a second session with its new paper ball.

'Watch it,' warned Kate. 'Your friend Paul's coming round again this evening. You'll have to be on your best behaviour. On the other hand, we don't want to encourage him to make himself too much at home.'

And she turned back to her work.

A selection of bestsellers from Headline

OXFORD EXIT	Veronica Stallwood	£4.99	☐
BOOTLEGGER'S DAUGHTER	Margaret Maron	£4.99	☐
DEATH AT THE TABLE	Janet Laurence	£4.99	☐
KINDRED GAMES	Janet Dawson	£4.99	☐
MURDER OF A DEAD MAN	Katherine John	£4.99	☐
A SUPERIOR DEATH	Nevada Barr	£4.99	☐
A TAPESTRY OF MURDERS	P C Doherty	£4.99	☐
BRAVO FOR THE BRIDE	Elizabeth Eyre	£4.99	☐
NO FIXED ABODE	Frances Ferguson	£4.99	☐
MURDER IN THE SMOKEHOUSE	Amy Myers	£4.99	☐
THE HOLY INNOCENTS	Kate Sedley	£4.99	☐
GOODBYE, NANNY GRAY	Staynes & Storey	£4.99	☐
SINS OF THE WOLF	Anne Perry	£5.99	☐
WRITTEN IN BLOOD	Caroline Graham	£5.99	☐

All Headline books are available at your local bookshop or newsagent, or can be ordered direct from the publisher. Just tick the titles you want and fill in the form below. Prices and availability subject to change without notice.

Headline Book Publishing, Cash Sales Department, Bookpoint, 39 Milton Park, Abingdon, OXON, OX14 4TD, UK. If you have a credit card you may order by telephone – 01235 400400.

Please enclose a cheque or postal order made payable to Bookpoint Ltd to the value of the cover price and allow the following for postage and packing:

UK & BFPO: £1.00 for the first book, 50p for the second book and 30p for each additional book ordered up to a maximum charge of £3.00.
OVERSEAS & EIRE: £2.00 for the first book, £1.00 for the second book and 50p for each additional book.

Name ....

Address ....

....

....

If you would prefer to pay by credit card, please complete:
Please debit my Visa/Access/Diner's Card/American Express (delete as applicable) card no:

Signature .... Expiry Date ....